TWICE SHY

GIL MASON
BOOK 10

GORDON CARROLL

For my eighteen grandchildren, including those in the heavenly arms of our Lord~

Chimney, Addison, Clementine, Elijah, Gabriel, Noel, Noah, Roland, Roman, Aislynn, Verity, Cillian, Amalie, Serena, Avery, Wonder, Grace, Evelynn

Twice Shy

"An unpleasant experience induces caution."
-Proverb

"He that has been once beguiled by someone else ought to keep himself well from the same."
-Aesop

PROLOGUE

The day was perfect, more perfect than she could ever deserve, thought Sarah as she stood behind the chapel doors, waiting for the wedding march to begin. Anthony Carlino stood beside her, giant and smiling, holding her arm. Her parents had passed years ago, her mother to cancer and her father from a broken heart, both far too young. And so, the once-Godfather of the Mafia, and more recently mentor and confidant to the blushing bride, was standing in as her surrogate father.

On the other side of the rich mahogany doors, Sarah knew Gil was waiting for her, dressed in a tuxedo, his groomsmen stretched out next to him, his father-in-law, Nathan, standing a step higher, preparing to officiate their nuptials.

Sarah was overjoyed that Nathan and Gil had mended their differences, just as she had come to terms with her own guilt and concerns, pushing them all away so that this day could finally come to pass. All that mattered now was to make Gil happy for the rest of his life. And she would do it. Nothing would stop her. Nothing would prevent them from living the life they deserved. Gil was so good. He had saved so many people and affected so many lives. Irmgard, her flower girl, was a testament to this, as were Billy, Tina, Nathan, and so many others.

All of Sarah's friends and remaining family were here—her sister, coworkers, and even Lisa Kaltz, her best friend since fifth grade.

Everyone.

After the reception, Gil and Sarah would leave for a two-week honeymoon in the Bahamas—no work, no worries, no snow. Sarah loved the beauty of snow but hated driving in it, not to mention having to scrape the windshield free of ice.

Glancing toward the windows flanking the main entrance, she saw gently falling flakes lightly powdering the church grounds. Colorado could be so beautiful. On this day, it looked like a postcard. Everyone said so—a snapshot set in time.

It was the most perfect of perfect days.

She couldn't have asked for more.

And she never would. She would be thankful and forever content.

At times, she thought Gil would never come around, that he'd never let himself be happy. His fears seemed destined to trap them, keeping them apart forever. His fear of loss, her coming to harm, and his enemies. But all that had changed. Gil had changed. He'd realized that love was worth the risk. Worth the danger. Worth anything.

Tears threatened to spoil her carefully mastered makeup, but Sarah fought them back bravely. Anthony Carlino patted her hand, smiling down at her.

What must he think of her?

It didn't matter. This was *her* day. Sarah's day. And she was going to live it to the fullest. No shame, no guilt, no fear. She would embrace it with her all, maybe even get a little drunk, something she never did, and give herself completely to Gil, now and forever. Overwhelmed with joy and anticipation, she basked in the moment.

And then the music started.

The doors opened.

And there they were. Everyone Sarah loved. Everyone she cared about.

The church was breathtaking, the steeple high, the stained-glass windows majestic, the wooden pews and walls ornate. Everyone was smiling—smiling at her—*for* her. She felt dizzy and almost stumbled, but Anthony Carlino steadied her with a strong, supportive arm.

And then she saw Gil proudly standing at the end of the long aisle. Suddenly, the dizziness was gone, erased by his smile—the flash of his teeth, the shine of his hair, the strength in his shoulders, the warmth and passion in his eyes. The colors of the sanctuary seemed to magnify, the sound of the music intensified, the atmosphere itself pushing her along. Gil, the man she loved, so handsome, strong, and good, stood there waiting for her—longing for her.

As she longed for him.

The walk seemed to last forever, an eternity, yet it was over before she'd had a chance to embrace it all. Anthony Carlino lifted her veil and kissed her on the cheek. He turned to Gil, shook his hand, and placed her hand in his. Sarah felt nervous, something she rarely experienced. Her lips trembled, but she cautioned herself to ignore the feeling so she wouldn't ruin her lipstick.

The two looked at each other—looked deep *into* each other. Overcome by the love they felt and the promise this day held, Sarah thought he might kiss her there and then. She wanted him to, but he held back, following tradition rather than his heart. The couple turned toward Nathan, who smiled, tears glistening in his eyes. Opening the Bible, he looked out over the crowd.

Flowers in hand, Sarah turned to look at her maid of honor, her bridesmaids, and little Irmgard. She returned her gaze to Gil. This day was so much more than she deserved, but, for once, she didn't care. It was hers and she would take it, accept it, live it, love it. She and Gil would be happy, and that was all that mattered. It was all that would ever matter. He was hers, and she was his.

Thank you, she thought. *Thank you to whoever—whatever—was responsible*. Gil's God? The universe? Luck? She didn't care. She was just grateful—*so* grateful. She was living a princess's fairytale dream, one from which she would never awake.

Her heart nearly burst as she looked out the big window behind Nathan. Delicate snowflakes continued to swirl silently, peacefully through the chilly air. She closed her eyes and listened to Nathan's gentle voice as he read from the Bible.

When she opened her eyes, there was no snow, no window, the beauty replaced by bodies and blood and carnage. Nathan was gone, and Anthony Carlino, too. The tears on her cheeks felt hot and sticky, and when she looked down at her hands, the flowers were gone—her fingers were red with blood. Panicked, she strained her neck to look for Gil, but he wasn't there. She realized she was kneeling, something hard and cold pressed against her head.

The man looking down at her was not Gil Mason. He pulled back on the hammer of the revolver, its double-click sounding as loud as death.

"One move, and she dies," he said.

1

BEFORE

The wedding was only a month away, and I hadn't even started shopping for a tuxedo. I knew that's what I should be doing instead of working the dogs, but dogs were more fun and easier by far.

The cat was a different story.

Doctor Steve, my veterinarian, had come up empty on finding a home for Atlas—at least for now. Of course, he had the added difficulty of keeping the situation largely undercover since I wasn't legally allowed to have a cougar. We both wanted to avoid the powers that be from taking him away.

Well ... usually, anyway. Days like today made me think that having him gone wouldn't be so bad. The idiom about herding cats had become all too relatable lately. Cats are not dogs. I mean, I know that, of course. Only now, I *really* know it.

I had four of the pups with me today—my Thor, nine-year-old Irmgard's Petros, Tina's Arrow, and my therapist Rick's Anna. Genetics told in all of them. They were all Max's, but they were also Viper's—Tina's K9—which was a good thing.

A *very* good thing.

The world couldn't handle four more Maxes. Max is too intense.

Viper's traits and drives lent moderation to that intensity. Of course, none of the four were as easygoing as my other dog—my old partner, Pilgrim. Even Viper's genes couldn't hope to moderate to that degree. Unlike Pilgrim, they weren't all bouncy and silly and always craving attention.

They weren't that.

Instead, they were a mixture of murder, mayhem, and joy, all mixed up and spread around, with each puppy inheriting different portions sprinkled throughout its character and disposition. Thor was most like Max. Next was Petros, then Arrow, and the nicest of the bunch, little Anna.

When I say *nice*, one must take into consideration the monster dogs that are her parents. I sported a white gauze bandage on my left wrist where sweet little Anna had latched and wouldn't let go during bite training. Ferocity is not a weakness of hers.

Irmgard and I had come up with the name Petros for her dog because of her love for Max. While still in the high mountains of Germany, she referred to Max as Petra—the name she'd given him when she didn't know his real name. Petra means *rock* in Greek, Petros—*little rock,* or *pebble*. Max is the rock, the Petra of the pack, while Petros is still a pup—a little rock.

All the dogs had basic obedience down by now, so I was working them on enhancing control under stress and in high-drive situations. Billy was with me, along with Tina, Irmgard, and Rick, followed closely by his two apprentices, *Frick and Frack,* the Enneagram and Myers-Briggs twins. Max and Pilgrim were there too, but they weren't training, just acting as spectators, and sometime drill instructors when the pups got too rowdy or tried to bounce away into the bushes and trees.

Sarah was back at the house, a hundred yards away, making wedding plans. I'd asked, and—*miracle of miracles*—she'd said yes. But that wasn't all she was doing. Sarah's a multitasker. She was also ordering replacements for all my property destroyed by the claws and teeth of the baby cougar.

I'd asked Sarah to take charge of that, too. After all, in a very short time, the house would no longer be mine alone—it would be *ours*. I have no eye for decoration or décor, but Sarah has a perfect eye—two of them.

It had already snowed a couple of times, but typical to Colorado, the sun had come out within hours or days and melted it all away. Today, the ground was cold and dry, the grass dead, and the bushes and trees brown and devoid of leaves. It could easily be depressing, but it wasn't. We K9 handlers have a saying—*The very worst day of dog training is better than the absolute best day of any other kind of work.*

And it's true.

Yes, there can be frustration, injuries, hardheaded dogs, harder-headed handlers, equipment issues, setbacks and drawbacks, and consternation over how to handle certain problems. When to motivate, pull back, or charge ahead. But that was all part of the game. Part of the fun and excitement. And when you make a breakthrough?

Such exhilaration.

And seriously, how can anyone *not* have fun working with such wonderful, loving animals?

I held out the three-foot lead (K9-ese for leash), to Irmgard who was standing next to me staring off into space, both hands in her hoodie pocket, fidgeting.

"Irmgard," I said. She jerked up, focusing on me with a strange smile. She took her hands out of her pocket. "You want to work Petros? You're next in the rotation."

With that same look she nodded without saying anything and took the lead. She ran Petros through his series of commands. Being German, she'd decided to use her native language for Petros's commands—go figure. *Sit, stand, lay, heel, retrieve, stop in motion, recall, bite, and release.* Bite and release were nearly constant because the reward consisted of a sturdy rubber ball with a rope attached, offered after every successful exercise. And, of course, you had to get the ball back afterward which meant the dog had to release. It's the first thing I teach every student and their dog.

Usually, I'd test the dogs before purchasing them for a department or agency to ensure the animal has high prey drive. In other words, the dog's genetic drive to chase prey—another animal, food, or a toy. I also look for the dog's tenacity—how long and hard it keeps after the prey.

One of the ways to test this is to get a puppy excited over a toy, then pop it under a milk crate and stand on it. The dog can see the toy through the holes in the crate but can't access it. If the dog gives up and goes off to smell flowers or pee on a tree after a short stint at trying to get to it, it indicates low prey drive, which is not suitable for a working dog. If, on the other hand, the dog digs and pushes, bites at, and scratches the crate, refusing to leave it until it succeeds, it's an indication of good prey drive.

If I deem a dog to have low prey drive, I pass on the purchase for the agency (which often costs upwards of ten grand, and that's for a green dog). It might still make a wonderful pet, or perhaps even a fine service dog, but it's not suited for military or police work.

In this case, though, since I wasn't buying these dogs—having unintentionally gone into the breeding business due to Max and Viper's shenanigans—I would just have to work with what I got. Fortunately, their offspring had all shown excellent prey drive, making training nearly a breeze—with one exception.

Releasing.

Hence the bandage on my forearm. Only Thor released on command from the beginning. I think he gets that from his mother. The others were a bit stingy with their toys.

The two easiest ways to get a new dog to release on command are a back-and-forth of Two-ball and Leash Lift.

Two-ball is a game that uses two balls attached to ropes. The handler starts by showing one ball to the dog, moving it around, and saying *yes* (the reward command), allowing the dog to bite and tug on it. Then, the handler shows the second ball to the dog, letting the first ball go still, then gives the release command just before making the second ball move and giving the reward command again. The dog finds the moving ball more exciting and releases the still ball to grab the moving one. The handler will repeat this process several times, incorporating a lot of play. The dog and handler will play this game thousands of times over a period of several days.

Leash Lift, on the other hand, is a straight obedience game. I put the dog in a sit on my non-gun side and give him his ball. I lift gently straight up on the pinch collar, high on the throat, and directly behind the ears, simultaneously giving the release command he learned in Two-ball. This maneuver activates the dog's gag reflex, causing him to spit the ball out.

I alternate between the two methods because Two-ball is all fun and games, whereas obedience alone gets tiresome for the dogs. They usually learn within a few sessions, but it can get a little tougher the more *in drive* they are.

When training, there is a progression in the level of difficulty. Training with balls is one thing, while a tug toy is a bit more challenging. A sleeve increases the difficulty further, and a bite suit takes things to another level. Real flesh, especially after the first bite when the dog experiences the taste of blood, the pheromone release, and the suspect's screams, can significantly heighten their drive. Therefore, practicing thousands of repetitions with these tools is crucial before allowing the dog to engage with a real person, if possible.

This is where I'd failed with Anna. I was slow and let her get me on the arm where she experienced her first taste of blood. Even so, she's still a sweet thing, and I think she will do just fine. Besides ... I didn't scream.

I finished the last set with the pups and handlers and looked at Atlas, the cougar. I dreaded taking him out for another attempted set, but a job's a job, and it had to be done. Reluctantly, I took up the chain leash. The others—the leather, nylon, and BioThane—were useless in that he bit through them in about a nano-second.

Sarah came walking from the house, talking on her phone. I looked at her questioningly. She shrugged her beautiful shoulders and mouthed *work*.

"Want me to do another set with Petros?" asked Irmgard, still seeming a little strange to me. I thought it might be because of Rick's interns. Irmgard can be a little shy with strangers.

I wanted to say yes, but I knew I would be stalling. It was Atlas's turn in the rotation.

"No," I said. "It's the kitty's turn."

Everyone grinned, ready for another episode of *Gil Gets Eaten, Scratched, and Frustrated*.

Sarah clicked off. "I've got to go. Sorry, guys, but duty calls. I may be gone for a while."

"Where to?" I asked.

"Baros County, south of Pueblo. A murder. They want some help with forensics."

It was my chance to escape. "Want company? I could stand a road trip with you."

She gave me a suggestive smile that would make Jessica Rabbit blush. "The state will only pay for one room."

I grinned. "Not for another month, young lady, so you stop that. I'll spring for mine."

"I'd love company," she said. "You can help with the wedding plans."

"Every man's favorite activity," I said. I looked to the others. "Sorry, you'll all have to wait until we get back to see me get shredded."

They all laughed. I laughed with them. So did Sarah.

We wouldn't have, had we known what was in store for us.

2

Steve Hearst, dressed in khaki shorts, a yellow and orange short-sleeved Hawaiian shirt, and blue Crocs with no socks, reviewed the screen in front of him. Sarah Gallagher, lead CSI investigator for the Colorado Bureau of Investigation, had written dozens of peer-reviewed articles on everything from DNA to quantum mechanics—world-class stuff. She was out of Steve's league, despite his two Ph.D.s and an IQ of 140. To be fair, forensic science wasn't Steve's field. Not exactly. Neither was crime scene analysis and investigation. Again—*not exactly*. However, Steve had witnessed more than his fair share of crime scenes. More than most cops and detectives, and way more than typical FBI agents, ATF, and DEA—more than most task force agents.

Witnessed the crime scenes—*caused* a good number of them as well.

Steve had graduated head of his class at the U.S. Naval Academy (USNA), did a nine-year stint in the Navy, first as a pilot, then as a Seal, and had participated in dozens of missions—leading a good portion of them. He never failed his objective, although there had been casualties. Injuries, close calls, shrapnel and bullets, and even a strike from a machete that came a fingernail's thickness from spilling his intestines. Lots of action. He'd been recruited from *there* to *here* … and *here* made his time in the Seals seem like a cakewalk. He was thirty-five, single, never married, no children, no girlfriend. His job had become his significant other and she was a green-eyed harpy, demanding his everything.

And he gave it to her.

The job was too important not to.

Turning from the computer screen, he sat back in his swivel chair, stretched his arms behind his thick black hair, interlaced his fingers, and watched the bank of monitors along the wall, each partnered with a technician recording and assigning designations for everything they saw.

Sarah Gallagher had arrived and was being escorted through the scene, but she hadn't come alone. She was accompanied by a man—a man with two dogs.

"Gil Mason," said one of the techs. "PI working out of Denver. Just sent what I have to your screen. More coming in."

Steve ticked an eye while sucking a tooth. "Why'd she bring a PI with her? And what's with the dogs?"

"Working on it," said the tech.

Steve had a long history with all five technicians. He knew them, and they knew him. Everyone meshed. They were more than techs—they were agents like Steve. Well, *sort of*. They were all bright and competent, warriors in their own right. They'd all been battlefield tested—blooded. They did what needed to be done.

Words flooded Steve's computer. He read them at a glance, and a name caught his attention.

Lance Kemp.

And then another. Kirk Sinclair. *Pappy?* Steve had worked with him in the pit—twice. Once, a while back, as a Seal and the other after Hearst had become a pilot. Pappy was a good man, exceptional, deadly, a great leader.

What was the connection?

"Get me the link between Sinclair and Mason. Everything."

"On it."

It didn't take long. It rarely did. They had, literally, the entire world's technology at their fingertips. Steve read it all, again at a glance. Speed reading was one of his many gifts.

"Get me FBI SAC Lance Kemp on a secure line."

Five minutes later, the call came through.

"Kemp."

"Hearst."

There was a pause. "What do you need?"

"What connection do you have with a private eye named Gil Mason?"

Another pause. "Who'd he kill this time?"

"Like that, is it?"

"You saw his record, I suppose?"

"Marine Corps, law enforcement. That stuff," said Hearst. "Seems competent, but there are a lot of competent vets in law enforcement."

"He's more than that," said Kemp. "Took out that OTA group for me all by himself. He was the one on the bridge, too."

"Bridge?"

"Royal Gorge Massacre? Don't tell me you didn't hear about it."

"I might have been out of the country at the time."

Kemp filled him in. "Took out Senator Marsh in Chicago, too."

"Marsh? The guy that was running for POTUS?"

"One and the same," said Kemp. "That was a bullet dodged."

"Reads a little edgy from the reports. Wife and daughter murdered. Let their killer get prison instead of killing him when he had the chance."

"Not for lack of trying," said Kemp. "Besides, he got him at the bridge. Tossed him over. Thousand feet straight down—plenty of time to think on the way."

Hearst rubbed at his stubbled chin, nodding silently. "Can he be trusted?"

"Depends. What are you up to?"

"Does it matter?" asked Hearst.

"It could. He's a Bible-thumper. Has a conscience. It's down deep, but it's there. Dig too far, and you might hit something. Do you have any leverage?"

"Not yet. You have anything?"

"Some," said Kemp. "I'd rather keep the OTA stuff out of it. I owe him. But I found something else when I was researching him. A buddy of mine in the DEA passed it to me after facial recognition matched him to a video feed."

"Send it," said Hearst.

"This puts me up. You'll owe me."

"Really? After all we've been through and meant to each other? You still keeping score?"

"Always," said Kemp.

"Okay, if it's worth it."

"Wouldn't have brought it up if it wasn't. One more thing."

"Shoot," said Hearst.

"Try not to get him killed. I like the guy."

It was Hearst's turn to pause. "Never heard you ask that before."

"First time for everything," said Kemp.

"Can't promise," said Hearst. "This could get messy fast. Very messy, but I'll do my best."

"You'll have it in ten."

It took seven. Hearst watched the video, complete with audio. It was dated over a decade earlier but was enhanced with modern technology. Hearst watched as Mason went through the *pollo house*. He saw the man with the hammer smash in the old woman's face and skull. Mason killed the man, went to the basement, and killed some more. Very efficient. He came back upstairs, tortured a wounded man, and was about to leave him alive—*until he made the comment about finding Mason and killing him and everyone he loved*. Mason shot him through the head.

Nice.

Hearst would have done the same, except he wouldn't have let the man live long enough to make the threat. Still, it was what Hearst wanted—needed. *Leverage*. Any court would call what Mason did murder. And in the political climate of today, Mason could easily go away for life.

Staying out of prison for life, especially for an ex-cop, was valuable leverage indeed.

"Might want to watch this," said another of the techs.

Mason was getting a dog out of his car.

Now, what was that all about?

An old-looking Shepherd eased itself out and limped to a bush, where it lifted a leg. A reddish-blond Mal stood at the door, looking up at the drone providing the video feed from five hundred feet above the scene. The machine was state-of-the-art, silent, about the size of a hornet. There was no way the dog could see, hear, or smell it.

Hearst felt an eerie and unaccustomed chill shiver up his spine.

He could swear that Mal was staring directly into his eyes.

3

I watched as Sarah surveyed the crime scene. A sheriff's deputy had been riddled with bullets, but that wasn't the worst of it. His throat had been cut, and his tongue pulled back and through the slit.

Classic Mexican necktie.

But that wasn't the worst, either. What they had done with his privates was the worst.

It was still warm in Baros County. No snow. Warm enough for flies.

In the winter—a mile-high—flies.

Five patrol cars from three different jurisdictions surrounded the scene. A fire truck, crime scene tape, and a few straggling lookie-loos were outside the perimeter.

We'd flown down in a private jet from Centennial Airport—*someone flexing their big bucks*—then drove down from the local airport in a rented SUV, Max and Pilgrim roaming freely in the back of the vehicle.

A patrol car pulled up, and a big man stepped out. He wore a khaki-colored shirt with Baros County Sheriff patches on his shoulders, blue jeans, cowboy boots, a five-pointed star on his left breast pocket, and four stars on each shirt collar. The stars signified that he was the head honcho—the sheriff himself of the county. He looked to be about six-five, maybe two-seventy, in his forties with graying hair at the temples, the start of a gut, and leathered brown skin—*partially Hispanic? Indian maybe?*

He didn't look happy.

An old-fashioned brown leather gun belt encircled his hips, and there was a long-barreled, silver-plated, wood-handled Colt Peacemaker in its holster, no safety thong—Marshal Dillon in *Gunsmoke* or Richard Boone in *Have Gun Will Travel*. A tie-down strap snaked around his thigh, keeping it tight and secure, the holster low, near the knee, like in an old gunfighter movie. Mirrored aviator sunglasses hid his eyes—*What we got here is a failure to communicate.* The wooden handle of his weapon was worn with use.

Sarah walked over to him, shook hands, and pointed to me. I saw him size me up. Slipping his sunglasses off, he let them dangle from his breast pocket by one arm, then waggled a forefinger at me, signaling me to come to him.

Seemed a little arrogant, like he thought of me as a servant—or maybe a dog—putting me in my place.

Still, this was his county, his turf, so maybe this was his way of staking it out and letting me know who was in charge right off the bat. A dog marking its territory, warning others. Holding my smirk on the inside, I walked over to him, obeying his summons, letting him feel free to lift his leg all he wanted. There'd be plenty of time to play *quien es mas macho* later if it came to that.

"Gil Mason," I said, holding out my hand.

Ignoring the gesture, he squinted down at me. "I know who you are. The guy on the bridge, right? Royal Gorge. That you?"

"That's me," I said.

"Well, I'm Sheriff Matt Adams. I guess you're savvy to cartel activity already."

"Some."

Using the same big, thick finger he'd used to summon me, he pointed at the body of his deputy. "What do you make of that?"

"A statement that your deputy was meddling in cartel activities. A warning to the rest of your crew."

"My men ain't no *crew*," said the sheriff. "They're a crack bunch and do just what I say. And *I'm* the law."

Apparently, the sheriff hadn't subscribed to the politically correct notion that there is no *'I'* in *'team.'* I decided not to correct him on it.

"Just an expression," I said. "No offense intended."

The sheriff nodded, still squinting at me. I was beginning to feel like I was in a spaghetti western. Clint Eastwood in *The Good, the Bad and the Ugly*. Sarah, sensing the tension, stepped in.

"Gil brought his canines. They can check for tracks, look for evidence that might have been missed."

"My people already been over it. We don't miss things."

"Then why'd you call for me?" asked Sarah.

His eyes swiveled toward her. "Didn't. Wasn't me. DOJ made the call. Guess they figure, like your friend here, that this may have started from over-the-border influence somewhere outside my jurisdiction."

"The Department of Justice? My office didn't mention them," said Sarah.

"Well, maybe you big-city agencies ain't all you're cracked up to be."

A black SUV pulled onto the scene. It looked a lot like my Escalade back home. The rental we got at the airport was blue. This one parked next to a fire truck, and a guy in a brightly colored Hawaiian shirt and khaki shorts got out. It was maybe only forty-five degrees out, not that I could talk. We were sort of dressed alike except that my monochromatic green shirt had long sleeves rolled up to my forearms, my jeans weren't shorts, and oh, my footwear was athletic rather than Crocs.

The man was lean and tanned, with good arms and broad shoulders. His super-white teeth nearly sparkled as he smiled at us, his cheeks dimpling. This guy would be a hit with the ladies. Definitely former military. Instinctively, I bladed my body to him. He registered the movement—I saw it in his eyes. His smile widened as he held his hand out to Sarah.

"Miss Gallagher, Steve Hearst. Thank you for coming so quickly." His eyes shifted to me, his hand still holding Sarah's. "Mr. Mason, glad to have you tag along." He looked to the sheriff. "Sheriff," he nodded his head, "sorry to butt in like this."

"Then why are you?" asked the Sheriff gruffly.

"I just do as I'm told. I'm not a boss like you, Sheriff. They tell me go here—I go here. Go there—I go there." He looked at Sarah, still holding her hand. "Worker bees. Right Miss Gallagher?"

Sarah smiled at him, obviously charmed. "That's what we do, Mr. Hearst."

Unconsciously, I looked at him, still holding her hand. My gaze went to his eyes, and I saw him smiling at me as if he'd just seen something he was maybe looking for. He let Sarah's hand go, nodding.

"Anyway," he said, "we've got a lot to go over. How close are we to being done here?"

"I'd like Gil to let his dogs search the area if that's okay?" said Sarah.

"Yeah, I thought I saw some heads bobbing around back there. I'd like to see them work." He grinned at me again. "That okay, Sport?"

"You're with the Department of Justice?" I asked.

"Just assigned temporarily. I do some stuff with the DEA and a few other agencies full-time. They asked us for assistance on this."

"Ain't no need for the feds to be sticking their noses in this," said the Sheriff. "It's a local brouhaha, that's all. I can handle it myself. Don't need no help."

Hearst did a strange little eye tick thingy while sucking at a tooth.

First, the sheriff's eye-slitting, and now this. I started to feel a twitch of my own coming on.

"I don't know, Sheriff," said Hearst, turning back toward the garish body of the deputy, "looks *cartel-ish* to me."

"Ain't saying it ain't," said the sheriff. "But since you feds won't seal up the border, they're everywhere—Texas, Arizona, Cali,

Colorado. Everywhere. Doing their drugs and robberies and whatever they want. Then, when we go to catch 'em, they just scurry back home out of reach. So, far as I'm concerned, even though this is your boys' fault, it's still local."

"I agree," said Hearst. "That's why we're here only as advisory assistance." He grinned bigger than ever.

"Yeah," said the sheriff, "advisory. Right." He looked back at me. "Go ahead and do whatever."

"No point in trying for a track," I said. "Your people have contaminated the scene's scent trails, and too much time has passed. Besides, from the tire tracks over there, it looks like they left in cars. We can do an evidence search, though."

"Sounds fun," said Hearst.

~

WHILE GIL WENT to get the dogs prepped, Sarah continued investigating the scene by collecting evidence from the deputy's body. Using a pair of tweezers, she reached between what was left of his upper lip and the bottom of his nose. Pieces of something white showed through the blood and flesh. Gathering several, she placed them in a plastic baggie, along with some larvae that would help seal the time of death. When she finished, she gave the go-ahead for the crime scene technicians to resume taking photographs and to cover the body for transport. The coroner had already pronounced and granted permission for removal, but Sarah had wanted a good *once-over* before anything was moved. After they lifted the body, she'd do a final inspection of the area under his body.

Sarah walked back to the sheriff. "Could I see pictures from when you first arrived on scene?" she asked.

Sheriff Adams motioned to a crime scene tech a few yards away. The tech ran right over, a high-end digital camera dangling against his chest. "Show her your crime scene pics."

The tech, a young-looking guy, gawked at Sarah as he handed her the camera. He edged close as she took it, only too happy to manipulate the touchscreen to show her what he'd captured.

"This is the first?" she asked, smiling.

"Yes, ma'am," he grinned like a schoolboy with his first crush.

"What time did you start shooting?"

"About five this morning. They'll be time and date stamped down there in the lower left corner."

"Thank you, …?"

"Jonny," he said, still grinning and staring.

"Jonny," repeated Sarah, flashing a smile that would conquer an army while holding her hand out to shake. He grasped it, holding on as long as he could before letting her take it back.

Sarah scanned through the photos on the screen for several minutes. "What was the temp when you started?"

"Twenty-nine degrees. It's warmed up a good bit since then."

Sarah held the screen so he could see. Displayed was a close-up picture of the dead deputy's face. "What's this ice from?" A splotch of crystals could be seen near the deputy's right nostril, destroyed lip, and cheek.

The tech shrugged. "Snot? Maybe separated plasma? Sweat? Some of his spit mixed with his blood from the gunshot?"

"Maybe," said Sarah. "Good job on the photos."

The kid beamed.

Handing him the camera, she returned to the body, took some additional samples, and then came back to Jonny and the sheriff, holding both baggies.

"I'm done," she said, "your people can finish up."

"What are those?" asked the sheriff, indicating the baggies and their morbid contents.

"Insect larvae," she said, holding up the first bag, "and bone fragments. Teeth, maybe? Not sure about that end one, but I'll know once I get it under a microscope back at my lab."

"You can do it at our office," said the sheriff. "We got a grant a couple years back. Upgraded all our CSI equipment. Got all kinds of fancy machines. We're like that TV show, *CSI*, we got so much stuff."

Sarah smiled. “I know how it is—you get new equipment, you want a chance to show it off, but we’re just staying the night. I’ll fly this back in the morning and have a report for you in the afternoon.”

Jonny looked noticeably disappointed.

The sheriff nodded, his big white hat bobbing. “Suit yourself.” He pointed at Gil, who was preparing Pilgrim for the evidence search. “Them dogs ain’t gonna bite my deputy, are they? Like I said, we’re a close group. Wouldn’t take to his body being desecrated any worse than’s already been done.”

Sarah shook her head, placing a hand on his wrist. “No, no. They’re very well trained. I’m so sorry for all of you. I promise to treat everything I’ve taken with the utmost respect. And I’ll use every skill at my disposal to find anything and everything I can to help bring the responsible people to account.”

The sheriff softened. Nodding, he put his big hand over hers, looking a little doe-eyed himself, like the young tech. “Thanks. Sorry if I come off gruff, but it’s been a long while since we lost one of our own.”

“No apology necessary. I completely understand.”

“Our stuff really is state of the art,” said Jonny hopefully.

“He’s right,” said the sheriff. “You sure you don’t want to use our crime lab? You can store your evidence, use the facilities and equipment—maybe save all the chain-of-custody paperwork for taking it and shipping it to us later.”

“No,” said Sarah, “thank you anyway. It’s probably nothing of evidentiary value—just bone and teeth fragments and a few swab samples for DNA testing. I’ll store the larvae in the cooler I have in the car. We’re heading back in the morning and the flight’s not long. But again, thank you.” She patted his hand and looked back toward Gil. “He’s just about ready. I’ll get your people out of his way.”

4

I'd allowed both dogs out earlier to empty—*potty break*. This time, I called on Pilgrim alone. Evidence searches were better done slowly, methodically—more Pilgrim's speed these days. I figured I would save Max for later, just in case. Sarah cleared the search area of police and medical techs. Pilgrim hopped out of the car, limping slightly.

"Looks like he's getting up there in years," said Hearst.

"Aren't we all. He's still got it, though. Watch." I gave him the sit command, then walked out in front of him, my hands to my chest, acting like I was holding a treat. We both knew I wasn't, but it was the setup for the search game, the pattern I'd set a thousand times over. I gestured, throwing something to the left, then to the right, and gave him the search word *finden*.

Off he went.

Pilgrim trotted here, then there, nose to the ground. He circled wide, then narrow, then wider. Fast-walking to another area, he stopped about twenty feet from the now-covered dead deputy, dug his nose into the dirt, and breathed deeply. He plopped down, nosing the dirt. I went over, and sure enough, he'd found a partially buried .45 caliber shell casing. I patted his head, told him what a good boy he was, then marked the spot with a little orange evidence cone I'd borrowed from the deputy taking pictures. I sent Pilgrim back out to search.

We continued like that for a good half hour, Pilgrim finding a total of seven casings, a bandana, a cigarette butt, a latex glove (dropped by a paramedic), and a brass token from a tourist attraction, partially buried for who knew how long. When I put him back in the car, he was spent. Scenting like that is hard work.

I took my items to Sarah. She was standing next to the Sheriff and a geeky-looking tech with a camera around his neck. I held up the baggie with the token.

"Any idea where this is from?"

The kid spoke up before the sheriff could answer. "That's from *Shooter's Showdown*. It's a movie prop ghost town about thirty miles to the west."

The sheriff gave him a look, like he didn't appreciate being upstaged.

"I saw that movie," I said. "It was fun. Good gunfights."

"They filmed the whole thing right here," said the kid. "When they were done, they planned to tear it all down, but a local businessman bought it from them at a steal and turned it into a tourist attraction. They finished work on the houses, fleshing them out some, and added a few rides and games. It's closed for the winter, but come summer, it brings some crowds." He thumbed toward his boss. "The sheriff here was even in the movie."

"Were you really?" I asked.

He gave the kid another of those looks, then turned to me. "Oh sure, I'm a big-time movie star. That's me."

"He's modest," said the kid, obviously proud of his boss. "Never saw his face, but he did the main character's stunt shooting. Turns out he was way faster than any of their hired stuntmen—a better shot, too. Didn't even need any special effects."

"Really? That's impressive. Maybe I'll get a chance to see you shoot sometime."

Sheriff Adams did the squint thing again, smiling at me. "Maybe you will."

I smiled back, handed the token to Sarah, and returned to Steve Hearst.

"Nice work with the dog," said Hearst. "Very nice. How about you and Miss Gallagher have coffee with me? We can talk."

"Talk about what?"

"Things."

"What kind of things?" I asked.

He turned his head to the west, then toward the sheriff by his car, then back to me. Shrugged, smiled. "Dogs, the desert, dead deputies, cartels. You know—things." He looked back toward Sarah. "If you don't want to join us, I can talk alone with Miss Gallagher. It is *Miss*, right?"

"We're engaged," I said.

He gave me that handsome grin of his, white teeth flashing amid tanned skin and dimples. "Is that right?" *Like he knew all along.* "Congratulations."

I nodded, trying to decide if I liked the guy or if I should shoot him. Charisma was his middle name.

He gave me that eye tick and the tooth-suck—so fast most people wouldn't even notice. *But I noticed.* I'd seen similar mannerisms from guys who had seen a lot of action—who'd witnessed a lot of trauma. *Hand tremors, bouncing leg, obsessive blinking, bobbing shoulders.* Little involuntary movements that help relieve stress. Things like the sheriff with his Clint Eastwood squint. Made me wonder what Hearst's real story was.

"Sure," I said, "I'd like some coffee."

5

Max watched as Pilgrim hopped beside him in the car. The old dog plopped down next to him and almost instantly fell into a deep sleep. Max did not sleep. Usually he would, even when he wasn't tired, *like he wasn't tired now,* conserving his energy for when he might need it.

Instead, he watched.

Taking in the sights ... the scents ... everything.

Max did not want to be here. He wanted to be back with Thor and Anna and Petros and Viper.

But here he was.

The cat was still there—the cougar. A kitten for now, but that would quickly change. How long before it would be a threat to his pack? Max didn't know, but he wanted to eliminate the danger before it was too late. Before he lost his children like he had lost his siblings.

The Alpha should know better.

Max knew better.

Max had learned the hard way.

~

By the time we reached the coffee shop, the temperature had dropped considerably. The place was small and local, deserted except for a single barista, and filled with the rich aroma of freshly ground beans. *I love that smell.*

"What'll you have?" asked Hearst. "My treat. Least I can do."

"Do they have tea?" asked Sarah.

"Not that kind of town," said Hearst.

Sarah smiled, shrugging, and gave him her order, *fluffy and sweet and sexy*—just like her. Hearst nodded, giving her the dimple routine. Sarah smiled kindly in return—a little too kindly for my liking. He turned to me.

"Same for you?"

"Black," I said, not smiling, "like my mood."

His eyebrows raised, but he kept the smile. "Dark, but okay."

Sarah and I sat at the rear near a wall and a window, my back protected by the barrier, leaving me a clear field of fire and a view of the outside or approaching danger.

Sarah gave me a look and put her hand on top of mine.

"Everything okay?"

I didn't say anything, just glanced toward Hearst at the counter getting our drinks.

"Are we jealous?"

"No," I said. "Why? Should I be?"

She laughed. "Oh, Gil, you know better. I've been chasing you for years, and now we're a month away from our wedding. No other man means anything to me. No other man ever will." She grinned at me, leaned over, and gave me a peck on the lips. I felt better, but not perfect.

Dimples.

"He is good-looking, though," I said.

She nodded. "I see *you* think so, and yet *I'm* not jealous."

"Funny," I said. "Dimples. Women go crazy for dimples."

"Not me. Weak cheek muscles cause dimples. None of your muscles are weak."

"And what's with the tan? It's winter, for crying out loud."

"Too much sun," she said. "Premature wrinkling."

"Perfect teeth."

"Too perfect," she said, "probably veneers."

"Charismatic," I said, "charming."

"I prefer the strong silent type. Not cocky or arrogant."

"Tall, good build."

She grinned at me. "Now *I'm* starting to get jealous. Stop looking at him."

Hearst came back with our coffees in porcelain mugs.

"Black enough for you?" he asked as I took a sip.

I had to admit it was good—mean and dark and deep—just how I felt.

"It's okay." I took another sip, watching him through the steam as he sat. "What did you want to talk about?"

Hearst smiled at me, then at Sarah. He sat loosely in his chair, completely relaxed, and took a drink before answering. "What did you think of the scene?"

"Of the crime scene?" asked Sarah. "Typical cartel retaliation."

I saw him tick, suck, look at me

"How about you?"

"Is the sheriff involved in some way? His other deputies, maybe?"

Sarah looked at me, surprised.

Hearst took another drink and smiled. "Why would you ask that?"

"He doesn't seem right—not mad enough."

Hearst shrugged. "Seemed upset to me."

"To me, too," said Sarah.

"At us," I said. "At *you,* Hearst. Not at the people who killed one of his men."

The tick and the suck.

"Far as I know, he's clean as snow, but until everything's settled, everyone's a suspect."

"But you think maybe?" I asked.

"I've worked with him a dozen times. Straight as an arrow. But who knows these days? The cartels have more money than the mint, and everyone has their price. The sheriff's got a spotless record, most of his men too, and he's caught more bad guys than I can count. Besides, he wears a white hat. Bad guys don't do that, do they?" He grinned even bigger, the dimples dimpling. "So, no, I don't believe he's turned. But, like I said, who can tell? Besides, it's not always money. There are other forms of leverage. I'll tell you this, though, that six-shooter he wears isn't just for show. I've seen him shoot. Maybe the fastest draw I've witnessed, and I've seen some pros."

"Good to know," I said.

"You've led men," Hearst said. It wasn't a question.

"Why do I get the feeling that you already know all about me? You shouldn't have even known I was coming until I got here."

"Not sure I know what you mean, Boss."

I leaned forward and set my coffee on the table. "I mean, I don't think you work for the DEA or the DOJ."

"Never said I did, Slick. Who do you think I work for?"

"CIA ... maybe some even darker organization ... maybe one I've never heard of."

Hearst raised his eyebrows a notch. "Dark, like your coffee? You *like* it dark, right? Dark doesn't bother you."

"Depends on the *brand* of dark," I said.

He smiled, no teeth showing. "I'm the good brand. The good guys."

"And what do you want from us?"

"I want you to help me stop the bad guys—the guys responsible for that deputy's death. His and a lot of other innocent people."

"That's why we're here," I said. "It's what we're doing."

"I want more ... maybe, anyway."

"More?"

"I want you both on my team ... *maybe*. There's still a little testing to do, but I think you're both solid. And that's a rare thing."

I turned to Sarah. She looked confused.

"He wants us to work for the CIA," I told her. "Or whoever—*whatever* organization he *spooks* for."

"You mean he's a ...," she turned to Hearst, "you're a spy?"

"Not exactly," he said, "but—sort of."

I stepped in. "We're getting married in a month."

"Yes," said Sarah, "yes, we are."

He shrugged again. "Okay, maybe not full-time then. Not just yet, anyway. Let's say part-time, see how it fits."

"No," I said.

"You'd be helping to save lives."

"We already help save lives. It's what we do."

"Small scale," he said. "I'm talking bigger—upper case—world-class scale. Thousands, maybe tens of thousands."

"That's your job," I said.

"Used to be yours too, Staff Sergeant Mason, United States Marine Corps."

"I did my time, played the big game. Now I'm ... *local*. Like Batman protecting Gotham."

"Senator Marsh wasn't in Gotham. He wasn't local. He was very possibly going to be the leader of the free world."

"He came to me," I said.

"And the cartel came here. What's the difference?"

"The difference is that I didn't know what I was getting into when I took the Marsh case."

"And if you hadn't, that little girl—Clair—*Keisha*—the one the big gangbanger kidnapped, she'd be dead. Would you do it differently if you had to do it over again?"

"Like I thought, you do know a lot about me," I said.

He smiled, again showing no teeth, and clicked up something on his phone. He handed it to me.

"Hit play," he said, then looked at Sarah. "You might not want to watch. *He* might not want you to, either."

I looked at her.

"Go ahead," she said.

Hearst handed me a set of earbuds. "Use these."

I almost handed it all back, unseen and unheard, but I didn't. I watched. I listened. It was me from years ago, just after Majoqui Cabrera murdered my wife and daughter—when I was searching him out.

"Where'd you get this?"

He picked up his coffee. "I break the cartels—catch the bad guys. It's what I do. It's what my team does. Sometimes things fall into my hands. Things like that."

I handed the phone and buds back to him. "Are you blackmailing me?"

The tick and the suck. A slight shake of the head.

I said, "Is this what you meant when you said there are other forms of leverage?"

"Just pointing out that *your dark* and *my dark* may be more alike than you think."

"I was a different man back then."

"We're all different men all the time. But you—you are who you are. Local or universal, you are who you are. And we need you. Both of you. The world isn't what it once was. It's not Beaver and Wally or *Father Knows Best* or even *Family Ties*. Now it's cartels and terrorists and bioweapons and nukes. So, I want you to consider this—you think you're local, Batman taking care of his city, but the bad guys, the really, *really* bad guys—they can come anywhere, anytime. And by then, by the time you see the truth and get on board, it could be too late. Even Batman joined the Justice League—Hawkeye, the Avengers. It takes pieces on the board to win the chess match. Without them, we all lose. Individually, the cities, the states, the countries ... the whole wide world." He finished his coffee, set it down, and stood. "You two think on it. Let me know." He pushed the phone back to me. "Keep it. It's not locked, and mine's the only number. It's secure. Just hit the send button, but don't wait too long. The plane leaves zero-dark thirty tomorrow morning."

"Plane? What plane?" asked Sarah.

Hearst grinned at her, showing the teeth and dimples. "The one that leaves in the morning. Get some sleep."

Sarah turned to me. I was about to tell her we'd talk at the hotel when I noticed the car driving slowly down the street toward us. It was beat up and old, rusted green. The windows were open ... *winter ... in Colorado ... the sun close to setting*. That's what first caught my attention. And then it was the four tatted men inside—pointing guns at us.

NATHAN ROAMED through the battered pages of his trusted and true New King James Bible. Five other translations sat on his desk, opened to various passages, each revealing clues to the meaning and guidance for successful marriages.

He set his glasses next to his tea and rubbed the bridge of his nose. There was a touch of pain, a lasting present from the torture he'd suffered at the hands of his kidnappers when Majoqui Cabrera had him taken. Nathan still had trouble with his sinuses, and the doctors said he probably would for the rest of his life. The bone had been badly broken along with the cartilage.

Some injuries couldn't be healed.

Some damages had to be borne and tolerated.

Some scars, a lasting reminder.

The tea was tepid now but still soothing. Nathan was looking for something, but he wasn't exactly sure what. He was looking for something *special*. When officiating Gil and his daughter Joleen's wedding, he used all the best lines about faithfulness, love, and patience. As he began writing this new set of vows, he worried he had already exhausted everything good and unique.

But, of course, that was foolishness. The Bible is like an onion—peel one layer and expose another. The first layer might offer a simple answer to a complex problem, but peel it away, and it reveals a wealth of information, often presenting new questions that require further exploration and understanding.

Nathan thought of when God commanded Abraham to sacrifice his son, Isaac, on Mount Moriah. Throughout the entire Old Testament, God vehemently denounced the sacrificing of children to false gods, stating that it was not only something He had never commanded but also declaring the very thought to be so heinous that it had never entered His mind. Why, then, did He suddenly want Abraham to sacrifice Isaac to Him?

It seemed strange on the surface, but it was a clue from God telling us to investigate—to start digging. Start peeling the onion. And he'd learned over the decades that the reward almost always pointed forward to Jesus. But where to start?

In the case of Isaac, Nathan had begun with God's command, *Sacrifice your first and only son, whom you love.* This command was in complete opposition to other commands, such as, *You shall not worship the Lord your God in that way; for every abomination to the Lord which He hates they have done to their gods; for they burn even their sons and daughters in the fire to their gods.* Nathan looked for other inconsistencies. *Was Isaac Abraham's first and only son?* What about Ishmael?

Nathan then compared Isaac's story to that of Jesus Christ, God's first son—sacrificed. But was Jesus God's first son? What about Adam? Those questions opened doors to the concept of substitution and what God refuses to demand of us, instead taking on the burden Himself. God interrupted the sacrifice of Isaac by providing His own sacrifice—the ram stuck in the thorns. Another incredible metaphor. Then came the question of location. Why Mount Moriah? Mount Moriah—the exact location where Christ would be crucified. The onion unraveling layer upon layer.

The marriage topic was no different—simple on the surface. One man, one woman, joined forever, forming a perfect union, seemingly straightforward. But, like the *Sham-Wow* guy on TV used to say, *wait, there's more.*

Israel is the bride. All through the Bible, God describes her that way. He courts her, woos her, proposes, and marries her. But when she cheats with other lovers, He divorces her. He *puts her away* from Him—something He hates. In fact, God hates divorce so much that He commands that once a man divorces a woman, he can never take her back. But God says He will break His own rule one day and take Israel back. Christ and Israel will one day be reunited. The Body, *Christians,* and the Bride, *Israel,* united for all eternity.

Again, the inconsistency. God commands that it never be done—

like eating flesh and drinking blood. But Christ says to eat His flesh, drink His blood—*a clue once again*. And so, the investigation begins anew. The digging starts—the reward waiting.

In the Book of Proverbs, God says that it is the glory of God to conceal a matter but the glory of kings to search out a matter. Nathan knew he was no king, but if kings could gain glory by digging, he could do no less. Taking another sip of tea, he put his glasses on and returned to his work.

He had wedding vows to write.

6

Max smelled the men, *the danger,* even before he heard the car, noisy as it was. The men were filled with poison —*drugs, alcohol.* They were hunters, and they had come to kill. Pilgrim slept on the seat, totally spent from the search, oblivious to the men or their intent.

Max checked the windows and doors, searching for an avenue of escape to attack, but there was nothing. He had broken through car windows before and could do it again. The side windows were easiest, he'd learned, but it would be difficult to gain the momentum needed with Pilgrim's body in the way. The back windshield was next, but this car had seats rather than a platform, inhibiting his run.

Deciding on the side window above Pilgrim's head and locking his sights on the bottom corner of the glass, he prepared his charge as the first of the men thrust his gun out the window.

Max bunched his muscles and launched forward, the glass shattering outward just as the car came abreast of him, windows open. The men, concentrating on the Alpha, were distracted. Shattered glass showered their faces.

They never even saw him.

~

PULLING MY SMITH &Wesson from its holster along my spine, I shoved Sarah to the floor and aimed at the men in the car. Realizing they had the jump on me, I prepared to take the first rounds, determined to absorb the hits. I wasn't wearing a vest, but I would return fire, killing the men before they could harm Sarah.

In my periphery, I saw Hearst register surprise at my reaction, but he quickly adjusted when he recognized the threat and reached for his gun.

We were both fast, but not fast enough.

They had us.

Only they didn't.

Because Max had them.

~

MAX WENT through his window and into theirs, his giant maw closing on the driver's face, his teeth shattering cheekbone, chin, and jaw. The man screamed, jerking the wheel and crashing into parked cars on his right, canting the angle and spoiling the other men's aim.

The impact whipped Max's hindquarters around and into the steering wheel, snapping it from its mooring and almost breaking his hip. A lesser animal would have lost its grip.

Max did not lose his grip.

He bit harder, splintering bones. The taste of blood flooded his senses, driving him to frenzy. He wrenched back and forth—a shark destroying its prey. The man stopped screaming.

The passenger seated next to him, and the men in the back were gathering themselves, pointing their guns into the front. Max released, then dove into the back, ripping at the rear passenger's throat. The man never had a chance to scream.

His partner, seated beside him in the rear, did have time. Screaming continuously, he repeatedly fired his weapon, hitting his compatriot several times but missing Max entirely. The front seat passenger turned and jammed his gun into Max's side just as the Alpha fired through the coffee shop's plate glass window. The rounds penetrated the windshield of the car at an off angle, catching the man three times in the face and killing him instantly.

Max bit at the gun hand of the last man, crushing his wrist. The man punched Max in the side of the head with his free hand, but because he was seated, he couldn't put his hips into the blow. Even so, it enraged Max further.

This man also had the time to scream. And scream he did.

The Alpha jumped through the shattered shop window and saw that the man still held a gun in what was left of the hand Max was savaging. He shot the man in the head and neck and then again in the head.

Max let the dead man's wrist go, hopped out, and came to a heel at the Alpha's side, scanning for danger.

But the danger, much like the screaming, had passed.

STEVE HEARST WAS IMPRESSED, and he wasn't a man to be easily impressed. What the dog had done and how he had done it—exploding through a closed car window, diving into a passing car, killing the men inside, *without even a command*. And Mason—getting Sarah Gallagher out of the way, shooting and hitting the man through two windows, killing the third man without thought or hesitation. *And that look...*

The look Hearst had seen when Mason turned back to him, his dog at his side, told him everything. Hearst had seen the look before ... sort of anyway. *Battle lust,* the blood madness that overtook some men. Only this time, in Mason, it was somehow more. Deeper, darker —*like Mason's coffee*. It had almost scared Hearst, and again, he wasn't a man to be easily frightened. Perhaps in Mason, it was something more than battle lust—more than *crazy,* even. Hearst had seen his share of both, but this was neither. He couldn't precisely identify what he had seen, but whatever it was, he liked it.

He'd wanted the Gallagher woman on his team because he knew her expertise would be a solid addition to their capabilities, but that was before he saw what he saw. Mason had only been along for the ride, but now he wanted him—the dog, too.

And he would have them.

SARAH SAT NEXT to Gil in the sheriff's office at the Justice Center, a combination of jail, courthouse, crime lab, investigation, and patrol sections. She was still shaking, unaccustomed to the aftereffects of the adrenaline dump that followed a near-death experience.

The office was ornate, featuring a rich leather chair behind a mahogany desk. Several shooting trophies glistened inside a glass display case. Mounted on the wall behind the desk was a gun belt, a Colt Peacemaker, twin to the one the sheriff wore on his hip but fancier due to its pearl handle, tucked in its holster. Silver-tipped .45 cartridges filled the bullet loops on the highly polished leather belt.

The sheriff wanted Pilgrim and Max to be taken and locked up by animal control, but Gil said no. When the sheriff looked like he was going to insist, Sarah was afraid of what Gil would do, but Steve Hearst intervened, and the sheriff backed down.

All three were questioned separately about the incident, but none was required to give a written account—*Steve Hearst again*. Sarah wondered if Gil might be right about him. A Drug Enforcement Agent wouldn't have the pull to account for their treatment.

There had been a gun battle on Main Street.

A car crash.

Men were dead.

"I guess you'll all be staying in my county tonight after all," said the sheriff.

"Just till morning," said Hearst.

"Longer than that," said the sheriff. "There's a lot to sort out."

Leaning against a wall, Hearst shook his head. "You have the story, and we'll be back. Might take a few days, though."

"We're getting married in a...."

The sheriff's head snapped toward Sarah. "Don't even," he said.

Sarah felt Gil react. He didn't tense—not exactly—but there was a *difference* in how his body felt next to hers. *Dangerous.* She feared for the sheriff and put a hand on Gil's knee, hoping to stop him.

Hearst stepped forward. "And you *will* get married, darlin'. Don't you fret about that. We'll have this all cleared up well before then." He turned to the sheriff. "Remember, partner, we're all on the same team. Those cholos were probably the ones who killed your friend. Once the ballistics check out, we'll know for sure. You want Miss Gallagher to run a check on the guns found in their car when we get back, that's fine." He looked to her for confirmation.

Sarah nodded.

Hearst grinned. "All settled then." He turned back to the sheriff. "Now, if you would, I need to talk with them alone."

The sheriff puffed up. "This is my office, my case."

"No argument, sheriff, but you know we have an interest. And you know who *we* are. I can make a call ... *if you want* ... but I'd rather we did this just between us. Like I said, we're all on the same team. And I doubt you're really upset about the bangers who murdered your deputy getting what they deserved. So, let me work this out, and my team will get you justice all around. We just need a few days, that's all."

The sheriff stared at him, at Sarah, at Gil—did his squint thing. "A few days," he said. He jerked his desk drawer open, sending a cascade of loose items to the front, including coins, bullets, and a badge. He pulled out a door keycard and shoved the drawer closed.

Tossing it across the desk to Sarah, he said, "That'll get you into the lab so you can store your evidence." He gave everyone another look and then left the room.

"He's not happy," said Sarah, taking up the keycard.

Hearst grinned at them. "Nice work out there, Ace. Good spotting. Good shooting. And that dog! How is that even possible? Never seen anything like that, not ever."

"Where exactly are we flying?" asked Gil. "And why?"

"Just a little briefing with my team," said Hearst, "for the job. It'll be good for you to get acquainted. You'll like them."

"Again," said Gil, "what job, and where?"

"I'll give you all that when I know you're in and when you need to know."

"You almost got us killed. I think that means you owe us."

"Me?" said Hearst. "They weren't gunning for me. They don't even know I exist. I'm a ghost, a phantom, a wraith. That's how we operate, you know that. Behind the scenes. No, they weren't hunting me—they were hunting you, Mason."

"Why would they be hunting me?"

"The cartels have a long memory," Hearst pointed at the phone he'd given him. "While you were playing with your doggies at the scene today, someone must have recognized you from the video—that or maybe retaliation for Majoqui Cabrera and the massacre on the bridge. Maybe MS-13 was playing footsies with the same cartel operatives responsible for the deputy's death. Either way, it means you're in their crosshairs now." He grinned. "I think you're going with us whether you like it or not."

"The cartels and MS-13 are two different animals," said Gil. "Both Majoqui and the pollo house were MS."

"That's what it looks like from the outside," said Hearst, "but there's plenty of cross-pollination when the money's right. Bees make honey wherever they buzz, Sunshine—hive mentality—very different from how we Americans think and act. But they all swarm and sting the common enemy. Cabrera was working with them way back when he took out your family and they've been doing deals together ever since. Well, until you tossed him off the bridge, that is." He pointed his gun finger at Gil. "You hurt them. Shamed them. They don't forget. They don't stop—not ever. The only way out is to burn them down, and that's what *I'm* all about." Hearst grinned a last time, showing teeth and dimples. "You too, I think. By the way, I cancelled your hotel rooms. I'm not taking a chance on them trying for you again. You're both staying at my base tonight. Your car's already there and I've got a driver and ride waiting for you outside. The plane tomorrow isn't as nice as the one you came in on, but it's free."

"So, where are we going then?"

Hearst winked at him. "I'll tell you tomorrow morning. Be ready at 0600." He stood. "Bring your dogs if you want."

Gil looked to Sarah, then back at Hearst. "Will it be dangerous?"

"Dangerous? Nah. No more than getting a cup of coffee and a free meal at a timeshare seminar." He grinned, dimples dimpling, white teeth shining. "You two get some sleep."

7

Billy, Tina, and Irmgard were playing a heated game of Risk. Billy was demolishing them. He'd already captured all of Europe, Australia, and most of the East. Alaska was next.

They were staying at Gil's house pet-sitting—if you could call it that. Glancing at Thor, staring at him from the corner, Billy had doubts about who was really in charge. Thor wasn't Max, but he wasn't Pilgrim, Viper, Petros, or even Arrow. Thor was *Thor*—very much Max in many ways.

Disturbing ways.

Thor could vanish and appear like Max. He was quiet and fast. But in other ways, he was different. Thor would play. And he wouldn't just attack, he would *think*—sometimes anyway. When he did stop to think, it was scary, almost like he was a person thinking—thinking about whether he was going to kill you or not. Billy could practically see the cylinders turning, like in a revolver during a game of Russian Roulette *—would this be the time the bullet snapped into place?* It was anybody's guess.

Petros was much friendlier. So was Arrow, the puppy Tina kept as Viper's replacement for when Viper eventually retired.

Thor and Petros had played and wrestled for hours after Rick, his interns, and Anna had left.

And then there was the cougar, Atlas. Now, he was a handful. Billy thought Gil might have finally met his match—bitten off a little more than he could chew. Gil had set up a training routine for Billy and Irmgard to follow for Petros, and they'd run all three of the dogs through a ten-minute set just before dinner. Irmgard had wanted to get Atlas out for a set, but Billy had quickly nixed that idea. The only big-cat training he'd ever seen was in a circus, consisting of a chair and a whip, and Billy had no intention of going that route. He'd seen what the baby cougar had done to Gil's house.

Billy watched as Tina placed her little yellow soldiers and cannons on the game board, laughing at Irmgard's comment about the cannons. Tina was so beautiful and so unlike any woman he'd ever been with. He hoped they would last. The thought of them breaking up brought an unaccustomed pain to his heart—another new for him. He'd never worried about his past girlfriends leaving him. If they left, they left. Billy always found another—not that many *had* left.

Billy was the leaver.

Almost always.

But if Tina left?

She was practically a mother to Irmgard. How would it affect her? The thought brought fear to him. Fear and anger. *How much pain would it cause Irmgard?* She'd already lost her mother once—her mother and her father. Could she survive losing another?

Irmgard put on a tough exterior, but Billy knew her in her more vulnerable times—her private times. The times she cried in her sleep and the nights when the dark attacked her like a stalking monster. *Or like a giant wolf.*

And whose fault would it be?

His.

Gil had broached the subject a dozen times, warning Billy that having Tina stay in the same house with them was wrong and dangerous. Knowing Billy's Catholic background, he'd used the Bible as leverage, reasoning that God didn't make rules against participating in physical intimacy outside the bounds of marriage because He was a party poop and didn't want people to have fun. Gil explained that God knows *how* and *what* He made us for, and multiple partners wasn't it—not for our physical bodies or emotional well-being. Gil also brought up the impropriety of their relationship and how it could negatively impact both Tina and Irmgard.

Inevitably, the discussions made Billy mad. He didn't understand why, but they always did, and he would either walk away or wave Gil off. Once, he had even told Gil that if he wanted to continue their friendship, he needed to leave the subject alone. Gil had responded that, as a true friend he couldn't. He'd said that love wouldn't let him —that allowing Billy to continue in behavior that could destroy him, Tina, and Irmgard, without advising against it wasn't love but rather apathy. Gil said he cared too much for them to take the cowardly way out. Billy didn't know how to respond, so he just walked away.

Lately, something else was bothering Billy. Things had seemed *off* with Tina ... even before Elio Colombo had tried to shoot her, hitting Billy instead. Billy didn't think it was their relationship, not exactly, anyway. She seemed to love him and wanted to spend as much time as possible with him, but something was wrong—some internal conflict. Billy didn't think it was the marriage thing. Unlike Gil, she seemed fine with their living arrangement. It was something else, but Billy didn't know what.

Billy's phone buzzed. It was Gil Mason. He answered.

"I could use some help," said Gil.

"Where and when?" Billy didn't even bother with the why.

DOMINIC ELKINS DREW and fired so fast his hands were a blur, and the three shots were like one slightly exaggerated trigger pull. Turning his head casually to the side, a smirk on his lips, his gun still extended downrange, he eyed the skinny, rumpled detective standing next to him.

"What? Did you forget we were shooting for time?" asked the younger police officer. It was nearly nine pm, and they had just finished a joint raid of a drug house. Dominic and his opponent, Sammy Rothstein, the shabby detective next to him, decided to stop at the firing range in the basement of the Gunwood Police Department for a little competition. "I'm taking this as a win. Just because you didn't hit the time mark and didn't draw doesn't toss this. You owe me a steak dinner. I told you I've been practicing."

Sammy pushed his thick glasses back up his nose with one finger, then used the same finger to activate the target silhouette motor so that it slid along its wire back to him.

Four holes were punched in the target, center forehead, a perfect diamond at fifty feet.

Dominic's eyes bugged. He shook his head and activated his own target. Two shots to the chest, slightly high and to the left—one to the face about lip level.

"It was supposed to be three shots," said Dominic.

"I had so much time left over I decided to complete the diamond before holstering."

"Funny," said Dominic. "Man! I've been hitting the range every day for a month. I never even saw you draw your weapon—or put it up. You sure those holes weren't already there?"

Without smiling, Sammy smoothly drew the snub-nosed revolver from its pancake holster on his belt beneath his suit coat, popped the cylinder open with one hand, dumped the four empty casings and two, still loaded, cartridges into the palm of his other hand, and held out the gun for Dominic's inspection. Dominic slid his own gun into its holster and touched the barrel of Sammy's gun with his index finger and thumb. The barrel was warm.

"I can't believe you," said Dominic.

"It's just reflexes and dexterity ... and a little math."

"Oh, yeah, right, that's all."

Sammy tossed the casings, again casually, and all four clanged into the fifty-five-gallon barrel reserved for empties. He thumbed in the other two, along with four fresh bullets, snapped it shut, and made it somehow disappear beneath his coat so quickly Dominic couldn't track it.

"Magic," said Dominic, "it's magic you're using."

Sammy's phone vibrated on his belt. "Detective Rothstein."

He listened, then said, "Text me the location." He listened again. "Dominic Elkins is here with me." More listening, then he clicked off.

"What was that about?" asked Dominic.

"Gil Mason. Used to work with Cherokee County."

"Yeah, my wife knows him."

"Can you get out of work?"

"I'm about to start my three days off. Is that enough?"

Sammy just stared at him, his savant brain working inside his skull. "It's Gil Mason, there's no way to know. But it's good enough to start. Want to have some fun?" Sammy pushed the button, sending the target back down range.

"What kind of fun?" asked Dominic.

Sammy's gun was suddenly in his hand, fire spitting from the barrel—four shots, faster than Dominic could register. The gun vanished again, and he pushed the button. Four new holes formed a cloned diamond, perfectly centered below the first.

"Our kind of fun," said Sammy.

Kirk "Pappy" Sinclair finished a shot of the finest whiskey in the world and set the empty glass on the bar. He took one of the pretzels from the bowl and slipped it to the Malinois puppy sitting obediently next to him. Dan Daley stoically took the snack and chewed it up, not a crumb reaching the floor.

Technically, both Pappy and little Dan were out of bounds. Pappy was a master sergeant, an SNCO (Senior Non-Commissioned Officer), and the E Club (Enlisted Club) was reserved for E5s (Sergeants) and below. That, and Dan Daley was a dog.

A Master Sergeant's insignia consists of three chevrons on top, three rockers below, and crossed rifles in the middle. A Marine Corps sergeant has three stripes up with no rockers below. As a dog, little Dan had no insignias at all, but he had teeth and had already proven he knew how to use them.

Social clubs are separated between officers and NCOs for several reasons. It affords a more stress-free environment between the higher-ups and the lower ranks, and when fights break out, it saves on demotions and time spent in the brig. Dogs are not allowed in either club for reasons of their own, teeth being one of them.

But Pappy craved the simplicity of the Enlisted Men's Club. Truth be told, he'd had never wanted command. He had never wanted anything but the thrill of combat and the camaraderie of his fellow Marines. But year after year, seeing substandard men hungry for power being promoted in rank (often due to politics) and incompetently putting him and his friends in harm's way forced him to seek promotion, for all their sakes. And he'd done his best.

He'd lost men—that was a part of war—a part of being a Marine that could not be helped. But he'd never failed a mission and had less loss of life, *on their side at least,* than any SNCO he'd ever worked with. Marines fought to be under his command. The kind of men who were here in the Eclub. In comparison, the Officer's Club was boring —like the Corps itself in peacetime. There were no American wars going on, not officially, anyway. Life in the Marines was reduced to training and classes.

Pappy looked down at Dan, or DD, as he often thought of him, after the comic book character Dare Devil. *He was certainly that*—and Pappy was thankful for him. Fearless. Forty pounds of sheer power and still growing. And so obedient. Tell him once, show him once, and Dan had it.

What a war machine he was turning into.

Pappy wished his Marines could be so sharp. The officers would never allow the dog to stay, and so, the NCO club instead of the other.

Besides, things tended to get rowdier here than at the O Club, and rowdy was what he was looking for just now—noise, drinks, fights.

What more could a Marine ask for?

A big Black guy pushed up to the bar, bumping into him. Six-four, broad-shouldered, lean hips, muscles on his muscles. He gave Pappy a once over, a little too drunk to take notice of the dog. "You might want to watch yourself gramps." His words were slurred, his eyes drooping.

Pappy gave him a grin and signaled to the bartender. "Another," he said, "and one for my new friend here."

Pappy felt a rumble from Dan resonate through his thigh, where the puppy rested his head. It wasn't quite a growl—more like an earthquake deep beneath the earth's surface.

"You don't even know what I'm drinking, old man."

Pappy gave him a wink, gently rubbing the dog's smooth dome. "After this, you'll never want to drink anything else again."

"You don't know me."

"Don't have to," said Pappy. "I know Marines, and I know the drink."

Two of the man's friends came up behind him, sensing a fight brewing, one Black, one White, both nearly as big. Neither of them noticed Dan either. The bartender set out two glasses of Pappy Van Winkle. The Marine picked up the glass and tilted it as if about to throw it into Pappy's face, the universal first punch in every bar fight in the history of bar fighting.

Pappy stopped him by placing a finger against the hand holding the drink. "Before you do anything rash, I want you to know that that's the best whiskey in the world and costs more than you make in a week. My advice to you is that you drink it, and we become friends. Otherwise, the night won't go well for you."

The Marine stood up, his chest puffed out, still holding the glass. He swayed, but only a fraction. Dan Daley tensed beside Pappy, ready to strike. Pappy rubbed his head gently, telling him it wasn't time, not yet anyway.

The Black Marine, who stood behind the Marine with the drink, gripped his buddy's shoulder. "Hey, hey Maurice, I know this guy. He's Pappy Sinclair."

At first, Maurice ignored his friend, but recognition began to work its way through the alcohol. "Master Sergeant Sinclair?"

"That's him," said his friend.

Pappy sighed. "No ranks here, Marines, not right now anyway. Not as far as I'm concerned."

"You don't look like so much to me," said Maurice. "Not like all the stories."

Pappy nodded. "Just an old man wanting to spend time with real men ... real Marines."

"Pappy Sinclair, Maurice." said the friend. "Don't be stupid. Drink the drink."

Maurice looked down at his friend. "He done put his rank on the table—said it don't apply."

The White friend, on his other side, spoke up. "Pappy Sinclair from that street battle we had in Kabul in 2018. If it hadn't been for him and his guys, me and a bunch of my buddy tankers would be dead. Drink it, Maurice."

"You think you tell me what to do?"

"He's also the guy who rescued Dashawn and Terrance in Fallujah when they were pinned down. Drink it," said his friend on the other side. "Or I'll punch you myself."

"Oh, you think so?"

"I'll punch you too," said the White friend.

Maurice looked back and forth between them, then at Pappy.

Dan Daly growled a cold rumble that vibrated through the floor and the air and into the drunk Marine. He looked down at the dog and saw his teeth and his eyes—those eyes—unflinching. Maurice was a little drunk, *but not that drunk*. He looked at the whiskey in his hand, drank, then held the glass out.

"Okay then," said Maurice, "that *is* the best drink I've ever had. I apologize, Master Sergea...."

Pappy stopped him. "Pappy," said Sinclair. "No ranks, remember?"

Maurice grinned. "Nice looking dog. Pappy it is. Pleased to meet you. Now that we're all introduced and friendly like, how about another round of that?"

Pappy looked at the gyrenes, shrugged, grinned, and motioned at the bartender. "Set 'em up." It was going to be an expensive night.

His cell vibrated. Gil Mason was calling.

It might be an even longer night than he'd planned. He'd need to find someone to watch little Dan for a few days.

8

Anthony Carlino had just pulled the covers over his chest and put on his reading glasses, ready to relax with a few pages of his book before drifting off to sleep. It was a ritual he'd begun with his wife decades earlier and made him feel close to her now that she was in Heaven. The book was *Tai-Pan* by James Clavell. He'd finished *Shogun* a week ago, opening a new world to him. Anthony was no fan of mysteries or police procedurals. *They always made the cops the good guys.* The thought made him snort.

It was guys like Anthony who made the world turn. The characters in Clavell's books seemed to understand that truth. It wasn't law and order or following rules—rules made by politicians who didn't follow them—that mattered. What decided the fate of the world was what went on in secret—deals, collaborations, and machinations. The gooks in Clavell's books understood this.

Not to mention, they were as clannish and tribal as the most hardcore Sicilian. They thought of all other races as dogs like the Jews used to—maybe still did. After all, God Himself referred to all other nations as dogs. That was before the Church, of course. The Church changed everything. Now, everyone was a dog in God's eyes

—*all the same*. At least until they decided, each for themself, to kiss the Don's ring. To come under His rule.

Respect.

The Asians in Clavell's books *got it*. Not the God part maybe, but the respect part. And the secrecy part. Oh, they were a sneaky lot, all right. Plans within plans within plans, sometimes taking generations to complete.

Anthony loved it.

The only thing he found wanting about *Shogun* was the lack of a great battle at the end. The book was as thick as the Encyclopedia Britannica, every page leading toward a giant fight at the end, and then—*nothing*. No blood, no fight.

Anthony liked action in books, and there had been plenty, so he was expecting the mother of all fights. But no, just a quick recounting of who won and how. *Sheesh*. Still, it was a great read. He and his late wife discussed it for hours and days. She didn't mind the lack of a good fight at the end. Liked it better, actually. That's how she was. For her, it was all about the relationships.

Bella didn't *really* talk to him—not in words—but she did in his heart. They'd been together for so long and were so close that Anthony knew exactly what she would say, even down to her tone. And so, they discussed everything they read. Not that they always agreed, but that was okay, maybe even better than if they did. The disagreements led to debates and discussions, and those led to understanding. Sometimes about the books, but more often and more importantly about each other. These discussions, where neither tried to prove a point but simply gave an honest opinion of how they understood what was written, allowed them to share their innermost thoughts and feelings in a very non-threatening way.

Bella never liked when he called other races names like *slopes* or *gooks*, but the guys in Clavell's books got it. They called Whites like himself the worst names imaginable. Who cared? Sticks and stones. The youth of today could take a page from that book. Besides, Anthony knew it was never the words that made for offense—it was the intent behind the words.

You could call a guy sir, or even Don, with a big smile plastered on your face, but the eyes—*oh, the eyes.* Those told the intent. Anthony had guys killed for what their eyes revealed. And he'd never been wrong. Not about that. The soul always showed through.

Slurs themselves could sometimes infer respect. Anthony admired the Asians in *Tai-Pan*. They were masters at the art of deception, the trade of guile, the architecture of deceit. They were a different kind of warrior. The characters in *Shogun* were samurai and emperors. In *Tai-Pan,* they were businessmen and politicians. All equally deadly in their own right.

If Anthony was still Don, he thought he'd like the chance to move in on the Asian markets. The Asians would have all the advantages—they'd been there from the beginning, had all the contacts, all the leverage, all the power.

What a battle it would be.

But those dreams were for a younger man. Anthony's time had passed. Now, it was Nick's time. He thought about encouraging Nick to read the books—at least the three—maybe even *King Rat*. That one was different, of course, focusing more on the American POWs rather than their Japanese guards in World War II, but the intertwining concepts and human truths were still basically the same.

Anthony had read Sun-Tzu's *The Art of War* about a year ago. His adopted son, Elio Colombo, had given it to him. He wished he'd read it when he was young. It would have made his rise to power easier. Tzu's wisdom in warfare set Anthony on a quest to read *Gai-Jin*, *Shogun,* and *Tai-Pan*.

His cell buzzed on the end table next to him. Setting his book aside, he picked up the phone and read the name.

Gil Mason.

~

NATHAN WOKE up and found himself still sitting in his recliner after leaving his desk hours earlier. He'd dozed. Glancing at his watch, he saw that it was nearly eleven. Stretching, he rose, picked up his cup, and went to the kitchen. He thought about drinking another cup of tea but knew he'd never get to sleep if he did, so he searched the refrigerator instead.

Having fallen asleep in the *narcolepsy chair* before dinner, he now felt hunger gnawing at him. He peeled a drumstick from the rotisserie chicken he'd gotten the day before, grabbed a cheese stick, poured a glass of water, and added a few ice cubes. Snagging a napkin on his way back to the chair, he sat down, put on his reading glasses, and picked up his Bible.

Where had he left off?

Oh yes, the *Bride* and the *Body*. Israel, the *Bride,* and Christians, *the Body of Christ*. God temporarily set Israel aside in the book of Acts, just as Jesus had warned in Luke 13:6-9 through the parable of the barren fig tree. But one glorious day in the future, there would be a reuniting of the two—a wedding. The old Heaven and Earth would eventually be wiped away, culminating in the creation of the new Heaven and Earth.

In some respects, it would be like this for Gil and Sarah. Their old lives—living alone, without love—would end. Their new lives—living as one, filled with love for one another—would begin.

Living as one, filled with love for one another ... that was the most accurate example he could think of for living sin-free lives. We wouldn't achieve this by following rules or commandments enforced by fear and willpower. No, it would come willingly because of our love for one another—the law of love realized.

Nathan set the book down, removed his glasses, and ate for a few minutes, pondering.

He missed Joleen, his daughter.

He missed Marla.

He knew they would both be happy for Gil and would be thankful to Sarah for helping alleviate his pain and loneliness. But still, he missed them. He missed them so terribly. It was like that sometimes, the pain sneaking up, trying to swallow him whole. The only thing that comforted him in these times was the knowledge that he would see them again and spend eternity with them. It was as though they had traveled to a faraway country that he had no access to, for now at least. But one day, the restrictions would be lifted, and he had only to be patient, to wait for that wonderful day.

His thoughts returned to the metaphor of the Bride and the Body. These reminded Nathan of other metaphors he had considered earlier in the night. The bread of life—*Jesus' flesh*—symbolizing His body that satisfies eternally. The wine—*Jesus' blood*—representing His sacrificial blood that cleanses us of sin. Jesus' first public miracle, turning water into wine, beautifully foreshadowed Jesus as the living water becoming the blood that would save us. Similarly, Moses' first public miracle, turning the water of the Nile to blood, symbolized what Jesus would one day do—sacrificing His own flesh and blood to save us.

Nathan closed his eyes in awe as he reflected on these things. All of history, the *Word* itself, *His-Story,* as written in the Bible—all pointing to Him—pointing to Jesus. Jesus, the blood, and the bread.

When Joseph, Jacob's son, was imprisoned in Egypt, he was housed with the Pharaoh's cupbearer and baker. The cupbearer represents the wine, the blood of Christ, while the baker represents the bread, the body of Christ. And what did Joseph say to the cupbearer as he was released from prison? *Remember me*—just as Jesus says at the last supper—*Do this in remembrance of Me.* The baker was hanged, showing that the flesh would die, while the cupbearer was freed, demonstrating that Christ's blood would set us free.

Nathan recounted Abraham's willingness to sacrifice his son Isaac on Mount Moriah. *There was so much more to that story.* God stopped Abraham at the last second by providing the sacrifice Himself, a ram whose head was caught in the thorns. Likewise, Barabbas, the murderer, was pardoned, while Jesus, a crown of thorns on His head, took his place—*our place.*

Mount Moriah, the mountain where God Himself provided a sacrifice in the place of Isaac, just as He told Abraham He would, was the very same mountain where Jesus was crucified in our place. Our God—what a wonderful, loving Father.

Nathan finished eating his dinner and went back to work.

He had wedding vows to write.

~

MAX STALKED the boar for nearly an hour. It was easy to track, but he had to be careful. The animal was enormous, at least two hundred pounds, with jutting tusks on either side of its face.

And it was aggressive.

Max had seen it kill a good-sized fox earlier—first goring it and then ripping it to pieces and eating it, leaving only a few bones and scraps of fur. The fox had had no chance against such a monster.

Max was not a fox.

He had never killed a boar. Never even seen one, but it smelled good, and he was hungry.

How to kill it?

The creature had no discernible neck, and the skull looked too massive and thick to crush.

Hamstrings?

Attacking its hamstrings would cripple, but not kill it. Still, once it was down, it would be far less dangerous, easy prey for hit-and-run tactics. The intestines would be fair game, and once the beast bled out enough, it would weaken so that Max could finish the job and eat. He would just need to be careful to stay away from those tusks—otherwise, it might be *his* intestines spilled on the ground.

The boar stopped in its tracks, snout lifting high in the air, scenting. Its head turned, eyes staring directly at Max, hiding behind a scramble of dead bushes. Incredibly, the boar had caught his scent, even downwind. The monster charged.

Max charged back.

9

"So, what do we do?" asked Sarah. We were in her room at the barracks. The base was small by military standards—a scattered assembly of planes, jets, jeeps, trucks, and thirty or so buildings. I estimated there to be no more than two hundred personnel. I hadn't spotted a name for the base—not anywhere—and the buildings I'd seen so far were all designated by numbers alone.

Sarah and I were housed in building eleven. We had separate but identical rooms right next to each other. The whole setup screamed clandestine operation. I recalled that the main character in the TV show *Stranger Things* was named Eleven. She'd been housed in a secret government laboratory in the desert, too. Coincidence?

I had worked numerous ops with Marine Corps Intelligence, several with the Drug Enforcement Agency (DEA), and even a couple with the FBI, but I'd never worked with the CIA before. I was pretty sure that was who we were dealing with in Hearst. This raised a lot of questions.

What did the CIA have to do with a dead deputy on the outskirts of Pueblo, New Mexico?

How had they come across a video recording of me taking out an MS-13 gangbanger years ago?

And what did Hearst really want with me and Sarah?

I had no idea, but I knew we were being kept in the dark for a reason. And I didn't like being kept in the dark. It wasn't that I didn't trust secret government agencies—it was just that … *I didn't trust secret government agencies.* I also didn't like the idea that they had gotten Sarah involved. That was why I'd made the calls.

"We play along … for now," I said.

"What does that mean?" asked Sarah.

"We go with Hearst tomorrow—see what's what. Then we decide whether to stick it out or bail."

Sarah shook her head. "So, who exactly is Hearst?"

"CIA, probably. That or another secret squirrel organization. But yeah, my money's on the CIA. Smells right to me."

"But I thought they couldn't work within the boundaries of the United States."

"Right," I said, "because secret government entities are known for following rules."

"That sounds cynical," said Sarah. "You were in the military, remember?"

"I still am … technically, anyway … on inactive status. Which is why I'm confident in that of which I speak."

Sarah gave a wry smile. "Oh, and aren't we proper?"

I grinned back. "Always." I was sitting on Sarah's bunk. She came over and sat next to me.

"Promise me we are getting married next month," she said, resting her head on my shoulder.

"I promise."

"Really?"

"Really. I won't let anything stop us."

"Not even the CIA?"

"Not even the whole government."

"Thank you," she said quietly.

"I love you," I said.

"I love you," she said, raising her head and kissing me softly.

I returned to my room and gave Pilgrim a bowl of dry dog food supplied by a soldier in a green jumpsuit devoid of military designation. I'd let Max out when we arrived, but there was still no sign of him. I hoped he hadn't killed everyone on the base. I thought it might come to that, but it would be a bit premature at this point.

In the morning, maybe.

I had work to do, so I took my go-bag and went looking for him. I wanted to bring him with me.

Outside, I noticed the towers, the lights, and the guns. It reminded me of a handful of bases I'd been to around the world. It also brought back memories of the OTA's compound—a nasty case I'd been involved in recently, which had also included my old friend Pappy Sinclair.

One of the men I'd called earlier in the night.

Max and I had an errand to perform. A secret errand. The kind that fit perfectly with the current Area 51-like surroundings. Of course, keeping my activities secret would require ... *secrecy*.

Whistling, I called for Max. I did it the old-fashioned way—thumb, index finger, lips, and teeth. The whistle was loud and high and carried much farther than my voice or Max's e-collar remote. I'd already tried the e-collar, but Max hadn't returned, therefore the whistle.

As to be expected, the base was surrounded by ten-foot chain-link fencing topped with razor wire, making it impossible for Max to escape or return unnoticed. There were also the guard towers, lights, and guns. I walked about fifty feet from building eleven and looked around. Nothing. No movement, not even a bald little girl with psychic powers. Only the darkness and the sounds of the desert.

And then, I waited.

It didn't take long.

~

MAX HEARD THE WHISTLE, finished gulping down a thick chunk of boar meat, tore another loose, gave it the same treatment, and then turned to join the Alpha. The rest of the carcass would not go to waste—Max knew that. He had heard the scavengers surrounding him. He smelled them.

They didn't dare move in while Max was present, but now that he was gone, they would converge on the meat, fighting amongst themselves to take what they could. It would be a feast.

And that was okay. Max had eaten enough.

The Alpha needed him.

Maybe they were going home—back to Thor—to Thor, Petros, Arrow, Viper, and the others. That was where Max wanted to be.

The boar had been easier to subdue than Max had initially thought. Going for the hamstrings had been the right move. In out, in out, so fast the wild pig never had a chance—although it tried.

Once it was down, Max realized he'd been wrong. The boar did have a neck—and, more importantly, a vulnerable throat. Although the creature could easily kill lesser animals, it had proved no danger at all to Max.

10

And there he was, materializing as if from nothingness, right in front of my eyes. As often as he'd played this trick, you'd think I'd be used to it, but inside, it still kind of scared me.

"You didn't scare me," I said. "I saw you coming a mile off."

Max didn't say anything. Then I noticed the blood. There was a lot of it.

"Who did you kill?"

Max just licked his lips, which was pretty gross. I shook my head. "How did you get off the base?"

He licked his lips again. I felt a little queasy, like when I went too many rounds on the Tilt-A-Whirl at Elitch's.

"No, really," I said. "I need to get past the gates, so how did you do it?"

He just stared.

Shaking my head, I turned and started walking. "Come on."

There were unmarked military cars parked up ahead. Having done a little scouting, I decided the only way to get to my Uber was on foot, but I'd need transportation just to get near the fencing—the base was that big. I'd taken note of the name of the road on the way in and called to get picked up, but we didn't have much time.

"And don't get blood all over everything. Real people pay for these vehicles with their hard-earned tax dollars."

Max burped, but he stayed beside me, eyeing for things to kill.

I picked the most nondescript car I could find, which wasn't hard since there wasn't much variety. It took me about fifteen seconds to jimmy the lock and another minute to hot wire the ignition. When I was comfortably seated inside, I looked back and saw a wide, bloody streak across the vinyl backseat. Max lay beneath it, facing me with a blank expression.

"Funny," I said. "You're going to clean that up."

Again, he didn't say anything.

Talk about frustrating.

I drove to an empty stretch of fence and slipped my wire cutters from my go-kit, along with a zip-lock bag containing a bunch of alligator clips attached to wires attached to other alligator clips. At the fence, I sectioned off a rough square about four feet by four feet with the clips and wires. I wasn't sure if the fence was equipped with touch sensors, but I thought it could be, this being a secret *Area 51-type* base and all. The surroundings kind of made me wonder if there were aliens stashed nearby. A picture of a dying ET holding a glowing finger up to a broken-hearted Elliott came to mind.

Next, I cut just inside the square with my trusty wire-snips, the clips and wires shorting the area outside the hole back to each other so there would be no break in the electric field's continuity. Most people unfamiliar with electricity think a *short* is a break between two wires, but that's referred to as an *open*, meaning no electricity can move past or through that break. A *short* is when two wires come together, or weak insulation allows two paths of electricity to merge, causing the current to flow along a different path or the same path but with too much strength, causing things to blow—*resistors, capacitors, fuses, transformers ... bigger things.*

I was trying to trick the sensors into thinking there was no newly cut hole in the fence by ensuring the electrical circuit remained intact, with no break detected. The fencing itself was not electrified—I'd already checked.

From there, I had Max jump through the gap. I followed. Fifteen minutes later, I was at the road. Fifteen minutes after that and farther down the road, the Uber showed up. It was a red 2020 SUV.

"Dude," said the man, who looked to be in his thirties, wearing a down vest and long-sleeved plaid shirt and jeans. He was White, had a thick black beard, wide shoulders, and wore a baseball cap. "I thought this was a prank. I almost didn't take it. But I love this area. I've seen all kinds of weird things out this way. Once, I saw three blue lights just whizzing around out here. People said it was probably drones, but it didn't look like drones. Looked like lightning, or those balls of blue fire the anime guys throw around." He stopped talking, turned his head in every direction, then asked, "Hey, where'd you come from?"

I considered pointing up to the sky but thought the guy might freak and leave me where I stood. "Got in a fight with my girlfriend, and she kicked me out of the car," I lied smoothly. Max had wandered off about ten minutes ago but suddenly returned out of the night, stalking slowly toward us, illuminated in the penumbra of the Uber's headlights.

"Hey! *Hey!*" cried the Uber guy, pointing toward Max. "What's that—what's that? A chupacabra?"

"Easy," I said, "it's just my dog."

"Your dog? What kind of a chick kicks a guy *and* his dog out in a creepy place like this?"

"A woman scorned," I said with a half grin. I could see he was on the verge of running. *Couldn't blame him.* Chupacabras have that effect on people. *Max would probably have that effect on chupacabras.* "But you're right," I said, "it is creepy out here. Mind if we go?"

"No, no, that's cool. Your—*uh*—*dog*—he potty trained?"

"Sure," I said.

"Is he—is he safe?"

The way he said it reminded me of the 1976 Dustin Hoffman movie *Marathon Man*, where Laurence Olivier's character, Christian Szell, tortures Hoffman using dental tools and repeatedly asks, 'Is it safe?' I felt as confident as the in-the-dark Hoffman when he answered, *"Yes, it's safe. It's very safe. It's so safe you wouldn't believe it. No, it's not safe. It's ve-very dangerous. Be careful."*

"Oh yeah," I said, "yeah, Max is very safe. Sure he is. There is nothing to worry about. Nothing at all." Something in my tone made the driver's eyes shift to Max.

"You sure he's not a chupacabra? I seen one not far from here once. Smaller than him, but not as nasty looking."

Max canted his head, the lights reaching deep into the soul of the animal as they do at night—*in the dark*—sparking green-red. The guy visibly shivered and stepped back, his hands moving up toward his mouth as if to stifle a scream.

"Better not to show fear," I said. "They can sense fear. Animals, I mean—dogs, cats ... whatever."

He looked at me. I gave him a twitch of the lips and a wink.

"Let's go," I said. I opened the door for Max, and he hopped silently into the back. I closed the door and went to the passenger side. "Mind if I ride up front with you?" The driver just nodded, and we both got in.

He adjusted the mirror so that he could watch Max. Max watched him back. The driver shuddered again and turned the mirror so he couldn't see him anymore. He looked back at me.

"Did ... did you see anything weird while you were waiting out there?"

Looking away, I nodded slowly. I was having too much fun now that I was inside the car and no longer in danger of being left on the road in the dark. "Some." I turned back to face him.

"Like what?" he almost whispered.

I gave him another twitch of the lips and turned away from him toward the window and the night. "Things you wouldn't understand. Things you *couldn't* understand," I turned back to him, lowered my eyebrows and my voice, "Things you *shouldn't* understand."

"Okay, okay," he said, looking away from me and stepping on the gas. He didn't say another word or even glance at me for the rest of the trip.

Again ... couldn't blame him.

~

THE JET TOUCHED down just before zero three hundred (three o'clock in the morning), and all my friends were there. Anthony Carlino had worked out all the logistics and handled everything. The mafia was, above all else, efficient.

They all carried their go-bags. Pappy extended a hand.

"Thanks for coming, Pappy," I said.

"Miss a Gil Mason shindig? Not happening."

"Did you all have a chance to get acquainted on the flight down?" I asked.

Billy walked up. "We did," he said. "We walking into WW III?" he asked.

"I'm not sure, exactly, but I like to be prepared."

Billy, Pappy, Billy's buddy Montgomery Byrne, Sammy Rothstein, and Dominic Elkins were all there. That made six of us … and Max, of course. The Uber driver stood outside his SUV watching as we talked. He looked scared. I'd taken the keys when we arrived … just in case. Everyone piled in.

"Back to where you picked me up, Jeeves," I said, checking my watch. "And an extra hundred dollars if we make it before zero four hundred."

"You guys," he stuttered, "you're—you're *ours*, right? I mean, you're not like aliens or anything, right?"

"You really think aliens would be shuttling around in a G5?" I asked with a grin. "That's your government tax dollars at work, my friend."

"You're military?" he asked.

"Way higher than military."

"Who are you here to kill?"

"Well, it ain't chupacabras."

He pointed up toward the ceiling, reaching toward the stars beyond. "You mean …?"

"Let's just say those blue lights weren't lightning balls or drones and that you won't have to worry about them after we're done, okay?"

The Uber driver turned toward the windshield, nodded, and stepped on the gas.

And, with plenty of time to spare, he made himself a hundred dollars.

11

Steve Hearst stood outside the barracks wearing a green jumpsuit and a bemused smile.

"Want to tell me what's going on here and why there are civilian trespassers on my top-secret government Air Force Base?"

I smiled back at him. "Given that there have been attempts on both my fiancé's life and mine since we met, and since you want to remain cryptic about our roles, I decided to invite a few friends to join us on this little field trip.

"Is that right?"

"That's right."

Hearst sucked a tooth, ticked an eye. He walked up and down, surveying the group assembled behind me, then stopped in front of Kirk Sinclair. "Pappy, good to see you."

"Steve," said Pappy, nodding his head. "Recruiting?"

"Trying to. He's not making it easy."

Pappy chuckled. "Gil never does. He won't go for it, so you're wasting your time."

"I remember when they said the same thing about you promoting."

"I suppose that's true," said Pappy. "You made a tactical error, though."

Hearst nodded. "The soon-to-be Mrs. Mason?"

Pappy held his hands out. "You never should have put her in danger."

"I didn't intend to. Things just took a turn."

"The kind of things you're involved in have a tendency to do that."

"It's the job," said Hearst.

Pappy shrugged. "I suppose so. Good luck with that."

"Thanks. I did get off to a bad start though, maybe it's not too late to fix it." Hearst turned to me. "Suppose we leave the beautiful Miss Gallagher behind today? I'm sure she can keep herself busy at the sheriff's office working on the evidence she collected. Would that square things between me and you?"

I nodded. "It might help—for today at least. Doesn't in any way obligate me to join up with you, though."

"Not at all, Sport. I got a feeling the mission itself will take care of that." He eyed the line of men. "Who else you got here?"

"You don't know?" I asked.

"Humor me," said Hearst.

"That's Bill, Dom, Sam, Montgomery ... and Pappy, whom you seem to know already."

"And you called for them ... why?"

"They're fighting men, and somehow, I get the idea we're going into a fight."

Hearst nodded. "Soldiers I've got."

"Yeah, but these guys I trust."

"You can trust me, Mason. Don't you know that yet?"

"I'm not sure what I know. You're a hard man to read."

Hearst grinned. "I take that as a compliment. Unfortunately, they can't come. They haven't been vetted—except for Pappy there. Him I know."

"Don't give me that," I said. "I don't have clearance. Neither does Sarah."

"I'm making an exception for you."

"Then make one for them too."

"It doesn't work like that," said Hearst.

"I have a feeling it works exactly like that. Either they come, or I don't go."

"Fine, you can all stay here—go home even. I'll take Miss Gallagher instead. She's who I wanted in the beginning anyway."

"Not gonna happen," I said, and something in his voice had changed—something in his voice and something in his eyes.

Hearst saw the same look he'd seen after the fight with the gang-bangers. He scratched at his hairline, ticked the eye, sucked at the tooth. "Alright, they can come. We'll probably see minimal action anyway. But if it gets worse, whatever happens to them is on you."

"I accept that," I said.

"Okay," said Hearst, "let's get your police officers and Mafia hit men on board and start this party rolling." Just then, a long van pulled up to them as if perfectly timed. "Oh, and where's your dog?"

I was a little taken aback that Hearst knew Dominic and Sammy were cops and Billy and Montgomery were Carlinos, telling me I'd been played all along. I'd decided to leave Pilgrim in his barracks, with instructions for his military aid to give him breaks and take care of his food and water.

"He's close," I said. "I'll need a minute to tell Sarah."

"She left for town about ten minutes ago."

Hearst was full of surprises, but now it was my turn. As Hearst waved a hand toward the van, his fingers swept across furry ears. Jumping back, he saw Max sitting just in front of him, eyes staring into his. For maybe the first time since they met, I noticed the grin was nowhere to be seen. Not the grin or even the dimples.

Hearst suddenly looked ten years older. I didn't think he was used to being surprised—sort of made up for my feeling played.

~

SARAH ENTERED the Baros County Sheriff's Office bracketed by two men Steve Hearst had assigned to her for security. Both men were lean and fit and wore ordinary clothes. No weapons were visible, but their eyes never stopped scanning. Knowing Gil the way she did told her these men either were, or very recently had been, soldiers. Elite soldiers.

Still, Sarah would have felt safer with Gil—not that she was in any real danger. After all, she was entering a Sheriff's Office where she would be surrounded by plenty of law enforcement personnel and lots of guns. However, she couldn't help but think of the scene in *Terminator* where Arnold breaks in, slaughtering everyone while looking for Sarah Connor.

Sarah Conner ... Sarah Gallagher ... coincidence?

In her mind, she could see Gil shaking his head at her silliness. These were the guys in white hats. Territorial, yes. Good old boy network, dripping with machismo and testosterone, absolutely. Still, they were all on the same side.

But was that really true?

After all, Sarah herself was mixed up with the Mafia. She was also a murderer—a fact she continuously fought to push out of her mind so that she could function. She was getting married in less than a month and would allow nothing to get in the way—not even her own guilt. After the wedding, she planned to spend the rest of her life making up for what she'd done by being the best wife possible for Gil. He deserved it. He deserved the best of her, and that's what she would bring to him. He'd saved her so many times already.

The night of the sexual assault flashed through her thoughts, making her physically wince—the horror, the feeling of absolute helplessness, the gritty reality of what that monster did to her. Unable to suppress the shudder that racked her, she struggled not to throw up. Sarah hadn't even thought of the attack in weeks—why now?

You know why.

Yes—yes, she knew. It all linked back to Gail Davis.

Guilt.

The guilt she felt from the sexual assault. Unreasonable, she knew, but still there. The guilt she felt over the murder. Reasonable, unavoidable, ever-present. But she would put it all behind her. Gil would help her do that. He would save her this one last time.

A deputy sitting behind a bulletproof glass shield buzzed Sarah and her bodyguards into the back hallway, and there stood Sheriff Matt Adams, all six feet five inches and nearly three hundred pounds of him. He was impressive and intimidating. Sarah felt a twinge of guilt flush her cheeks as if this man of the law could see right through her façade to the horror hidden deep inside.

"Where's your boyfriend?" He gave her a once over, but not in the way Sarah was accustomed to. Most men swept her with lustful or admiring glances. This, she thought, seemed fatherly, as if checking for injuries. Somehow, it put her more at ease, a thing for which she was thankful.

"He's off doing things with Steve Hearst," she said.

"I thought you were both going."

"So did I. Last-minute change, I guess."

"Where?"

"Nobody told me—just that I was needed here and that I should start analyzing the evidence."

The sheriff eyed her two bodyguards. "You guys staying all day or heading back?"

The one on the left spoke up. "If she's staying inside, we can go until she's ready for a ride back. If she needs to leave for lunch or anything else, we need to be with her."

Sheriff Adams looked at Sarah. "I can have food brought in. If you need to smoke, we've got a recreation yard attached to the jail. Up to you."

Sarah smiled and shook her head. "I don't smoke, and I'm fine eating lunch here. I'll call when I'm done. Might be late, though."

"At your service twenty-four seven, ma'am," said one of the men. "You sure you don't need us to stay?"

"How many deputies are in the building?" Sarah asked the sheriff.

"Off and on, ten or more patrol. Another thirty jail deputies and ten or so detectives—and me, of course."

"Close to fifty altogether," said Sarah, "and the sheriff himself. I think I'll be fine, thank you."

A flash of Arnold Schwarzenegger robotically sweeping through the police station, killing everyone in sight, crossed her mind again, making her wonder if she should keep the bodyguards after all.

But, of course, that was silly, she thought as the two men walked away.

12

The C130 was huge—it isn't called Hercules for nothing—but it wasn't as luxurious as the Carlinos' G5. And it was loud. So loud it rattled the bones. We left from the airbase where we were lodging and a few hours later landed in California, again on an air base—another secret one. *How many secret bases are there, and how do they keep them secret?* I could almost hear *The X-Files* music theme.

Steve Hearst had his men usher me and my friends into a hangar where about twenty other elite military guys were kitted out, milling around, getting coffee and water, and shooting the breeze, apparently waiting on us. Behind a podium was a large monitor hooked up to a computer. I guessed we were in for a mission briefing—*so much for just meeting Hearst's guys.* I was suddenly thankful Sarah wasn't here.

"Look familiar?" asked Pappy. He handed me a cup of coffee, black of course.

"Just like old times," I said. "You seem pretty tight with Hearst."

"Not really. I've worked with him a few times, back when he was a Seal, and later after he started doing whatever it is he actually does now. Spook stuff, but I don't know who for. He's a good pilot though, I can tell you that."

Pappy took a sip, steam rising. "This would be a lot better with some whiskey in it."

"Any idea where we're going?"

Pappy chuckled. "You can read the signs as good as me. We're practically at the border, and after what happened with you at the restaurant and what you told me about the dead deputy, I guess you can dope it out."

Same old Pappy.

"Yeah," I said. "I've seen *Sicario* about a thousand times. Never expected to be here with Thanos himself, *living* it though."

"Thanos?" asked a puzzled Pappy.

"Yeah, you know. Josh Brolin? *Avenger's Infinity War* and *End Game*?"

"What are you talking about, Mason?"

"No! You can't be serious. Two of the greatest movies of all time."

"What? Those stupid comic book guys flying around in the sky and stuff? Greatest movies of all time? You gotta be kidding me, Mason."

"Okay, how about *No Country for Old Men?*"

"You're a weirdo, Mason."

I couldn't even think of a response, so I just shook my head.

"Anyway, the last thing I want is to go into Mexico and shuttle some drug lord back to rat off his amigos, even if they did kill that deputy. Our inept justice system would probably just let him go with a fat paycheck anyway. If that's the play, Hearst can count us out right now. I don't trust the Mexican military or their police."

"Well," said Pappy, "looks like we're about to find out." He pointed his coffee cup toward the podium where a full-bird colonel was now standing.

Turned out we weren't going to Mexico to arrest or extradite anyone.

The mission was to kill the enemy.

And that, I could get on board with.

~

IRMGARD WAS STAYING in a two-story cabin in Estes Park. Her great-grandfather, Anthony Carlino, was inside. He'd driven up early this morning and had breakfast with her. Tina was at work, needing to appear in court and conduct a K9 demonstration at a high school before she could head up to the cabin, which wouldn't be for several hours.

Irmgard's great-grandfather had the cabin equipped with a series of kennels for the puppies. Arrow was outside with Petros, wrestling in the patches of snow and pine needles, tumbling and bumbling over, under, and around each other. Irmgard loved watching the puppies. They made her laugh. They were sweet and wild and so cute. But they were also a handful, and she was tasked with cleaning up after them. The job kept her busy, which was good because it took her mind off the places it tended to drift.

The bad places.

The scary places.

The places where evil men wanted to do bad things to her—like what they did to her father in Germany and to Billy, Tina, and her Uncle Gil. Irmgard tried not to think about those things and those men, but she couldn't help it. Her stupid mind kept going there.

Blood and darkness and the wolf and the terror. Her mother so thin and weak, and the deep-dark circles under and around her eyes. Her poor fingers so thin, the green-blue veins bulging and twining across her knuckles like spongy ropes. The anger at her mother for not playing with her, wishing she would just die and be done with it, and then begging her to wake up when she wouldn't and knowing it was her fault that she'd died—that she'd killed her with her wishes.

Tina had told her it wasn't her fault and that it had just been a coincidence. She'd found Irmgard crying in bed one night, and they had talked about her fears. Irmgard told Tina she believed her.

But Irmgard didn't believe her.

Sometimes, you just had to tell grownups what they wanted to hear so they would leave you alone. Irmgard's mother dying was her fault. She'd wished it, and it happened, just like her father's murder was her fault. She'd heard the cars, seen the men, and snuck into the living room when she wasn't supposed to.

She hadn't eaten the peas.

And then the man shot her father in the head.

Why hadn't she eaten the peas?

It was such a little thing, but now it was too late. That's just the way life was ... always too late.

And then the wolf.

Petra saved her from the wolf. Irmgard didn't deserve to be saved, but Petra saved her anyway. And then there was the smelly man with the tattoos who stole her from Billy and Tina, and after him, the nicely dressed man who tied her to the chair and said he was going to blow her up with a bomb...all because Irmgard was angry with her mother for being too tired and sick to play with her one morning.

Irmgard was bad. She knew she was bad. She didn't want to be bad—didn't mean to be bad—but she was.

Petros and Arrow bounced over to her, chewed at her feet, and pushed their cold noses and flicking tongues into her palms, demanding to be petted, rubbed, and played with. She complied because she loved them ... and they loved her back ... even though she was bad.

TINA FINISHED HER COURT APPEARANCE, a drug case involving Viper, who had sniffed out a dozen kilos of meth. The meth was so fresh it was still wet inside the individually wrapped cellophane packages hidden in Tupperware containers in the trunk of the rented car. The three suspects tried to run—two of them anyway—the ones not yet in handcuffs. The first guy made it about ten yards before Viper hit him in the left butt cheek, dragging him around and down, screaming and crying and saying he surrendered. The second guy got plowed by two task force members as big as linebackers and about as fast.

She had waited two and a half hours to give her testimony but spent only about twenty minutes on the stand. After being sworn in, she stated her credentials along with Viper's credentials and certifications and provided her account of the events. The evidence was introduced, which included the drugs, pictures of the suspect's injuries, and the doctor's reports—all in all, twenty minutes. Not bad.

Of course, it didn't always go so smoothly. Sometimes, Tina endured hours, even days, grilled by the defense. They could be brutal, challenging everything—a ridiculous waste of time. Still, it was all part of the game. At least it was over, and she had plenty of time to make it to the K9 demo at the school. And after that, the cabin and Irmgard.

Irmgard. Tina realized she was falling more and more in love with that little girl every day. She might even love her more than she loved Billy, which was saying a lot. But she was scared. What if she and Billy didn't work out? They had had problems lately, arguments—the conflict with her job.

If things didn't work out, if they did break up, she would lose Irmgard. The very thought frightened her. But more frightening was the thought of Irmgard losing *her.* What would that do to the child? She'd lost so much already. How much could one little girl take? How much loss could she absorb before being crushed by the weight?

Tina tried to shake it off, knowing there was nothing she could do about it right now. When she reached her car, she slipped her fingers through the holes in the plexiglass covering the back window of her police cruiser. Viper licked her fingers, whining with happiness and excitement at her return. Being with Viper always improved her mood.

As she got behind the wheel, her thoughts returned to Irmgard.

Irmgard and Gil Mason.

Gil had warned her—her *and* Billy—several times, telling them that what they were doing was dangerous, even destructive, for Irmgard's mental well-being. Playing house without the commitment of marriage was like playing a game of Russian Roulette, with the heart and mind of the little girl at stake.

Gil could be such a prude.

At least, that's what she had thought at the time. Now, she wasn't so sure, especially after realizing that her relationship with Billy was at odds with her professional life and might cost her her job—possibly even more—maybe even her freedom.

As she drove out of the court parking lot and headed toward the school, her head started to throb. Behind her, Viper stuck her head past the partition and licked her ear and cheek. Smiling, Tina rubbed Viper's snout and ears and under her chin.

"I love you too, baby."

13

"So, what do you think?" asked Sheriff Adams.

"Very nice," said Sarah, "I'm not just saying that either. Your people put the grant money to good use. In fact, I'm a little envious of that new electron microscope. It's state of the art. Better than what I have at my lab. Maybe I should talk to whoever put together your grant request—get a few tips?"

"Candace Walsh," he said. "She's on maternity leave—little boy—her second. But I'll give her your number when she gets back. She'll enjoy talking to you. She's pretty proud of the whole set-up."

"She should be." Looking around, Sarah spotted the refrigeration section. "Who else has access to this area?"

Adams pointed to the glass doors, which could only be unlocked via keycards. "We can program the lock so that your card alone has access. Like I said, Candace is out, and if we need to get any evidence for court, I'll have my evidence tech ask for your help. You remember Jonny—the young tech with the camera you met at the crime scene?"

Sarah nodded, holding the cooler containing her evidence. It was sealed with a long strip of evidence tape to maintain the chain of custody. The night before, she had placed the cooler in the refrigeration section using the keycard given to her by the Sheriff.

"Good enough for me," she agreed. "I'll need you to initial the tape once we cut it, and also note the time stamp on returning it to the fridge."

"No problem," said Adams.

He seemed much more amiable than he had during their earlier meeting. Maybe it was the absence of the other men, or perhaps he felt more comfortable in his own castle. Or ... it could be that they were alone together. She knew she had that effect on men. It wasn't something she tried to do—it was just nature taking its course. It could be annoying, but it could also be useful.

"Any idea when Gil will be back?" she asked.

"Can't help you there. I called Hearst a few minutes ago, but he tends to be pretty tight-lipped." He pointed to the keycard she wore on a lanyard around her neck and indicated the access pad. "Want to put it in now, or do you want to lug that cooler around all day?" he asked teasingly.

That nature thing again.

"Thank you," she said, smiling back, knowing from experience the truth behind the adage that you can catch more flies with honey than with vinegar. Sarah touched the card and stood aside as Sheriff Adams pulled the door open and held it for her.

"After you," he said, giving her another once over. This time, it didn't come off quite as fatherly.

"It's nice to see chivalry isn't completely dead." Sarah entered the room and set the cooler on a counter stocked with sticky-backed evidence tags, packaging materials, heat-sensitive plastic bags of various sizes, permanent markers, sealable plastic cylinders, ties, an assortment of sign-in/sign-out manila envelopes, and a three-foot-long heat-sealer. *Almost like home,* she thought.

"There's still a few old timers like me who remember, even in your America," said Adams. "But we're a dying breed."

"I'm hoping for a revival," said Sarah, smiling. "A teenage boy actually held a door open for me at the store last week."

"Good to hear, but I wouldn't count on a revival. Once respect is lost, it's hard to get back. It takes a strong hand, and I'm not sure this country has enough of those to bring it back."

"Strong hands?"

Adams nodded. "You know the old saying, *Hard times make strong men, strong men make easy times, easy times make weak men, weak men make hard times.* Men these days—so weak. Man-buns, fingernail polish and earrings. I can only imagine how hard times will have to get before they toughen up."

"Oh, I think there's still strong men out there," said Sarah.

"In America? Not enough to turn the tide. This place is as good as dead—run by crooks, women, perverts and children. And it's spreading like a plague to the whole world. No, America's through. A decade left—maybe less. No hope here. Drugs, crime, deviants. People think the invasion is just starting when, in reality, it's already happened. The weak men *let* it happen. Maybe the invaders will be stronger—at least for a while."

"The invaders?"

"The cartels. Survival of the fittest. Strong invaders kill weak men—then they take over. They live in the dead men's houses, murder their children, and rape and impregnate their women with future warriors of their own. They turn everything the weak men have into theirs. Happened to the Greeks, the Romans, the Aztecs, and the Indians. Everywhere and every when, since the fall of man, and now it's happening here. Despite all its high and mighty boasting, America lasted less time than any of them—a couple of hundred years. Rome lasted *two thousand* years. It's the way it's always been, the way it will always be."

"That's very ... pessimistic," said Sarah.

"Only for the losers. The ones who can't or refuse to adapt."

Sarah shook her head. "But in your scenario, isn't everyone a loser? I mean, wouldn't we all be killed or enslaved?"

The sheriff cocked his head, looking at her, not saying anything. It made Sarah feel a little afraid. They were here alone in the evidence department, and now that she thought about it, she hadn't seen anyone else since her bodyguards left.

Something about the way he was standing there—maybe his posture or his stance—suddenly reminded her of the Double Tap Rapist who had assaulted her so long ago. She didn't know why or what it was about him, but the slight fear she had begun to feel suddenly flared. She took an involuntary step back. He was such a big man, so imposing. He could easily grab her up, clamp a giant hand over her mouth, throw her to the floor—do whatever he wanted to her.

Do what *he* had done to her.

And there was no Gil to protect her. No Pilgrim. It was just the two of them—alone.

"Hey," he said, reaching a hand toward her shoulder. She slid under and away from his grip. "Hey, easy. I get a little caught up in discussions like this. I don't mean anything by it. I just want people to know the situation—so they can be prepared. That's all. I've had to deal with our failing culture and values and this border stuff and its consequences for a long time."

Sarah bumped into the counter, halting her retreat. "I'm sorry," she said. "It's not you, it's me. I had an incident ... years ago. I don't like to be touched, even now."

The sheriff looked at his open palm, then at her. He nodded. "Those bad men I spoke of. No chivalry. I'm sorry for whatever happened to you, but you're safe with me. I'm *not* a weak man. I'd kill anyone who tried to hurt you."

To prove his point, he turned to face the wall and, as if by magic, his gun appeared in his hand. Just as magically, he holstered it, then drew it again. He twirled it around his finger—holstered it—drew it again—twirled and spun it, then back in—back out, too fast to follow. She'd seen such feats in movies—old westerns—but never in real life. It was amazing. Even Gil couldn't hope to compete with him.

"You're completely safe with me."

Sarah nodded, impressed. But, for some reason, Gail Davis flashed to mind, making her feel unworthy of his chivalry.

Blinking several times, she turned to the cooler. "I guess we should get this into the freezer so I can get started."

The sheriff thumbed open a pocketknife as long as his palm and sliced through the evidence tape sealing the cooler. He handed her an evidence transfer card.

"Got a pen?" he asked.

14

Nathan sat across from Rick and his two interns outside a small diner advertised as having the state's best-pulled pork sandwiches. Nathan wasn't sure if it was the best, but it was certainly close. They were on Morrison Road, just east of Kipling Boulevard in Lakewood. The afternoon crowd was beginning to thin as customers finished their late lunch breaks and shoppers headed home before their spouses beat them to it.

"How do you come to that?" asked Rick. "If God is omniscient—all-knowing—meaning He knows everything, then logically He must know everything, past, present, and future. This means that before He created the world, He knew we would be sitting here having this conversation at this exact time and in this exact place."

Nathan shook his head as he wiped his lips with a napkin. "God is all-powerful and all-knowing, but we must examine these concepts in the context of correct biblical meaning, not man's fallible philosophical interpretation. And to do that we need apply the same rule to both assumptions. God *is* all-powerful, yes, but that doesn't mean He can do absolutely anything. It means that He can do anything *doable*. For instance, God can't make a rock so big He can't lift it. The creation can never be greater than the Creator. Even more compelling, consider this—God cannot make Himself never to have existed. That doesn't make Him less powerful—it makes Him real. He *does* exist, has *always* existed, and always *will* exist."

Rick put down his sandwich, wincing as he reached for his drink. "Whoa! That hot sauce is hot." Both of his interns, Enneagram and Myers-Brigs, nodded in agreement.

"Okay, let's say I buy that logically. I'm not saying I do—I need to digest the notion first to see if I can punch holes in it. But, for the sake of argument, let's say I do. How does that equate to the *all-knowing?*"

"Same way," said Nathan. "God knows all things that are *knowable*. He knows, or at least He *can* know all eternity past and present."

"Past and present ... why not the future?"

"Because it doesn't exist yet."

"Doesn't work," said Rick. "I accepted your challenge to read the Bible and am currently reading the Book of Ruth. Your theory fails when it comes to prophesy. How can God know anything about the future if it doesn't already exist?"

The sounds of traffic buzzing along Kipling at a steady pace surrounded them as they sat at a wooden picnic table outside the diner. The sun, still a few hours from setting, was inching toward the mountaintops. Overhead, a scattering of fluffy white clouds contrasted against the brilliant blue of the mile-high sky.

"God *tells us how* in the book of Isiah. You haven't gotten there yet, but you will, and it's a lot more powerful than someone sneaking a peek into the future. It's not like the guy who previously records a football game and then acts like he can guess what will happen. In Isaiah Forty-six, God proves to Israel that He is the only true God. To do it, He talks about this very topic ... *His knowledge and His power*. He says:

> 'Remember the former things of old,
> for I am God, and there is no other.
> I am God, and there is none like Me,
>
> *declaring* the end from the beginning,

and from ancient times, things that are *not yet* done,
saying, 'My counsel shall stand,
and I will *do* all My pleasure,

calling a bird of prey from the east,
the man who executes My counsel from a far country.
Indeed, I have spoken *it;*
I will also *bring* it to pass.
I have purposed *it;*
I will also *do* it.'

"Take note of a few key points here. First, God says nothing about looking into the future. He says He *declares* the end of an event from the beginning, like when He proclaimed that Lucifer would bruise *Jesus' heel*—a flesh wound, as we talked about before—but that Jesus would bruise Lucifer's *head*, a fatal wound. Next, God tells exactly *how* He declares such a matter. He says His counsel shall stand, and He will do all His pleasure. He has spoken it, and He will *bring* it to pass. He has purposed it and will *do* it—not that He has *already* done it in some rigidly set future that He visits or peeks into outside of time. He says *He will do it* when the time is right."

"I don't get it," said Wayne *Enneagram* Lederman, "what's the difference?"

Nathan held up his pulled pork sandwich. "It's like this—in five seconds, my sandwich will be out of my hand and on my plate. Five, four, three, two, one ...." Nathan dropped his sandwich, and it fell to the plate. "See? I just brought to pass what I declared from the beginning of my statement to the end of the event. I put the sandwich back on the plate, but did I look into the future to do it? No, I said it and brought it to pass by *doing* it.

"Of course, I could have had a heart attack on the count of three, or you could have knocked it out of my hand onto the floor, but nobody's going to stop God. If He says He will have a son born of a virgin in a town called Bethlehem on a certain month, day, and year, then He can do it. No one can or will stop Him."

"Okay," said Rick. "I concede that's one way God could fulfill prophecy, but I don't see how that's the only way. I mean, why couldn't He look into the future?"

"Because the future hasn't happened yet. It doesn't exist. Only the present exists. The past is a memory, and the future is yet to come. Time is a function of God—like love. God didn't create love—it's part of who and what God is—just as time is a part of who and what God is. God experiences time, and so we experience time."

"And you can prove this how?" asked Rick.

"It's how God portrays Himself throughout the entirety of the Bible. He is always *in* time, working with us. He never goes back in time. He never goes into the future—never even says He's *looking* into the future. He says He will *make* things happen in the future at a time He determines, like me with my sandwich.

"Additionally, there are instances when God's prophesy does not come to pass due to our reactions. For example, He sends Jonah to tell the people of Nineveh that He will utterly destroy them in forty days for their wickedness. The people believe Jonah and repent, so God spares them, changing His mind in response to their actions. Jonah gets mad at God for making him look like a false prophet, saying that's why he fled from Him in the first place. Jonah knew God was loving and merciful and thought this might happen, making him look foolish. Besides, Jonah wanted the evil people of Nineveh to perish.

"From the passages, it sounds like Jonah knew God pretty well, and if *he* thought God might change His mind and give Nineveh another chance, he certainly didn't think the entirety of the future was set and immovable. No, the story shows God working *in* time with us, as He does throughout the entire Bible. Also, notice that in the Genesis account—which you've already read—God never says anything about creating time. He tells us exactly what He *does* create —matter, energy, and life ... nothing about time."

"Then how did time get here?" asked Rick.

"As I mentioned before, time is simply a function of God—part of who and what He is. Like love, it's intrinsic to His character and being. God isn't outside of time, existing in some imaginary realm, because He can't be outside Himself. God isn't outside of love. Love and time exist because God exists."

Rick plopped a potato chip into his mouth. "You have other examples?"

Nathan picked his sandwich up off the plate and smiled.

"Lots."

15

Things had gotten off to a good start ... but that didn't last long. We split into three teams—a combination of Delta, SEALs, and Rangers, with some of my guys interspersed throughout. The actual military guys didn't like it, especially the team leaders. They were afraid we'd get them killed.

Couldn't blame them.

I was a little afraid of that myself—except for Pappy, of course. He was a legend, even among these guys.

However, fire teams are usually composed of individuals accustomed to working together, which minimizes the need for communication during combat and allows them to function like a well-oiled machine. Because we had no prior training with these men, our coming on board could quickly turn bad—gum up the gears. Hearst seemed to understand this, so he relegated us to the rear, where we would watch the others' six, meaning we'd be responsible for covering the back of the formation. Sort of a testing/learning mission for us.

After the briefing, as we were preparing to board a Boeing CH-47 Chinook helicopter, one of the team leaders, a tall, lean SEAL, leaned in close and whispered, "You mess us up, and I'll do you myself."

Seemed like a nice guy.

There was really nothing to say to that. I felt my lip twitch at the corner, held off the smile, and boarded the copter.

It was around eleven at night when we entered the mansion proper. The SEAL team leader guy was three men ahead of me as we traversed a dark hallway, rifles out and pointing. Hearst had sent a picture of our target, Agustin Cruz, a drug lord and the boss of bosses, to our phones.

The SEAL team leader guy glanced back at me, still not looking happy. *He should have been looking for the enemy*. A bullet struck him in the throat, spraying the walls and the men around him with a geyser of blood.

Wasn't me.

His troops returned fire, but they were shooting blind, even though we all wore night vision goggles. The initial round had come from an unidentified sniper in an unknown location. A second bullet struck the soldier behind the fallen team leader, tearing through a portion of his Kevlar helmet and embedding itself in an expensive-looking painting depicting a matador thrusting a sword into the neck of a massive bull, the matador's red cape draping one of the bull's horns as the man dodged.

We'd just started and already our team had one man on his back, bleeding, and another taking a knee to get his wits about him.

My men and I were quickly being advanced toward the front.

I'd taken note of the direction of blood spray from the first round —*an obvious exit wound*—as well as the path traveled by the second round, deducing the general proximity of the sniper's roost. I aimed in that direction, but before I could fire, Sammy Rothstein sent a single round downrange, striking the hidden figure in the head and taking him out.

Sammy looked at me. "Good spotting," he said, "but you were looking a little to the right."

"Did you see him?" I asked.

"No, but from the angle of the shots, he had to be there."

"Did he?"

"Of course. *Math* doesn't lie. *Geometry* doesn't lie. You knew it, too. I saw you aiming that way—close anyway. You just forgot to carry the seven." He tossed me a quick wink.

The guy who took the helmet hit must have been a medic because he stayed on his knee, working on the team leader. One extra man stood over him for cover while the rest of us continued forward, searching out our objective—Agustin Cruz, the leader of the Cruz Cartel. According to Steve Hearst, this organization, one of Mexico's most brutal criminal groups, was responsible for encroaching into the U.S. and killing Sheriff Adams' deputy.

Up ahead, the team turned left and ran straight into a gun battle. Our weapons were suppressed—theirs weren't. The narrow confines of the walls amplified and echoed the sounds of the exploding gunpowder as the cartel soldiers fired into us.

There were too many of them for this not to be a trap.

"It's a trap!" yelled one of the men near the front as he stayed his ground, shooting fast.

"Observant," said Sammy sarcastically as he killed two men before I could even get off my first round.

Being trapped in a corridor with shooters at the other end sending an unending stream of copper-jacketed death at you is a bad situation, with really only two options—run *or charge.* And running wasn't an option because we had an injured man down behind us. Sammy must have had the same thought because he was right beside me as I broke past the SF guys, who were taking the brunt of the fusillade.

The bad guys were kneeling behind a three-foot wall of sandbags piled at the end of the hallway, with only their heads and shoulders visible.

Looked like about seven of them.

Usually a lucky number, but not this time ... not for them anyway.

I killed two, the first with a shot through the face and the second dead center in the upper chest. Sammy sprayed three, putting them all down. The last two turned tail, staying low as they fled before turning another corner.

"Max, here," I called quietly.

I'd left him pretty far back, but he was with me almost instantly. I didn't see him, didn't hear him—I *felt* him. *"Packen."* I pointed to where the men had run, and Max shot past us.

It didn't take long.

Screaming ensued.

And then other sounds.

Horrible, guttural, raw, terrifying.

Music to my ears.

I looked back at the SF guys and saw fear engulfing their faces. They were hard men, experienced and blooded, but what they were hearing ... affected them.

Couldn't blame them.

The man closest to me had a bullet wound in his thigh. The third in line had blood dripping down his jaw and several holes stitched across his armor.

"Let's go," I said. And we did, all of us.

We broke out of the corridor into a spacious living area with a massive fireplace, plush couches and chairs, and even a statue of a conquistador dressed in armor. Above the fireplace, easily ten feet high, was a display featuring a bullwhip, a set of pearl-handled Colt Peacemakers, and a black cowboy hat. I almost expected to see a matador's red cape, sword, and maybe a set of horns—they would have fit nicely with the painting we'd passed that now sported a fresh bullet hole.

Exiting the enormous room, we came to another branch of corridors. We might have been stymied as to which way to go, but Max had left breadcrumbs for us to follow.

Sort of, anyway.

Breadcrumbs Max style ... in other words, bodies ... and pieces of bodies.

He'd killed the first man about fifteen feet down the corridor and was still working on the second, tearing at his spinal column near the base of his skull. Splinters of bone, globs of yellow fat, red meat, and blood flew in every direction as the man screamed. I approached and fired a bullet into the back of the man's head. He stopped screaming and flopped limply. Max dropped him, his eyes bright and excited.

"*Foran.*" I sent him out scouting ahead. Looking back at the SF troops, I said, "No more traps. Max will make sure of that."

They looked at each other, *nodding*, then back at me, brief smiles crossing their lips.

And away we went.

MAX DROPPED the body of the man the Alpha had killed and, at his command, ran ahead, leaving the others to follow. He moved fast, darting this way and that, turning corners, taking in the scents as they drifted to him on the currents of air that flowed and wavered, spiraling and rising, drifting and collating, always leading toward his goal.

Targets.

Men.

Prey.

A man hidden in an alcove behind a plant took a shot at him, but Max knew he was there and sprinted straight in, spoiling the man's aim and ripping into his stomach and chest. The man dropped his weapon and tried to flee, but his hiding spot blocked him in on three sides. All he could do was collapse and curl into a fetal ball, leaving his head and neck easy targets. Max swiftly dispatched him while the Alpha and the others brought up the rear and moved on.

Max took out three other attempted ambushes and ended his run at an open door at the back of the mansion, where two men were entering a car as another vehicle sped away. Launching, Max followed the driver into his seat inside the car and crushed down on his face. The passenger tried to shoot Max but, despite firing several bullets, only managed to kill the driver. Max clawed his way over the dying driver and attacked the passenger, who, in hindsight, should have saved a bullet for himself. His death was far worse than being shot.

As Max finished with the man, the Alpha and the others arrived, immediately opening fire on the fleeing vehicle. They hit it with such concentrated firepower that it swerved, crashed, flipped over, and burst into flames.

Max vaulted out of the car he was in, leaving everyone inside dead or dying. The now Maxless, driverless vehicle careened forward and crashed into a tree. Max tore straight for the burning wreckage of the other car, leaving his companions in his dust.

The prey might still be alive.

16

Dominic Elkins felt the bullet slide across his neck, just below the jaw, so close the heat burned him. In response, he dropped the empty rifle, letting it hang by its three-point strap, and drew his pistol. He fired five times, hitting and killing four men—one of them twice. *Hitting him twice, that is.* He only died once.

"Take that, Sammy," he said under his breath. It wasn't that Dominic was competing with Sammy—it was just that *Dominic was always competing with Sammy*. They were on separate fire teams, but afterward, there would be a tallying.

The trap had almost worked. Four of the Special Forces guys on Dominic's team had been put down before they even knew they were under fire. But Dominic, at the back of the line with Billy, had time to react.

Shifting his aim, Dominic emptied a magazine into a corner section of plaster behind which the other two men were hiding. One man fell forward into the open hall, bullet holes dotting his head, face, and neck in an uneven line. Dominic inserted a new mag and, ducking at an angle, rounded the corner. The second man was running as fast as he could.

He didn't make the corner.

One of the soldiers clapped Dominic on the shoulder. "Man, that's the fastest draw I've ever seen. You pulled our fat out of the fire. We were sitting ducks there."

"It's not over," said Dominic, feeling the old battle lust burning bright. Until this moment, he hadn't realized how much he'd missed the days of near-constant combat—going on nightly raids, taking out terrorists, fighting his way out of cities swarming with the enemy. "This way," he said, pointing with a nudge of his chin.

"Can't let you do it," said the SF man. "I have orders to keep you safe. Back of the line. Sorry."

Dominic grinned at him. "Not my style." He turned and ran in the direction the dead man had been heading, holstering his pistol and loading a new magazine into the commando rifle as he went.

Everyone else, including Billy, followed.

BILLY RAN ALONG behind the other men. This Elkins guy was a friend of Gil's. Like Gil, he'd been a Marine and then a cop. Billy still had a hard time with the whole cop thing, even though he was in love with one, but the military guy had been right—Elkins had saved their bacon for sure.

They'd been moving along just fine when they were suddenly pelted from the end of the hall, trapping them with nowhere to turn. At least three men took bullets—maybe more. They didn't all go down—they were tough—but it wouldn't have taken long had Elkins not emptied his rifle, taking out a slew of them. And that bit with the pistol at the end? *Crazy*. Billy had only seen one other man as fast—*maybe as fast*—Elio Colombo, the Ghost.

He kind of wished Elio was here now—they could use him. That Hearst guy had made it sound like this would be a simple in-and-out operation—kill the drug lord responsible for the death of the deputy Gil and Sarah were investigating and then go home. This thing had turned into anything but.

Cage fighting was one thing, but Billy was no soldier. This kind of melee was way outside his skill set. He'd killed men in the service of the Family—been in some hairy spots—but this? Nothing like this. Even the battle with the bikers near Black Hawk hadn't been like this. This was *war*—actual war.

And Billy didn't think he liked it.

~

MAX GOT to the burning wreckage of the second vehicle far ahead of the soldiers running behind him. The men inside were all dead and burning.

The battle was over.

The Alpha reached him first, but Max had already turned and started for the car he'd jumped out of—just in case.

Arriving behind him at the car Max jumped from, I looked inside and saw the carnage—carnage that had not been caused by crashing into the tree.

I gave Max a nod of approval and touched his neck with an open palm. As the others joined them, they saw what Max had done and, one by one gave Max a nod. I turned, and the other men and I headed back to the mansion.

Max by my side.

~

STEVE HEARST WASN'T HAPPY. Things hadn't gone as planned. *They'd been waiting for them.* An ambush. That meant someone in the chain was dirty. *One of his?* Maybe—maybe not. Could be an SF, or, more likely, someone on the Mexican side—a cop, a prosecutor, a politician. Because of the money, influence, women, power, and threats the cartels could bring to bear, anything was possible. Anyone could be turned, no matter how sure you thought you were of them.

One of Steve's favorite reads when he was young was Frank Herbert's *Dune* series. In *Dune,* Dr. Wellington Yueh's Imperial Conditioning—signified by a black diamond tattooed on his forehead—ensured he could never betray House Atreides ... *but he did.*

It was no different with the cartels. They were simply too brutal, too rich, too powerful. The only ones you could trust were those with personal tragedies. *Personal stakes*. Wives, daughters, fathers, brothers, sisters—*kidnapped, tortured, raped, murdered*—by the cartels. Only those willing to die in the pursuit of vengeance could be trusted, and even then, who could be sure? Like *Dune's* Dr. Yueh, the right leverage still might work.

The only thing Steve could be sure of was that *someone* was dirty. And whoever it was, he'd find him.

But not tonight.

Tonight was a bust.

The target hadn't been there, and they'd suffered severe casualties, one of them possibly fatal. Kevin Dawkins, one of the team leaders from Delta, took a bullet to the throat. Whether he'd make it or not was a flip of the coin.

On the plus side, they'd killed a lot of cartel soldiers. But even that paled compared to the wounds his men—*some of them his friends*—would have to live with. They were all in this together. They were all warriors. They knew the risks and the dangers, but still ...

The only other good thing to come out of this was what he'd learned about Mason and his men. Not Pappy, of course—apparently Hearst trusted him—but the others.

Mason was the shining star. He and his monster dog had saved their team. Still, Rothstein and Elkins had been pleasant surprises.

A lot to think on.

Once they were back across the border.

Once they were home.

17

When I woke up in the morning, I was sore. A bullet had grazed my left shoulder, just outside the protective strap of my outer vest. In the heat of combat, I hadn't even felt it. But later, I did—first in the helicopter when one of the guys noticed the blood, and even more so back at the base in the infirmary. There, several of us were treated by very competent doctors and nurses. My wound ended up needing about thirty stitches, so it was technically more than a graze, but it was nothing compared to what some of the other guys had endured.

Not to mention, the mission had been a failure.

No dead cartel drug kingpin.

We did a quick debrief in the infirmary while the doctors worked on us, but it was cut short due to the medical staff being all prissy about germs and contamination and the risk of infection—silly stuff like that.

So here we were now, minus the Delta team leader guy who took a round in the throat and a few other less seriously wounded soldiers who hadn't been released yet. The same full bird colonel who briefed us yesterday was up front, getting ready to speak. Steve Hearst stood beside him, wearing shorts, a short-sleeved, untucked Hawaiian shirt ... oh, and the crocs.

Sarah had been knocking on my door at sunrise. I'd been asleep for about twenty minutes. She asked how everything went, which led to a half-hour recounting of the night's events. Afterward, she insisted on checking my wounds and kissing them to make them all better. I think it helped.

She told me she'd fill me in about her day when she returned from the sheriff's office that evening. There were test results to review, and she had a full day's work ahead, having sent DNA to two different labs she'd told me about. I was okay with that because I figured the debriefing would take at least several hours. I wanted to go for a quick breakfast with her, but she wisely ordered me back to bed, where I got roughly five hours of hard sleep. And now here it was, almost noon, the debriefing just starting.

A Special Forces operator named Larson handed me a cup of coffee. He was a tall, lean guy with blond hair, green eyes, a light mustache, and a beard. Before the raid yesterday, he'd been aloof, but now, after the night's events, he seemed to accept me as an equal. That's the way it is with warriors. The proof comes from action, not words, and once you've been tested and found fit, you're accepted into the brotherhood.

Pappy walked with me to our seats as the colonel adjusted his computer on the podium.

"Larson there thinks you walk on water," said Pappy. "I could hardly get him to shut up about you. I think he wants to ask you on a date."

"Not my type," I said, sitting down, "beards tickle."

"I'd ask how you know that, but I'm afraid you might tell me." He chinned toward my shoulder. "How's the boo-boo?"

"All better. Sarah kissed it for me."

"No tickle?"

I gave him a look. "No tickle."

"You started it."

"Yes," I said, "but you know she has no beard."

He looked up to the colonel. "So, what do you think? We gonna get reamed?"

"What for? It wasn't our plan, and the rat wasn't one of us."

"You and me know that—doesn't mean *they'll* believe it." Looking around, Pappy leaned in. "You see your boys Elkins or Rothstein anywhere?"

I'd been secretly scanning for them since I arrived, but no joy yet. I shook my head to the negative.

"That usual for them?" asked Pappy.

I shook my head again, locking my eyes on Steve Hearst. "What are you thinking, Pappy?"

"CIA guys—a scary lot in some ways."

"What sort of ways are we talking?"

"Oh, you know—isolation, waterboarding, sleep deprivation, enhanced interrogation. Those sorts of ways."

I felt the change in my blood. "That would be a very bad move for Mr. Hearst."

Pappy must have heard the change in my voice. "This is his base. He seems to have considerable resources."

"Wouldn't be enough," I said. "Sammy and Dominic are here at my request. I'm responsible for them."

"Yeah, that's what I figured."

In the distance and from outside the hangar, I heard a series of gunshots ... and then another ... and another. Very fast.

I stood.

Steve Hearst saw the movement and tossed me a half grin. "It's okay, Ace, nothing to worry about. Your two buddies are working with a few of my men—*giving them some pointers*. Never seen shooters like them ever before. I've got them schooling a few of my best. Maybe they'll rub off. And don't stress about them missing the debrief. Me and the colonel met with them earlier and filled them in."

Take your seat," said the colonel. He was maybe fifty, a no-nonsense kind of guy, blocky and powerful, with a perfect high-and-tight, white-walled haircut. I sat, reassured by Hearst's assurance but still just a little wary. Like Pappy, I, too, held an inherent distrust of secret government institutions and their minions.

For the next three hours, we listened as the colonel reviewed the entire night's activities. He began with an update on our injured—everyone was still alive, for now. Then, he provided a brief outline before diving into the details. Both he and Hearst asked numerous questions, and we all shared our points of view, regardless of rank or designation. In most SWAT and Special Forces briefings and debriefings, there's a rule that allows lowly privates to challenge or dispute anyone, even a general, regarding tactics and deployment. Success is always the mission, and bad ideas can get everyone killed. The only requirement was that you had to be able to adequately defend your position.

When there was a lull, I stood and said, "So, who ratted us out?"

The colonel looked a little irritated. "We don't know we were ratted out just yet."

"It was a trap, clear as day," I said. "The only way they could have known we were coming is if one of us ... *or one of you* ... talked."

There were murmurs, all in agreement, throughout the room of seated warriors. None of us were rookies. The men in this room were the cream of the crop, and our experience told us the truth.

Steve Hearst scratched his forehead and, walking a little closer to us, smiled. "Thanks, Sport, I'm looking into it."

"Looking into it?"

The smile turned into a grin. He gave me the eye-tick, *almost a wink*, and sucked at a tooth, making a *kitching* sound. He held out his hands. "That's what I do."

"And is that what you're doing with my friends, Rothstein and Elkins? Looking into them? Because if it is, you're looking in the wrong place. It wasn't me, and it wasn't anyone I brought with me."

"I know that, Friend. I've already *looked into* all of you." He eyed everyone else in the room. "All of you too. Those of you who've worked with me in the past know how I do my job, so you can trust me to find the leak. The cartels have lots of assets, lots of sophisticated equipment, and people on both sides of the border. We had to work with higher-ups in the government of Mexico and their military—shut down or at least *turn* a few cameras on certain satellites and radar sites our government has given them access to in past joint agreements. Lots of opportunities for loose lips. But thanks to you, your friends, your fur missile, and everyone else in this room and the infirmary, they still couldn't sink our ship this time. So, like I said, I'm looking into it."

I gave it a thought, nodded, and sat back down. Forty-five minutes later, the meeting ended. I walked up to Steve Hearst.

He was waiting for me.

18

Steve Hearst decided it was time to take Gil Mason to the next level—see where exactly he stood and what potential there was for making him a concrete offer instead of a tentative one. He'd seen enough. As Mason walked toward him, he decided to make his pitch—no time like the present, after all.

"I thought you might want to talk," he said.

"Got me all figured out, do you?"

"Working on it, Slick. Have to admit though, you've got some sneaky little hitches I'm still fuzzy on."

"I'm not that deep, Hearst. Just ask, and I'll fill you in. I don't talk in riddles—not like some people. Not like you. See?"

Hearst grinned, sucked at his tooth, let the eye *tic*. "Yeah, well, it comes with the job. Still, I kind of doubt you're as easy and straight as you think you are."

Mason shrugged his shoulders. "Charles Caleb Colton once said, *'Nothing more completely baffles one who is full of trick and duplicity himself, than straight forward and simple integrity in another.'*"

Hearst looked up at the sun, turned, and started walking, with Mason at his side. "Did you use that simple integrity to go straight forward to the police to turn yourself in after killing those gang-bangers at the pollo farm in the video I showed you?"

"Not quite the same thing," said Mason. "You and me, we're on the same side, or at least we're supposed to be."

"Maybe," said Hearst. "I want to be, I can tell you that. So, you want it straight, I'll give it to you. I want you on my team. You, Sarah, Rothstein and Elkins."

"Your team? What exactly is your team?"

It was Hearst's turn to shrug. "You know the old phrase, *'If I told you I'd have to kill you?'*"

"I've heard it."

"It applies," said Hearst. "Until you say yes, anyway. Then I can tell you everything."

"Without having to kill me?"

"Theoretically."

"CIA?" asked Mason.

Hearst squinted an eye behind his sunglasses and tilted his head from side to side. "Kinda-sorta. What's your pal Billy's story?"

"My apprentice," said Mason.

Hearst grinned, did the tooth suck *click*, pointed a finger at him. "See? Right there. Not so straightforward when you think it might get someone you care about in trouble. Billy Carlino, nephew to the Godfather of the entire Italian Mafia. Not the brightest upstairs maybe, but seems like a good kid. Still, a good kid in the Mafia probably has a past. Bodies buried, skeletons in the closet. Things like that. Just looking at him I can tell. Kid's an open book, and I'm a quick study. But then, I think you know all this already, you being the world's greatest detective and all. And yet, you didn't bring up his family connections."

Mason's expression didn't budge, but he didn't say anything either.

"Nice poker face. I only brought it up to show you we aren't so different, you and I. You have your secrets, I have mine. But I'll give you what I can for now. I'm part of a very secret, very elite unit called the ATAC."

"ATAC. You guys and your acronyms."

Hearst grinned. "Governments consist of kids who grew up on Ovaltine, alphabet soup, cereal, and TV shows—Mission Impossible with its IMF, SHIELD, UNCLE, CONTROL, KAOS...."

Mason held up a hand. "CONTROL and KAOS weren't acronyms, just funny-sounding organizations."

"Unlike the ATAC," said Hearst. "It is an acronym, but it ain't even close to funny."

"Let me guess, another, *'You'd tell me what it stands for, but then you'd have to kill me.'*"

"Only if you don't come on board."

"I'm not coming on board."

"You don't know that—not yet."

"Yes, I do. There's no sense in wasting your time."

"I never waste time, Kiddo. I told you I was a quick study, and even though you're not nearly as open a book as your new assistant, Billy, I think I have a read on you. I know the kind of man you are—quick to action, competent, effective, high moral standards that don't always correspond to the law of the land, which means you work by your own set of rules. In a lesser man, that would make you useless to me, but in your case, I think it might just work out fine."

Mason shook his head. "Our government changes hands—*as much as you can say it changes hands*—every four to eight years or so. And, as such, it changes its mind and morals at least as often, and almost always on a downward trend. I won't take or follow evil orders."

"Evil?" Hearst grinned. "I'm offering you the chance to *fight* evil on a grand scale, not just your local Gotham City criminals we talked about before. With us, you might be the one to stop a nuclear or biological offensive, an EMP, the sorts of attacks that can affect an entire nation, maybe the whole world."

"Or be ordered to start one," said Mason. "I know how the best intentions and organizations can be corrupted."

"No, sir, not with us. That's not what we do. We don't start things. We're not the aggressors. We don't participate in nation-building or destroying. Our job is pointed in one direction and one direction only —the safety and security of *this* nation, America."

"Today," said Mason, "*maybe*. But tomorrow, all that could change. When you work for the government, *for the bureaucracy*, you're always subject to taking orders, and the more individuals issuing orders, the less they feel accountable for them. It's like Mel Gibson's character Benjamin Martin said in the movie *The Patriot*, 'An elected legislature can trample a man's rights as easily as a king can.' I think we've seen ample evidence of that in the last hundred years or so. No, I'll do what I can on *my* scale. I'll be Batman. You go ahead and play Justice League all you want, but don't get in my way."

Hearst just looked at Mason, his expression unchanging, no tooth suck, no eye twitch. "Well, I guess I'll have to go with my first choice then, the beautiful Miss Gallagher."

"No," said Mason.

"How's that, Champ?"

"I said no. You leave her out of this."

Hearst shook his head, removed his sunglasses, and put them in his pocket. "This ain't the fifties, Bucko. Women these days get to make up their own minds."

"You're good at talking people into doing things, and Sarah has a soft heart. You were going to have her go on that raid with us—a raid where super-trained Special Forces and SWAT heroes got shot and blown up despite being the best in the world. What might have happened to her?"

Hearst looked to the left, then to the right. "I wouldn't have let her get hurt. She would have stayed with the copters until after the cleanup. I wanted her for evidence preservation and future insight, that's all."

"That's your story now, but that's not even the point. We both know nothing is safe when it comes to the cartels. You said it yourself. They have connections and plants in high places—police and military assets. They could have taken our copters down with SAMs or grenade launchers or a dozen other surface-to-air missiles. I'm not going to allow you or anyone else to put my wife in danger."

"Not your wife yet, Slick."

Mason stepped closer. "Don't push it, Hearst."

"Not pushing anything, but national security takes precedence over personal love stories—yours included. I've got a job to do, and I'm going to do it, even if it interferes with your life."

Several soldiers, including Pappy and Billy, came around the corner of the building and saw the two men.

Mason said, "You took off your sunglasses a second ago, a clear sign you think this could turn violent. You're not wrong, so stop now. Sarah and I are leaving. You stay away from her."

"Or?"

Mason punched Hearst in the liver, right below the floating rib. It was hard, fast and precise. Hearst took the hit and started to swing back, but his body suddenly folded in on itself. He collapsed, landing in the dirt on his side, the world spinning and dust clouding his face.

"Stay away from her." Mason stepped back as Pappy and the others, maybe five in all, ran toward them. Hearst tried to stand but couldn't. He struggled to gain an elbow and knee, where he rested until others pulled him to his feet.

Mason turned to go.

"Hold up there, Jack." Hearst shrugged off the hands. "No way you get to sucker punch me and then just walk away without giving me a chance to respond."

Mason turned back. "You had plenty of warning, and this isn't high school. You asked, '*Or what?*' I answered. If this goes any further, you could end up hurt bad, maybe worse."

"Stand down, Sgt. Mason," said Pappy. "This man outranks us both."

"Not me, he doesn't, Master Sergeant—not here, not now. I don't work for him. I don't work for anybody."

"No rank," said Hearst, "but if I win, you agree to join the team."

"I already gave you my answer."

"I'll sweeten the pot," said Hearst. "I'll throw in Miss Gallagher. You win—I'll never speak to either of you again."

Mason shook his head. "Hearst, you said you were a quick study and that you could read people. Do you really think I'm going to cave? If you do, then you haven't read me at all."

"Now I'm thinking maybe you're just scared."

Mason's lips twitched. "Max, here," he said quietly. Max broke from behind Hearst, where he had appeared as if by magic ... sitting ... watching. He spun to a heel at Gil's side. None of the men had seen him come up behind them—not even Pappy.

Hearst's eyes grew big, but he said nothing.

Mason and Max turned together and walked back to their barracks.

19

Sarah had the evidence laid out on several tables. Blood samples were pressed between slides under microscopes, and shell casings were separated and suspended inside a glass box, where a mist of vaporized superglue coated their copper surfaces to reveal hints of finger or palm prints. She had blood type testing in progress, gunpowder analysis, metallurgy, DNA growth matrices, and familial database searches underway. Sarah would still rather be back in her own lab, but she had to admit Adams and his staff had an incredible setup.

Hearst had told her that Agustin Cruz, the drug lord they had failed to kill in the raid, had been arrested in the past, and his DNA was on record. This gave Sarah an idea. There were two leading organizations structured to map, analyze, and crossmatch DNA markers for identifying victims, suspects, and relatives—Parabon and Othram. She sent samples to both.

These labs performed their magic by mining human DNA to identify biomarkers of forensic significance and then generated leads by combining genetic genealogy, DNA phenotyping, and kinship analysis. They then ran the data through a sophisticated computer program. In Parabon's case, the program was called Snapchat

Advanced DNA Analysis, which delivered the closest composite sketch possible.

The sheriff keyed himself in with his card. "Any luck with the evidence?"

"Just got started, really. There was a lot of prep, even after yesterday. I should have results before end of day, though."

"End of day," echoed the Sheriff. "You talk like a tech."

Sarah grinned. "I am a tech, but I think you mean a geek or a nerd."

"You don't look like any geek or nerd I ever saw. Not a tech or a scientist either. A movie star, maybe." He walked over to the table where teeth and bone fragments were laid out next to the glass box containing the shell casings and token. "Or a beauty pageant or homecoming queen." He pointed at the casings. "Anything on these?"

"They're still cooking, but it's not looking promising." She walked close. "You can see nothing's popping out—no ridges or swirls. But, like I said, it's still early. Maybe a small partial will show."

"If they're from over the border, prints won't help much anyway," said the sheriff. "Not a lot of consistency in gathering useful information like fingerprints. Too many small villages and cartel-run regions. As for the token, they're everywhere around here. Shooter's Showdown is our most popular tourist attraction. In the summers, we get nearly as many weddings at the church up there as an Elvis chapel in Vegas."

"Sounds charming," said Sarah with a grin.

"It is. Very traditional—a little rustic, but not flashy like in Sin City. I was only speaking quantity, not quality. In fact, when I get married, that's where it'll be."

"Married? Do you have a date?"

"Not officially, but very soon. Anyway, I only brought it up to say the likelihood of one of our suspects dropping the token is a long shot."

"We'll just have to keep our fingers crossed," said Sarah.

"Yeah, that and ten bucks'll maybe get you a cup of coffee." He grinned at her. "Speaking of which, you want to take a break and have a cup with me?"

"No offense, Sheriff, but the last time I went out for coffee in your town, I almost got killed."

"Yeah, well, about that, I wanted to make it up to you. And this time, you'll have a police escort."

"Thank you. That's sweet, but really, I've got to finish this. I'm not sure how long I have or when Gil will be finished with whatever he's doing with Steve Hearst. If I hurry, I can do as you suggested and leave everything here, saving us all the chain of custody issues with transporting things back and forth."

"See?" he said, "I had one good idea anyway. Okay then, I'll let you get back to work. You need anything, I mean anything, you let Marcie or the deputy up front know, and they'll get it for you."

"Thank you, sheriff. I think I'll be fine."

But then she saw Gil walking towards the glass doors, and from the expression on his face, she realized she might be wrong.

I WAS STILL in a mood when I reached the sheriff's office. I thought Hearst might order me secured to the base or something like that, but he didn't. After being let in by the deputy at the front desk, I saw Sarah with Sheriff Adams in the lab.

From Adams' pose, smile, and proximity to Sarah, not to mention how he was leaning in toward her, it looked like he was hitting on her. *Man, was I being jealous?* I shook my head and pushed it aside. I pointed at the door, asking Sarah to let me in. She walked over and used her card.

"Everything okay?" she asked.

I forced a smile and kissed her lightly. "Fine, now," I said. "But it's time for us to leave."

"Now? I can't. I've still got work to finish."

"How long?"

"Several hours at least. I'm waiting on DNA results from Parabon and Othram. Why? What's the hurry?"

"I think I've overstayed my welcome," I said.

She gave me a look. "What did you do?"

Shrugging, I said, "I sort of punched Hearst."

Her mouth dropped open.

"Good for you," said the sheriff. "I've wanted to punch that guy for years. Those stupid dimples and that tan. I mean, really?"

"Exactly," I said.

"Did you put him down at least?"

"Oh yeah," I said, "he hit the ground hard."

"Nice."

Sarah looked at both of us like we'd lost our minds. "Why on earth would you punch Steve?"

Steve?

"He ... well ... he," I couldn't remember what exactly led to what, and nothing came to mind that didn't make me look like I was in the wrong—even though I knew that I wasn't. "You sort of just had to be there."

"Well, I wasn't there," said Sarah, "so you'll just have to explain it to me." She was starting to look a little angry.

"It's a man thing," broke in the sheriff. "Being a woman, you wouldn't understand. It's best to just let it go and accept that if Mason here thought it necessary to punch that smarmy G-man, it probably was."

She looked at him, her jaw dropping even further. "For a man that's getting married, you might want to rethink how to phrase things to a woman."

I started to feel a little afraid for the sheriff. "You're getting married?"

"He thinks he is," Sarah said to me, before turning back to Adams, "but with that kind of attitude, you might not make it to the altar. Telling a woman she wouldn't understand something just because she's a woman is about as bad as telling us to calm down." She turned back to me. "He says they're getting married in the church at Shooter's Showdown."

"It's beautiful," said Adams, "You'd love it."

"Hey," I said, "maybe we could ...."

Sarah gave me a harsher look than the one she'd given me after I told her I'd punched ... *Steve.*

"Don't even," she said coldly.

"How about a cup of coffee, Mason?" continued Adams, either not registering Sarah's expression or just ignoring it. "You can tell me all about the fight, and I want details."

"I could use a cup," I said, seizing the opportunity to make a clean getaway.

The sheriff clapped a giant hand on my shoulder and carded the glass door as he held it open for me.

"Let me know when you're done, and I'll come pick you up," I said to Sarah, taking the sheriff's cue and pretending I didn't notice her expression. I knew I'd have to pay for that later, but she did have work to finish, and besides, as wiser men than I have noted in the past, retreat is sometimes the better part of valor.

WE MET at the same coffee shop where the shooters had tried to take us out. A big plywood rectangle covered the hole in the window I'd shot out and busted through. If another car full of thugs came for us, I wouldn't be able to see them ... but then again, they wouldn't be able to see us either.

The sheriff drove his department vehicle while I took my rental with Max and Pilgrim in the back. On the way, I texted my guys—Billy, Pappy, Byrne, Sammy, and Dominic—and asked them to meet me at the coffee shop. Billy got there before we did. The others were still at the base and would take a little longer.

"How's the shoulder?" asked Billy as we sat down.

The sheriff was getting our drinks. My punching Hearst seemed to have put him in a good mood. And for some reason, his good mood put me in a better one.

"Fine, thanks. Why were you on the way to town when I called?"

"Looking for you," said Billy. "That was a sweet punch. That liver shot! *Fast!* So fast I barely caught it."

"I shouldn't have hit him," I said.

"Yeah, right. You've been wanting to hit him since I got here. Let me guess, it's those dimples, right?"

"And the teeth and the tan," I said. "You see how he acts around Sarah?"

"Oh, I see it," said Billy.

The sheriff came to the table with the drinks. "Hey, you didn't start without me, did you? I want to hear everything."

Right then, Pappy, Dominic, and Sammy entered the coffee shop. Sammy and Dominic immediately noted the sheriff's holster and gun.

"You any good with that?" asked Sammy.

I saw that the sheriff had taken note of their taking note.

"Good enough," he said neutrally. "You two shooters?"

"We've been known to throw some lead," said Dominic. I saw him wince immediately after he said it, realizing how stupid it sounded.

The sheriff didn't burst out laughing, but it was close. He grinned, "Maybe the three of us will have to try out my shooting range. State of the art." He looked at me. "Another of those fed grants."

Pappy didn't say anything—he just watched and took it all in.

"The sheriff's a movie star," I said. "He did all the stunt shooting for that film Shooter's Showdown. He was faster than the special effects team."

"Really?" said Dominic. "I loved that movie. Great fights and shooting and that twist ending. Awesome."

"Shooting range," said Sammy. "That could be interesting."

"We got us a date," said the sheriff, "but first, I got a war story to hear." He looked back at me.

I held out my hands. "They were all there."

Dominic looked as though he was about to talk but held back, perhaps remembering how silly his last comment had sounded. Billy, nonplussed, started in, mindless of how he might sound to the older men.

Ah, the simplicity and boldness of youth.

Before Billy could complete his first sentence, the sheriff's phone buzzed. Interrupting Billy, he held up a hand and listened. His jaw flexed, and when he looked up, he stared right at me.

"Something's happened. Someone has taken your woman."

My woman?

Sarah.

20

Max watched as the men poured from the shop. Pilgrim was sleeping. Max had been asleep, too, but before the doors even opened, he caught the enhanced scent of the warriors and was instantly on his feet, looking for danger. The Alpha jumped into the front seat, and they sped away, taking corners so sharply that Pilgrim was nearly thrown to the floorboards. The bigger dog looked at Max with a startled expression but then had to fight for purchase as they rounded another corner far too fast. Max barely swayed with the vehicle's movement.

The Alpha usually drove with extreme care for Max and Pilgrim, but not this time, and Max could smell fear radiating from him ... *fear* ... and something else.

Rage.

The ride didn't take long.

~

THE LAB WAS IN SHAMBLES. The glass box containing the shell casings I'd seen less than an hour earlier was smashed on the floor. Evidence bags were scattered, and forensic equipment was destroyed. Two deputies were inside, while a few others buzzed about. The card access lock had been smashed open, shattering one entire glass panel. Surprisingly, the glass door itself was still intact.

Sheriff Adams stood next to me, his expression mirroring the way I felt. This was his castle, and we were his guests. Someone had invaded the source of his pride and stolen his treasure right under his nose.

"Security cameras," I said in a voice that sounded dead to my ears.

Adams nodded. "Central Control, through the corridor into the jail section. Follow me."

"How many suspects?" I asked as we moved.

"Differing reports—three, maybe as many as five."

"Five men were able to breach your headquarters—do all this? Take Sarah and get away without getting shot to pieces? Tell me how that's possible."

Sheriff Adams tossed me an angry look. "We'll know in a minute. But remember, the bulk of my troops are unarmed jail staff. I've got less than thirty road deputies for the whole county, including those who are off-duty. And those at work don't hang out here—they have patrol duties."

From my own experience with the SO, I knew what he was saying was true, but it did nothing to ease my fury.

Our group was buzzed through several security points until we finally entered Central Control. Inside, two deputies were watching numerous monitors in a darkened room about the size of an average living room. A row of handheld radios rested in their charging cradles, and a line of large brass keys hung on pegs along one wall. Across from these was a thick plate of bulletproof glass with a tray at the bottom featuring a push-pull drawer and a section cut out for receiving radios and keys from changing shifts.

"Play it," said the sheriff to one of the deputies, a thin Hispanic girl in uniform. She had dark hair pulled back into a tight bun, wore thick glasses, and looked like she was maybe fifteen years old. With a push of a button, the main monitor showed an outside camera view.

Two carloads of gangbangers pulled up out front, and five guys emptied from their doors. They all looked like doppelgängers of the men Max and I had killed outside the coffee shop a couple of days ago. One driver stayed with each car. The rest ran straight through the front doors, each armed.

A tall, thin, White male deputy with a receding hairline burst through a door to one side of the front desk's bulletproof enclosure, gun drawn. He was instantly obliterated by a hail of bullets fired from fully automatic weapons. Without hesitation, the men then fired into the desk officer's bullet-resistant glass, denting its front plating but not breaking through or hitting him.

The deputy they'd shot dropped to the floor, and before the door he'd entered from could close, the men leapt over his body and burst inside—running the halls, ignoring the deputy hiding under his desk inside his battered but impenetrable enclosure.

The camera switched angles as the men moved through the complex, and it was apparent that the Control Room deputy had sequenced the video before we arrived so we could see the exact route the men had taken.

No one challenged the killers as they made their way to Sarah. I felt rage building inside but fought for control. I had to pay attention, look for clues, take everything in. Sarah's life depended on it.

And then they reached her.

There was a short burst of gunfire, devoid of audio, followed by a kick and a bash with the butt of a rifle, and they were inside. One of the men, muscular and about six-one with a shaved head and covered in tattoos—mostly gang symbols, except for the Virgin Mother on his right shoulder—grabbed her. Sarah scratched him across the face, and he punched the side of her head, knocking her unconscious. He tossed her over his shoulder and stood there as the others destroyed the lab. They were fast, destructive, and thorough, but they were also something else—*selective*. I don't think anyone else noticed—not Pappy, Billy, or maybe even Sammy—but I noticed.

When the men were done, they retraced their route through the halls and exited through the front doors of the SO, again unchallenged. The big guy tossed Sarah, the woman I love, the woman who means more to me than anything else in the world, into the backseat like she was a piece of luggage or a bag of trash—*like she was nothing*—of no value at all.

I memorized his features, his tats, his scars, the line of his jaw, the set of his shoulders, every detail. I would meet him face to face one day—*but only once*—and then he would never meet anyone again.

I watched the video feed of the cars driving away to the west, everyone else watching me.

IRMGARD WAS STILL at her great-grandfather's cabin. She loved it here, and to make things better, Tina was with her—Tina, Viper, and three of the pups: Petros, Arrow, and Thor. She was on a walk with the dogs while Tina finished up some work on her computer and kept an eye on Atlas. Irmgard wanted to take the kitten with her, but Uncle Gil had made her promise to wait until he was back. Only Tina was allowed to be out alone with the cat. At all other times, he was confined to his cage.

Viper kept the pups in line, ensuring they didn't stray too far as they followed the winding dirt road to the mailbox. Some of the pups, especially Arrow, liked to wander off the path into the mountain brush, darting through dirt and rocks and circling trees that stretched toward the sky like spires. Thor would run after Arrow, throw him onto his back, and lead him back to the pack. When Thor couldn't manage, Viper would bite Arrow's scruff and drag him back to Irmgard, as he was now too big to pick up. Arrow would behave for a few minutes before forgetting and chasing after a squirrel, chipmunk, or bird, and the cycle would repeat.

Irmgard thought it hilarious.

She was happy.

The sun was shining, and the air was cool but not cold. White, fluffy clouds drifted across a blue sky while a mild breeze carried the scent of pine and flowers in gentle waves. The mountain was alive with wildlife, creating an orchestra of nature.

An image of the gray wolf flashed across her thoughts so fast and unbidden that she stopped in her tracks.

Her heart skipped a beat.

And then it was gone.

Petros nudged a cold nose into the palm of her dangling hand, and she almost jumped. She looked down and saw his warm, caring eyes and slicked-back ears. Realizing where she was, she knew that everything was all right. Petros was worried about her, having sensed her unease the way dogs do. Petting his head, she smiled at him, fighting to control the shivers running through her—shivers that had nothing to do with the temperature.

It was getting worse, and she didn't know what to do about it.

And that scared her.

The images—the thoughts and feelings of darkness—used to come only at night, in her dreams and nightmares, but that was before that man, Elio Columbo, kidnapped her and strapped her to the chair. He hadn't hurt her, but he'd been so cold, so calculating, like a robot in a movie that had gone bad—like Arnold in *Terminator* 2.

Irmgard knew all about Arnold because Billy—her dad—watched all his movies. Also, Arnold was from Austria, reminding her of her native Germany. That man had been like the Terminator in the movie—robotic, merciless, unstoppable.

Almost.

Max could stop anything, even that man, *even a Terminator*. But Max wasn't here, and for now, Petros was too small and young to save her. And now, even the entire pack, with Pilgrim and Viper's help, couldn't shield her from the thoughts and images that assailed her.

The darkness was too deep.

It made her feel bad.

Made her think of doing bad things.

Bad things to herself.

If only she'd eaten her peas.

Using her finger and thumb, she pinched her forearm, digging her nails in as hard as she could, then twisted. It didn't bring blood, not this time, but it hurt enough to drive away a little of the darkness. She didn't know why it worked, but it usually did—sometimes anyway. Sometimes, it would take a little more force. She'd have to pinch harder, twist further, dig deeper.

A week ago, before coming to the cabin, she'd taken a knife from the kitchen. It wasn't big, just a little paring knife, but it was pointy and had a very sharp edge. She had it in her coat pocket now. She kept it with her always.

She didn't understand why she had taken the knife. Tina had been in the other room at the time, and when Irmgard saw it, something suddenly told her to grab it—grab it up and hide it so Tina didn't see. *So that Tina and Billy wouldn't know*. And she had, just in case. She didn't know what *just in case* meant, but for some reason, it seemed important—as if maybe the pinches and fingernails wouldn't work for much longer, that she'd need something more.

And she'd been right. Sometimes the pinches still worked, but sometimes they didn't. So, she started cutting herself—nothing serious, just thin little lines on the insides of her forearms. And she only did it when the scratching and pinches didn't work—when they weren't enough.

Like now.

She remembered her mother, so thin, so weak, her eyes dark and glazed with pain, hurting too much to play with Irmgard. And the thought followed, *Why don't you just die?* She didn't want to think it, tried as hard as she could not to, but there it was.

She tried the pinch, the scratch. They didn't help. Then other thoughts came, so dark, so mean, so scary. Irmgard needed more—something with an edge. Something with a point. She pressed her finger against the tip of the knife. It slid through her skin with little effort. The pain made her start so abruptly that Petros growled at her side. Thor ran to her, looking for something to kill, something to protect her from.

But there was nothing—nothing they could do to protect her. Nothing they could see or hear or attack. There was only the edge. There was only the point.

There was only the knife.

21

Nathan had spent the morning talking with the elders of his small congregation. Four elders, including himself, oversaw an attendance ranging from about a hundred to a hundred and fifty, depending on the week. Their church's mission wasn't to grow their roster or their funds. In fact, they didn't even take a weekly collection, relying instead on a drop box at the back of the sanctuary where people could leave money and checks if they felt able to contribute—no tithing required. Tithing was part of the law and members of the Body of Christ were free from the law. Free to serve God and others through love rather than rules and fear of the eternal consequences of sin.

It wasn't that Nathan had no interest in bringing new people to the Lord—on the contrary, it was his primary personal goal. However, as a pastor, his job was to nourish and strengthen the flock. He focused on teaching, discussing, and seeking ways to deepen their understanding of God and His Word. He aimed to uncover God's true meaning in the scriptures and understand His character so that everyone could better emulate those divine qualities.

After the meeting with the elders, Nathan spoke with a newly married couple of about five months, counseling them on the best way to handle minor disagreements according to Biblical principles. He ate lunch, then returned to his house to work on the wedding vows.

But the words just wouldn't come to him.

He'd prayed, read, studied, and then prayed some more, but nothing that came to him seemed special or unique enough. He thought of his conversation with Rick and the two interns—they were smart men, very smart, maybe too smart.

Too smart for their own good.

Men like them could easily intellectualize themselves into an eternity in Hell. Nathan liked them and hoped to be able to continue their friendship and discussions for all time. He wanted them in Heaven with him, his wife, his girls, and Gil.

Gil.

Nathan worried for him. He seemed to be doing better, but he was still confused, still filled with rage. Still at war with what had happened to Joleen and Marla. Still at war with the thought that Majoqui Cabrera was now in Heaven.

Nathan feared that Gil's inability to understand and accept the requirements of the law of love would inhibit his and Sarah's chances of having a successful marriage. He had hoped something inspirational would come to him—something that might plant a seed in Gil's soul. Something that, with careful nurturing, might grow into understanding. But nothing had come.

Shaking his head, he reflected on his discussion with Rick and the interns. Rick asked for other examples in the Bible that illustrate God's knowledge of time and the idea that the future does not yet exist. Staying within the texts Rick had already read, Nathan decided on the incident involving the golden calf in Exodus 32. Despite witnessing the ten plagues of Egypt, the pillar of fire, and the parting of the Red Sea, the Israelites rebelled against God, demanding that Moses' brother Aaron make them an idol to worship. God was so furious that He told Moses to stand aside so He could *utterly destroy* them and start over again with Moses. However, God's love for Moses was so great that Moses was able to talk God out of destroying the Israelites. In Jeremiah 15, God reinforces the idea that He can change His mind based on His children's actions and needs. He declares that even if Moses and Samuel stood before Him, He wouldn't change His mind in this case, indicating that His love for them had influenced Him to change His mind in the past.

Nathan's cell buzzed. It was Rick.

"I have you on speaker," he said. "My interns insist on hearing your answer."

Nathan smiled. "Your question?"

"Earlier, you said the Bible clearly states that God changes His mind, but I've found several verses that contradict that claim."

"Okay, before you go through those, let's look at a few facts. Remember the first rule when studying a book or participating in a conversation—evaluate the information within context. When information is taken out of place without context, it can be twisted to mean anything. To discover the truth, we must evaluate a matter in context with what is being spoken about and what has already been established. For instance, in Jeremiah 18, God speaks to the prophet and tells him to go down to the potter's house. Jeremiah does, and God shows how the clay is marred in the potter's hands ... not because the potter wanted or made it be marred, but rather because of its own instability. God explains to Jeremiah that if the clay doesn't work for the vessel the potter intended, he can decide to make it into another vessel that seems good to him.

"God explains that *He* is the potter in this analogy, and Israel is the clay. He warns Israel, through Jeremiah, that He can do the same to them. Consider this quote from Jeremiah 18:7-11 '*The instant I speak concerning a nation and concerning a kingdom, to pluck up, to pull down, and to destroy it, if that nation against whom I have spoken turns from its evil, I will repent of the disaster that I thought to bring upon it. And the instant I speak concerning a nation and concerning a kingdom, to build and to plant it, if it does evil in My sight so that it does not obey My voice, then I will repent concerning the good with which I said I would benefit it. Now therefore, speak to the men of Judah and to the inhabitants of Jerusalem, saying, 'Thus says the Lord: Behold, I am fashioning a disaster and devising a plan against you. Return now everyone from his evil way, and make your ways and your doings good.'*

"In this passage, God makes it clear that if He promises to do something good for someone, but that person takes advantage of it or becomes evil, God is no longer obligated to fulfill His promise. Conversely, if God declares He will destroy a nation, like Nineveh, but that nation turns from its evil ways and repents, then God will change His plan and not bring about the destruction.

"It's kind of like telling your nine-year-old son that you'll take him to a waterpark because he got an A on a test. However, if the day before the trip he throws a tantrum and kicks his mother, you wouldn't take him to the waterpark. Doing so would be bad for him and teach him the wrong lesson. God always aims to teach us lessons that are good for us, even if they are painful or difficult.

"Also, note that everything God says in this passage is in the present tense. He doesn't say it like it happened in a future that already exists—one that He looked into to see what would happen to Israel. No, what He says is, '*Behold, I am fashioning a disaster and devising a plan against you.*' He then proceeds to tell them how they can avoid the disaster. '*Return now everyone from his evil way, and make your ways and your doings good.*' The obvious meaning here is that if they do, He won't have to go through with the disaster He is planning against them.

"This alone shows that God is working in time *with* them and will gladly change His mind and not punish them if they turn from their evil, harmful ways and instead do good, which is all He wants in the first place. God says over and over that He desires mercy, not sacrifice."

"That's a lot," said Rick. "By the way, full disclosure, I'm recording this."

"Perfectly fine," said Nathan.

Lederman's voice came through to Nathan in the background. "See, I told you he wouldn't care about being recorded—typical Five."

Jules Harrow came right in, "Classic INFJ."

Rick continued, "I'll shelve my verses on that subject for now until I can go over them with the stipulations you just emphasized, but one quick point—in those verses, you used the word *repent* in relation to God. My Bible app says *relent*."

"The quick answer is that the translators didn't believe God repents, so they changed the word *repent* to *relent*. The Hebrew word *nacham* means *to change one's mind, be grieved, repent.* In Genesis 6:6, God says He was sorry that He had made man on the earth. The root word used here is, again, *nacham*. In fact, God says He *nachams* or *repents* over twenty times in the Book of Genesis. The word *relent* is actually weaker, but translators likely found it more palatable to use than *repent* because *repent* is frequently associated with the need for human repentance."

"Wait," said Rick, "what about the verse in Numbers where it says God doesn't repent?"

"Numbers 23:19 ... context," said Nathan. "When we read the context, we see that Balaam is speaking to Balak. He's saying that God is not a man—*like* Balak—who lies, nor a son of man—again *like* Balak—who repents. In other words, God doesn't lie or repent the way humans do—the way Balak does for his own personal interest or to harm others. God does everything for the overall good of His children. Men often lie to hide their wrongdoings or evil plans, and when they repent, it's usually because they feel guilty for their bad actions. In contrast, when God repents, He does so in response to what His children have done, whether good or bad. When God lies, it is to thwart evil or to protect His children from harm."

"Wait, you're saying that God has lied?"

"Way too deep to get into here, but again, the short answer is yes. It sounds heretical, but the *truth* is the only thing that matters, and if it's Biblical, then it can't be heretical. Theologians will fight this to their dying breath. They will come up with various ways to explain the verses away, but theologians are just men, and like all men, are often wrong. And you can usually tell they're wrong when they start going into philosophical arguments or begin using fancy, hard-to-pronounce words or phrases like *anthropomorphic* or *the panoply of scripture* to explain away the obvious intended context of the verse in order to prove their point.

"Despite everything I just said, I firmly believe that God generally hates lying. In a perfect world, like before the fall of man, lying wouldn't be needed or allowed. But we live in a fallen world, and things are different now. Similarly, God hates divorce. In a sinless world, divorce wouldn't happen, but in our fallen world, it is sometimes necessary because there are worse things. For example, if a man beats his wife or cheats on her, then as bad as divorce is, staying with him might be worse because of the harm and danger to the wife and family. So, while God hates divorce and lying, He allows these things when necessary.

"To prove my point, I'll give three examples. First, in 1 Kings 22:19-23, God sends a deceptive spirit to mislead Ahab's prophets, ultimately leading the king into disaster. Second, we see God rewarding the Hebrew midwives for their deception of the Egyptian soldiers. They claimed that Jewish women gave birth too quickly, allowing the children to be hidden so that they wouldn't be put to the sword, thus saving baby Moses. Third is the story of Rahab, who concealed Israelite spies in Jericho and then lied to the soldiers who were searching for them. God approved this lie so greatly that He included Rahab in the genealogy of Jesus Christ Himself—not a lot of honors greater than that one."

"Wait-wait-wait," Rick broke in, "doesn't one of the Ten Commandments say, '*Thou shalt not lie?*'"

Nathan clarified, "Actually, it states '*Thou shalt not bear false witness against thy neighbor*.' This specifically targets perjury—a legal definition concerning falsely accusing someone of a *crime*. Jewish law even goes further, stipulating that the punishment for perjury matches the severity of the false accusation, aligning with the potential punishment the accused could have faced."

"That's a lot to go over," said Rick. "A lot to take in. I'm glad I recorded it."

"My turn," said Nathan.

"Like I know anything about the Bible."

"No, it concerns your field. I'm struggling to come up with the sermon for Gil and Sarah's wedding. You know Gil well, maybe even better than I do, and you've at least met Sarah. I could use your help."

They talked for another ten minutes, and Rick told him what he could. When the call ended, Nathan thought he might just have it.

22

We were in the SO's conference room on the second floor, adjacent to the Investigation Section. The room had a large table, numerous chairs, and several computers and monitors. Sheriff Adams was there, along with Billy, his mafia buddy Montgomery Byrne, Pappy, Sammy, Dominic, Steve Hearst, and other uninjured participants from the raid. They'd all volunteered, insisted, really, and I wasn't about to say no—Sarah's life was at stake.

A map outlining a twenty-mile radius was displayed on a seventy-five-inch monitor.

"The inner perimeter is set one hundred yards around this building," said Hearst. "Mason and his dogs have already checked the entrance and exit the perpetrators used, as well as the parking lot, looking for evidence and clues. His Shepherd lost the track right where the video feeds show them getting into their car and driving off." He looked at me. "You find anything useful?"

I shook my head to the negative—a lie—which wasn't exactly ethical when dealing with partners in an endeavor. But having examined the scene, I knew that someone in this room, or at least very closely associated, had to be on the take. When I found out who it was, I'd shoot him dead ... *after* he told me where Sarah was.

Pilgrim had led me to three shell casings scattered along the escape route, still sticky from the superglue mist. He also found a torn, bloody tie, likely from the dead deputy at the original crime scene, and two empty, clear plastic zip-lock baggies with blood stains inside.

Hearst continued, "We've set the outer perimeter in standard ring formation varying from yards to miles. All major roads have been locked down—and I mean locked down. Every car coming in or going out is being hand-searched. The sheriff has enlisted help from other agencies across the region, securing the smaller routes and even foot trails. All my assets are in play and some of you here know how considerable those are. Our best bet is that they're heading to the border through Texas, Arizona, or New Mexico."

"Why?" Billy asked, his voice and face revealing his rage. "Why did they take her? What reason could they possibly have? She wasn't even involved in the raid!"

Hearst gave a half shrug. "To send a message. That's how the cartels operate, always sending messages. It's like in the movie *The Untouchables* when Sean Connery explains the *Chicago Way* to Kevin Costner. He tells him, '*They pull a knife, you pull a gun. He sends one of yours to the hospital, you send one of theirs to the morgue. That's the Chicago Way.*'

"It's like that with the cartels, only times a thousand. If they think we have a spy in a town, they'll just wipe out the town, every man, woman, and child. Life means nothing to them. We played their game back at them—tried to send a message after they killed our deputy—but we failed. Now they're doubling down on us—marching into our HQ and stealing Miss Gallagher from right under our noses. Simple as that."

It was a good speech, delivered with force and sincerity, but I knew it was a lie ... or at least wrong. They weren't sending a message, not this time. Sarah knew something. She'd discovered something during her investigation. I didn't know what it was, which meant she must have uncovered it today. Otherwise, she would have told me.

And she hadn't.

However, I saw something on the video feed—something the gang members did after they grabbed her—that left me with a puzzling question. Why didn't they just take what they wanted and kill her on the spot? This information could be crucial in finding her, but I couldn't share it with anyone outside my team. If others knew, we would all become targets, complicating our efforts to recover Sarah in time.

Before they didn't need her anymore.

Before they killed her.

There was a positive side, though. Whoever planned this had to have done it on the fly, which meant they couldn't have covered all their bases. They probably hadn't had time to develop elaborate escape routes or detailed runs for the border. Sarah had to be close by.

My last case, involving an assassin named Elio Columbo, taught me that, in desperate situations, there were often only two possibilities. Either the gangbangers were running full speed toward the border with all the roads closed and guarded, or they weren't.

We'd issued BOLOs with several pictures of the car, the suspects, and Sarah to every county and jurisdiction within a six-state area. So far, there had been no sightings—not of the bad guys, their car, or Sarah, all of whom were easily identifiable, especially Sarah. No one who saw Sarah could fail to notice or remember her. Not ever.

She wasn't on her way to the border, not yet anyway.

No, it was like with Elio Columbo.

Sarah was close.

She was close, and I would find her.

PILGRIM WAS EXHAUSTED. Learning from Max, he dozed lightly in the back of the car. Pilgrim was conserving his energy, something he rarely did or even thought of doing. Intuitively, he seemed to understand that he would need his strength in the very near future.

He'd searched the area around the Sheriff's Office and jail, discovering most of what he found in the dirt and grass near the sidewalk and a few things in the parking lot.

That was after he'd lost the track.

The track had been easy. Multiple suspects always made it easier, leaving lots of ground disturbance, even on concrete and asphalt. This track had been even easier.

Sarah.

He knew her smell, knew it well.

Pilgrim loved Sarah.

He had killed protecting her.

Her scent told him many things. She'd been hurt, bleeding.

She was scared.

Pilgrim would find the men that had taken her.

He had their scent.

He would have their scent forever, locked and sealed in his receptors and in his memory.

And when Pilgrim found the men who had hurt her—the men who had made her scared—he would kill again.

THE SHERIFF WENT LAST. He was mad. *Couldn't blame him.* The bangers had killed his deputy, shot up his town, stormed his castle, killed another of his men, kidnapped his guest, and then gotten away scot-free.

Only they wouldn't get away. I would see to that. Traitor or no traitor, nothing would stop me from saving her.

We would have to address the issue concerning our marriage later. Being close to me had once again placed her in danger—maybe even worse. *What kind of a fool was I, thinking I could ever have a normal future with a woman? With a family?*

I pushed the thoughts away. I had a job to do, men to kill, Sarah to find.

Nothing else mattered.

Nothing.

Sheriff Adams outlined the roadblocks and the air and ground support, which were considerable but still inadequate given the size of the area. I only half-listened, focusing instead on faces, postures, and glances. The traitor was here in this room. The more I thought on it, the more convinced I was. How else could they have known about the raid, the dead deputy, the layout of the Sheriff's Office, the lab, the evidence ... Sarah?

I played everything back in my head, starting from the beginning. Who was it that had called us down here in the first place?

No, not *us*. Not *me* ... just Sarah.

Steve Hearst.

I looked at him. He looked back at me. We stayed like that for maybe thirty seconds. *I was wasting time.* There were others to study.

I examined each of the soldiers in the room—all that had been on the raid—mentally calculating the pros and cons, the possible motives. I replayed every interaction I'd had with them, as well as any I'd witnessed them have with Sarah.

I supposed I could just nab them one at a time and torture it out of them—I was sure to get the guilty party sooner or later. I had almost reached the point where I might try it, but they were hard men, strong men. It would take time, and time was a luxury I didn't have ... *that Sarah didn't have*. Not if I was going to get her back.

And I was going to get her back.

I needed to leave. We were wasting time. I had to meet with my men—tell them the plan I'd devised after studying all the possible characters in the room while listening to the speeches. I can multi-task when I have to—I just don't like it.

When the briefing finally ended, the sheriff, Hearst, and all my guys looked at me. I chucked my head towards the exit and started that way. Steve Hearst was waiting for me at the end of the row of chairs.

"I'm sorry this happened," he said. "We'll get her back."

"Yes," I said, feeling my lips twitch at the corners, "we will."

"I need you to come with me. I have something to show you."

"I have to talk with my friends," I said.

"This first. It won't take long, I promise."

More wasted time? I almost said no, but then I decided he might actually have something.

And if he didn't ... what better time to start the torturing?

23

Anthony Carlino stood at the sink, finishing the dishes while watching Irmgard through the window. She was playing outside with the dogs, but something was bothering her. He didn't know what it was, but he'd read people for far too many decades not to notice. Of course, Billy was away, so that could be it, but it felt ... more. Tina had also been on edge.

Problems in the relationship?

Very possible, thought the old man. If Tina and Billy were to break up, many problems would be solved. His son, Nick, wasn't comfortable with their relationship. A breakup would make him very happy. The same could be said of many of Nick's lieutenants. None of them wanted a cop that close to their dealings. There'd been talk. *A lot of talk.*

Initially, Anthony wasn't thrilled with their relationship either, but after getting to know Tina, he saw how good she was with Irmgard and how happy she made Billy. However, Nick wasn't wrong. Even though Billy was technically out of the family business, he was still part of the *Family* and could never truly be out. It just wasn't possible. He knew too much—such as where certain bodies were buried—a lot of bodies. He would inevitably be privy to information that could endanger other Family members. And if it was impossible for him, a member of the ruling Family, to avoid such information, how much more impossible would it be for a non-member—a cop?

Sooner or later, someone would get scared, mad, or even just think she'd spilled the beans—ratted on someone, even if she hadn't —and take her out. What would Billy do then?

It would cause chaos in the ranks. Chaos presented an opportunity for other factions that would only too quickly seize whatever advantage they could to wrest control from the Carlino clan. And that wasn't even considering the possibility that the feds might pressure Billy to turn State's evidence against them.

Ordinarily, Billy would never go against the Family—Anthony knew this in his heart. Billy loved them, loved him. But if it came to a choice between the Family and Tina, maybe even Irmgard, a man would have to make a choice, and a choice like this might well go against the Family. Anthony wouldn't blame him.

So, while it was true that Tina being gone could be a good thing in many ways, that possibility had a hard side. A bitter side. A *bad* side. Because if she left, she couldn't be allowed to live. She'd seen too much—been too close. Billy should have thought of this, but he was young and stupid and had allowed his heart to lead him rather than his head. It was the story of youth.

The thing of tragedies.

But it was what it was.

Just the way it *had* to be.

Like many things in the life of a Mafioso, Billy may have started it, but the Family would finish it—a sad reality of the right he had been born into. As an old soul, Anthony understood how things were and how they needed to be, but it was still hard—painful—even after all these decades. They were left with the hand they'd been dealt and the cards they'd played.

Irmgard would be heartbroken for a time, but kids were tough. Resilient. A new pet, maybe a bike, the passage of time. Time helped everything—blunted the pain. Anthony knew all too well. His wife's passing still hurt. It would always hurt, but not like it had.

It would be more difficult for Billy unless he and Tina broke up first, especially if she jilted or cheated on him. Not that she would—she wasn't the type—but perhaps it could be made to look like she had.

Anthony shook his head. Nah, Billy was too sharp to believe in two connected setups. *One would be hard enough.*

Because there would have to be at least one.

Making her death look like an accident was essential—there was no question about it. Otherwise, Billy might lose his mind, perhaps even completely turn on the Family and Nick. That was something Anthony couldn't allow, no matter what. The real challenge lay in creating a scenario convincing enough for Billy to accept the *possibility* of an accident. With his experience in the Family, suspicion was bound to arise, but if there was enough doubt to keep him guessing, he could carry on, willfully submerging the truth in an effort to stave off the pain.

A loving wife, pretending her husband isn't cheating on her.

A fair boss, thinking his employees wouldn't steal from him.

A trusting father believing his son's excuse for the drugs in his pocket.

Everyday life, everyday lies. People doing what people do so they can survive.

Through the window Anthony watched as Arrow dropped the ball in front of Irmgard. She picked it up, gave it a look, and stayed that way as if lost in thought, her free hand reaching inside her pocket, fidgeting with something.

What was she doing?

Anthony didn't like it. He was about to go outside and see what was wrong, but then she turned and looked at him. She didn't smile. She didn't wave. Instinctively, Anthony looked toward the road, then the woods, searching for danger but saw nothing.

No, not nothing.

There was the look on her face—the almost glazed stare of

someone facing death. Anthony had seen it before many times. He felt a shadow glide through him. Arrow barked, and Irmgard threw the ball, the game resuming. Anthony shrugged his big shoulders, shook his head, and returned to the dishes.

Everyday life, everyday lies. People doing what people do so they can survive.

~

ARROW DROPPED the ball in front of Irmgard. She picked it up and looked like she was going to throw it for him but suddenly stopped. She seemed to be looking at him without seeing him—as if she were seeing through him—past him. Her hand went to her pocket.

At first, Arrow thought something had scared her. He turned and scanned the area, searching for danger, ready to attack, ready to fight.

But there was nothing.

Nothing in sight or within hearing or scent range.

Thor and Petros were still off playing in the trees. Arrow could see them dancing back and forth, growling playfully. If there had been some form of danger, they would have alerted and come to them—or taken care of the problem themselves.

No, there was no danger, not out there. The danger—as real as a bear, a bobcat, or a rattlesnake—was *inside* Irmgard. Arrow could feel it, hear it, smell it. He sensed a change in her pheromones, the adrenaline dump, cortisol pumping through her veins, heartbeat racing, teeth grinding. Arrow would have attacked whatever was threatening her, but he didn't know how, so he did the only thing he could.

He barked.

Startled, Irmgard left what she had been touching in her pocket, took a deep breath, and threw the ball. She was all right, for now at least.

Arrow chased after the ball.

~

TINA TYPED the final keystrokes on her computer, completing a report on the narcotics Viper had found during their last vehicle stop. She rocked her head from side to side and back and forth, easing the tension that always built up in her neck and shoulders from contorting her body to work on the computer while sitting in the driver's seat of her patrol car.

Viper chewed noisily at a Kong toy in the back, producing horrible sounds that momentarily reminded her of the night Max saved her from the bikers who'd invaded her house. Tina was thankful for the rescue and his protection, but she still experienced an occasional chill when recalling the incident.

The fight with the big biker, the walk down the dark hallway, what she had seen, heard, what Max had done.

Her mind flashed back to Gil, shoving streams of wadding into the bleeding hole in her stomach, his eyes hollow and robotic, devoid of emotion, sympathy, or worry—just blank, not even human.

Shaking the memory from her head, Tina heard a call for assistance on the radio. It wasn't directed at her specifically, but she tuned in since it might involve a K9 deployment. The dispatcher was sending county cars to help Cherry Hills PD with a 911 call. A concerned neighbor reported seeing someone sneaking around an open garage. Cherry Hills PD units were preoccupied with a multi-car accident on the far side of the city. Tina was a little way out, and it was close to the end of her shift, but she called in anyway, saying she would respond to the incident.

The houses in Cherry Hills were nice—expensive. The neighborhood was home to many lawyers, doctors, sports celebrities, and even a few actors. They had nice cars and big money. The gated community had its own security. Tina knew the two guards on duty today—a fifty-year-old lady who smoked three packs a day and an older, overweight man whose gun belt would likely fall around his ankles if he had to run.

Tina was just about to put her car in drive when her phone vibrated. It was a text from Billy saying that Sarah had been kidnapped and he would fill her in as soon as he could, but that he wouldn't be home tonight.

Kidnapped? Sarah?

Tina would have called him and demanded more information, but that would have to wait until after the call.

She had police work to do.

24

Steve Hearst opened the door to the control room. It was like something out of a secret agent movie.

Go figure.

I'd followed him back to the base from the SO in my rented SUV. The room was filled with banks of monitors, rows of manned computers, and a huge screen at the front displaying streamed drone footage from high in the sky. Different controllers played at their screens, causing the feeds to zoom in and out.

"In addition to this," said Hearst, "I've allocated three space-based satellites to help cover the area. We *will* spot them. We will get her back." He looked at me, the tooth suck and the eye tick completely absent. So were the *Slicks, Sports, Champs,* and other little nicknames he liked to throw in as part of his schtick. He was all business now, and for the first time, I felt like I was seeing the real Hearst—not the agent, not the act, but the man's naked soul.

"No," I said. "You won't. Not like this."

"What do you mean?"

"She's not moving. She's not out there where you're looking. She's stationary. And so are the men who took her."

He stayed silent for a few seconds, processing what I'd said. He looked at the screen and then back at me.

"Spill," he said. "Tell me what you know."

"I know this wasn't retaliation for our raid. I know this wasn't a message. The bad guys were looking for something in the lab. Evidence. They found it, took it. I'm positive that you and your men had things set up too fast for them to have made it past your perimeters. They're still here—*close*—probably holed up in a stash house or a pollo holding pen like the one in the video you have of me where I killed the banger.

"What I don't know is why they took Sarah. But that's not important right now. We need to focus on getting her back, and to do that, we have to act fast. But we can't use your guys or the sheriff's men. Someone's compromised. I don't know who, not yet, but someone. I trust my men, so we'll have to do this ourselves."

Hearst rubbed at the stubble covering his chin and jaw. He head-bobbed toward the door, indicating we should step into the hallway, which we did.

"You say you know your guys? Well, I know my people in that room," said Hearst as he shut the door. "They've been vetted a thousand times over, and I have them surveilled twenty-four seven. They're all good—solid. The leak isn't on my end."

I nodded. "Okay, that leaves someone higher in your organization or someone in the Sheriff's Office."

"Or," said Hearst, "any one of a thousand in the Mexican government or ours."

"No," I said, shaking my head. "Has to be someone here, now, close enough to know that Sarah was onto something. That leaves whoever *you* might have spoken to or the SO. There was no way for anyone in the upper echelons of the Mexican government or our own to have that information and then act on it in real-time."

Behind us, the door opened, and a guy with a headset leaned out. "Agent Hearst, you're going to want to see this."

We re-entered the control room and saw a video feed showing about a dozen marked sheriff's cars surrounding the suspect vehicle we'd seen in the attack on the lab. At least twenty guns were pointed at the men inside the car.

"Where is this?" asked Hearst.

"I25, just north of the border to New Mexico," said the man who had called us into the room.

"Let me hear everything," said Hearst.

Instantly, live audio was piped into the room from an advanced stereo system, sending garbled and overlapping police chatter to bounce off the walls. A confident-sounding female dispatcher's voice overrode everything.

"Channel One is on emergency traffic only for officers and deputies involved in the felony traffic stop. All other radio traffic go to channel two until further notice."

A male voice came across, "B42 is giving verbal orders for the driver to exit the vehicle." In the background, we could hear a voice issuing orders through a loudspeaker. For several seconds afterward, there was silence.

"Non-compliant," said the first deputy. "Second set of announcements being made now." More loudspeaker orders echoed through the room.

"Still non-compliant, but there's furtive movement from the suspect in the backseat. Driver and one other male visible in the front seat. No sign of the female victim. Third set of announcements being ... *stand by*. Rear suspect exiting to the west ... running. We need K9 to the scene *ASAP! GUN! GUN! HE'S GOT A GUN!*"

A series of overlapping cracks reverberated across space, filling the room and our imaginations. Those of us who had been in similar situations relived our personal experiences. I felt it, saw it in their eyes, heard it in their silence—but for me, it was more. If Sarah was in that car, she was in imminent danger. And if she wasn't in the car, I needed at least one of the suspects to live so I could force her location from him.

The drone footage was superb—digitally perfect and color-enhanced. The red and blue strobes of the police lights flashed as the guns of the suspect and at least nine officers fired, their gasses and bullets passing each other in flight. Sparks pinged off and into a police cruiser. Bullets from law enforcement did *not* bounce off the suspect, and the drone's color enhancement displayed his life's blood in vivid brilliance as he danced a short jig before falling to the dirt.

The driver and the front seat passenger came out shooting, one from each side, using their partner's escape as an attempt at distraction.

It didn't work.

Both men were sprayed with rounds from AR15s, pistols, and shotguns. The driver got off one shot, hitting himself in the foot—the passenger maybe three—before being obliterated.

Steve Hearst turned to me. "Looks like you were wrong. They were still moving, after all. Sarah's probably on the floorboard or in the trunk."

But Sarah wasn't in the car, not stuffed down on the floorboard or stashed in the trunk.

Her shirt was, though—torn, bloody, and partially burned.

STEVE GAVE me the rundown as we drove to the scene. They found her body about nine miles to the north. The driver led them there. He was shot in five places—twice in the right leg, once in the side, once low in the ribs, and the last in the right shoulder. None of the wounds were life-threatening, but the shock and loss of blood might do the trick.

Sheriff Adams arrived at the scene of the shootout before we did. He ordered the paramedics to drive to the location where the suspect said Sarah was, hoping she might still be alive. While en route, the paramedics continued to work on him, one of Hearst's men continuing the interrogation.

Totally illegal.

The suspect had played the Sgt. Shultz game of *I know nothing*, until Adams told him they weren't leaving for the hospital until they found Sarah. Adams told him the paramedics would keep taking wrong turns and getting lost until he took them to her.

The suspect broke, telling Adams and one of Steve's men, an agent who had made it to the scene and rode in the ambulance with them, that they had taken the woman because of her beauty. He said they had their way with her while hiding in the woods until the helicopters and sirens sounded far enough away, and then shot her in the head and burned her body. They said they had attacked the Sheriff's Office as a message from the cartel to those who would attack them and that as long as there was no further retribution, the matter between them would be deemed closed.

The body, a charred, unrecognizable mess, was about Sarah's height and build, wearing her shoes—what was left of them—and a small fragment of her pants. Next to the body was a five-gallon gas can. They'd piled sticks, still smoldering, under and over her.

Adams came up to us, shaking his head. "I'm so sorry, man. We got here fast as we could. Suspect took a little convincing."

I nodded, the stench of burning hair and human flesh stinging my nostrils. "Thanks for the bluff. It worked, at least. Might mess things up in court, though."

"Wasn't a bluff," said the sheriff. "I'd have let him bleed out. He still wasn't talking, though. Sang out once I put my finger into the hole in his leg. Sang real pretty then. As for court ... he won't make it to trial. Not even arraignment. You got my word on that. She was a classy, beautiful lady."

Hearst stood next to me, nodding silently.

"It's not Sarah," I said.

"It is, though," said Adams. "I know it's hard, Son. These things always are. There was another gas can in the car, and we found a section of a map marked from here to the dirt roads, the highway, and on to New Mexico. We discovered the map stashed in one of the dead suspect's pockets."

"No," I said. "No, it's someone else."

Steve shook his head. "I'm sorry, Mason, but wasn't it you who said they didn't have time to plan this thing out properly? How did they happen to have a woman of Miss Gallagher's height and weight and wearing the same clothes? Not to mention finding her shirt in the car and the blood? I'm sorry."

"No," I said again.

Adams stepped up to me and held out his closed hand. "There's one more thing." He opened his fist.

Resting in his palm was the engagement ring I had given to Sarah.

25

Tina parked down the block behind a county car. She opened the rear door, where Viper obediently stood waiting for her. Tina slipped the nylon harness over Viper's head and front leg, snapping the clasp under her chest. She then attached the lead to the agitation collar around Viper's muscular neck and gave the command for her to hop out. Viper jumped, landing silently on the asphalt, ears high and perked.

Tina pulled her nine-millimeter handgun from its holster and wedged it in a downward angle against her chest. She commanded Viper to heel and walked to the far side of the large, two-story house. A county deputy and two security guards, who had been standing behind a bushy pine, joined her.

"What have you got?" she asked the deputy. She'd worked a couple of calls with him over the years—young kid, big in the shoulders, small at the waist. Pretty good-looking. Competent. Last name Trebek, first Rob or Bob or Bobby—something like that.

"Security got the alarm, responded, saw a guy inside but lost sight of him. White male, late twenties to early thirties, baseball cap. Said it looked like he was looting the place."

"Bobby, right?"

"Rob," said the kid.

"Right. Owners?"

"Elderly woman. Passed last week. Funeral was yesterday. Adult children have been in and out of the place but left after the funeral and told security they wouldn't be back until next week. Debbie, the female security officer here," he pointed at the smoker lady, "says they called the executor—one of her kids—and he says no one should be inside the house. He gave us permission to enter and check it out. He gave us the door code."

"Works for me," said Tina. "You have another car on scene?"

"Dillon's around the back. He's got a trainee, so there's two of them. I can go with you."

"Good. We'll leave the guards to watch the front, and you can cover me while I give instructions." She turned to the security officers. "You two good with covering the front while we make entry?"

Debbie spoke up, her voice sounding like she was gargling nicotine-stained shards of glass. "We got you covered, honey." She drew her gun, a massive .357 with a six-inch barrel. She waggled it at shoulder height, pointing toward the sky. "Me and Hank here will make sure no one escapes."

Hank, the fat man whose pants looked like they might drop, was pale and did not draw his weapon.

"Okay," said Tina, hoping that Debbie didn't blast all of them by accident. "Let's go, Rob."

Tina, Rob, and Viper jogged up to the front door and noticed it had been kicked in, its doorframe splintered and lying just inside the hallway. *So much for needing the door code.* They both stood to the sides, peering through the windows that framed the doorway.

Tina keyed her mic, informing dispatch she was making K9 announcements and asking for emergency traffic on channel one. Using her deepest, loudest voice, she shouted through the doorway, "This is the Colorado State Patrol K9 Unit. Anyone in the house, identify yourself now and come out with your hands up, or I will send in a police-trained K9, and you will be bit!"

There was a noise from inside, possibly chairs being thrown and furniture breaking.

Over the radio, Deputy Trebek advised dispatch and everyone else that they'd heard something while Tina gave her second set of announcements. The sound of glass shattering reached them. Tina usually gave three commands before sending Viper, but since the suspect was obviously trying to escape, which meant he'd heard her, she decided that two were enough.

She gave the command, sending Viper in.

RICK BREWED a fresh cup of coffee and took it to his desk. His patient, a Mrs. Ellen Bassett of the Longmont Bassetts, was lying on the leather couch, her head and feet propped comfortably on opposite ends. His interns were probing and prodding her with complementary questions, each designed to sort and categorize her traits according to their specialized fields of study in psychology. Seventy-two-year-old Mrs. Bassett loved the attention—*a trait worth noting*—as she gave them reams of data for future analysis.

"So," asked Jules, "would you say shyness played a part in your decision not to speak at the convention?"

"Oh no, my dear boy, shyness has never been a characteristic of the Bassett personality. To be frank, it was the décor. Beige sets an awful tone. I warned the organizers about it before previous engagements when they asked me to speak, but they refused to do anything. Just as I predicted, there I was amidst a dreadful turnout because of that awful color. This time, the head of ceremonies promised they would change it before my appearance. But when I visited a month before the scheduled date, nothing had been done. And you know the old saying, once bitten, twice shy. There was no way a person of my stature could endure another humiliation due to their incompetence."

"Certainly not," agreed Jules, canting his head toward his compatriot, Lederman. "Classic ISTJ," he whispered.

"And classic tendencies toward Type One," said Lederman.

"Did I say something interesting, boys? Perhaps controversial?"

"Simply keeping within your breeding and stature," humored Jules.

Rick had to admit that the two were becoming very skilled at seeing through the fluff as they did a deep dive into the true nature of their subjects. People put on so many airs. Defenses. Protections against the wounds delivered throughout a lifetime—armor built up to ensure survivability. *Once bitten, twice shy indeed.*

He allowed them to continue while he sat back, listening, sipping his coffee, and contemplating his ongoing conversation with Gil's father-in-law, Nathan. Nathan had a unique preaching style and held unconventional ideas about God and His nature. Rick had to admit that Nathan's ideas and points seemed to align well with the scriptures he read. Every interaction between God and man in the Bible appeared to occur within the same timeframe rather than in a separate, dimensional realm outside Heaven. So far, Rick had found no evidence in the Bible to suggest otherwise.

Heaven. According to the Bible, there were three of them—the sky above us, outer space, and the supernatural realm, where angels and some deceased people seemed to reside. One might well describe *that* Heaven as possibly existing in another dimension. Either way, Nathan had shown him several passages indicating that there is time in Heaven. For instance, in the Book of Revelation, Chapter 8, verse 1, John mentions there was silence in Heaven for about half an hour. Rick had researched several online commentaries refuting the notion that God exists within time, but they all seemed to use circular reasoning, which he found to be a load of balderdash.

Working with cops as he did, Rick had picked up on a couple of their adages, such as *KISS—Keep It Simple, Stupid*—and *If it doesn't make sense, it isn't true.* There were exceptions to almost all rules, of course, but by and large, things were what they seemed. It wasn't like in movies and TV shows where everything leading up to the conclusion pointed you in the wrong direction so there could be a big surprise reveal at the end. In Rick's experience, abductive reasoning suggested that when it looks like a duck, walks like a duck, and quacks like a duck—it's probably a duck. Even in his profession, where people often pretend or bury the root of a problem deep beneath layers of conflict, the adage proved true far more often than not.

It was because of this that Rick counseled Nathan the way he had concerning Gil and Sarah's marriage vows, pointing out exactly why Gil was having such a difficult time accepting the idea of marrying again. In this respect, Gil was not so different from Mrs. Bassett lying on the couch. Gil had been bitten once—badly bitten—losing Joleen and Marla right before his eyes, helpless to stop their murders. It was no wonder he would be doubly careful about risking that kind of pain and horror again. The secret, Rick confided to Nathan, was that Gil needed to be shown that the risk, no matter how great, was worth the prize. Rick had no idea how Nathan might incorporate the concept into the wedding ceremony. Still, he felt it addressed the core difficulties the couple might face as they entered the bonds of matrimony.

Despite being an unbeliever, Rick had found his and Nathan's discussions about God stimulating and mind-expanding. He considered the pastor a worthy opponent, at least for now. Additionally, since he had religious patients, the gain in insight was valuable—it wasn't a complete waste of his time.

However, when it came to science, Rick was confident that Nathan's arguments would inevitably fail. Being well-versed in the sciences, Rick knew that in a battle between magic and logic, logic always wins.

26

I scooped the ring from the sheriff's palm. It was blackened, covered in soot, and still warm to the touch. There was no mistaking it—it was *the* ring. The same one I had put on Sarah's finger such a short time ago. Clutching it tightly in my fist, I turned to the charred body, searching for any recognizable features, but aside from the patches of clothing spared from the blaze, there was nothing.

"I'll get samples," said Steve Hearst, standing next to me, "have them sent for DNA testing. My boys will rush it."

"Already underway," said the sheriff. "There goes my lab tech, Jonny, running lights and siren back to the lab. We'll know quick—quick as humanly possible. I'm truly sorry, son. I feel responsible. I know it was Hearst that called for her, but it's my county. You came here to help us. I can't believe something like this could happen."

"We'll get them," said Hearst, "all the way to the top. We missed the first time—we won't miss again. I give you my word. I won't rest until we bury them and everyone remotely responsible."

The words went on and on, and there were others—Billy, Pappy, *others*, hands touching my shoulders and back. But it was all nothing, gibberish that meant and did nothing.

This wasn't Sarah—my Sarah. *It wasn't*—no matter what they said.

My heart told me it wasn't. I'd know. I'd know. Please, God, I'd know—wouldn't I?

~

TINA HEARD the scrabble of paws and claws scratching across hardwood floors and rugs. Then came a commotion of scattering furniture and what sounded like someone climbing the stairs. There were a few seconds of silence and then a scream—and another—and another.

"Okay," said Tina to Trebek, the county mounty, "let's go."

They entered the house, guns drawn—Tina with her nine-millimeter handgun and the deputy with an AR. They carefully checked each hallway and opening as they went, mindful of an ambush. Even though Tina was confident that Viper would have alerted them to any earlier or closer dangers, safety still had to be observed. Despite the screaming, crying, and begging that could be heard from upstairs, they needed to ensure they weren't bypassing a possible threat—a second suspect who might not be as detectable as the first one.

Unlikely, of course, but possible.

The great Gil Mason himself had once taught a class she attended years ago about how K9 handlers and their cover officers had to steel themselves against the cries of suspects engaged with their K9s, no matter how pitiful or frightening, due to the potential danger posed by other suspects lying in wait. To drive the point home, he had shown numerous body cam videos of K9 handlers who had failed to follow this advice, becoming fixated on the need to rescue the suspect or protect their K9 companion from possible harm, thus becoming victims themselves. This tunnel vision left them vulnerable to attack.

The videos showed horrific injuries. Guns, knives, and even bombs often causing grievous wounds, and sometimes even death, to the handlers and their dogs or both. Tina had been a handler and trainer long enough to become immune to the cries and screams, mentally acknowledging that whatever happened to the suspect was on him. She'd given plenty of warnings. And besides, he shouldn't have been burglarizing a poor, dead old lady's house anyway.

Trebek, his face pale, eyes wide, gave her a look and pointed upward, where thumping, growling, and blubbering could be heard through the ceiling. Tina understood, he wasn't callused like her. She would have to be hard for him. She waved him off and pointed toward the kitchen ahead. He understood, gathered himself, and they finished clearing the immediate area before coming to a long, winding staircase cluttered with overturned chairs, pillows, a nightstand, and a broken lamp. The burglar had apparently tossed things onto the stairs during the announcements in an effort to slow down their pursuit. Unfortunately for him, it hadn't worked to slow Viper. Doubly unfortunate for him—it *had* worked to slow Tina and Trebek. They had to carefully clear the way of obstacles while still covering their passage up the stairs with their guns, which meant the bad guy was stuck dealing with Viper alone.

It didn't sound like he was dealing very well.

By the time the two of them made it to the top, Tina saw the bad guy, exactly as described, now with a blood-stained shirt and pants. He was lying on his back with Viper on top of him, gripping his forearm with her teeth. They shifted back and forth, the suspect trying unsuccessfully to throw her off.

Trebek called out calmly, "Suspect, stop fighting the dog and let me see your hands."

"I can't, I can't, I can't! Get him off-please!"

"Stop moving, and I'll call her off," said Tina.

"I can't! Help!"

"Not until you stop fighting and stay still," said Tina in a very relaxed tone.

"Ahhhh-ahhh! I can't! Get him off!"

"Stay still if you want her to come off. Otherwise, we'll be here like this all day, and it's going to hurt real bad."

In response, the suspect stopped uselessly flailing at Viper and stayed as still as he could while his body was jerked about by Viper's head shakes.

"I can see both hands," said Trebek, keeping the suspect covered with the muzzle of his AR. "You're good."

"I'm calling her off," said Tina. "Don't move, or she will re-engage. Do you understand, suspect?"

"I understand! I understand! Oh, please get him off!"

Tina gave the release command. Viper gave a final tug, released, and spun around so she could face the suspect while lying between him and Tina."

"Don't move," said Tina.

The man instantly sat up and reached his uninjured left hand to his belly, pulling up his shirt and reaching for something tucked in his waistband.

"Stop, or I'll shoo... !" yelled Trebek.

Before he could get the last word out, Viper had already struck with the speed and force of her namesake, gripping a sizable portion of the man's belly in her jaws.

The man shrieked, screaming that he gave up—*again*.

"Not this time," said Tina. "Not until you put your hands over your head and stop resisting."

"If you don't do as instructed, I will shoot you," said Trebek.

The man screamed a final time, then shot his arms up over his head.

"You got him?" asked Tina.

"Go ahead," he said. "If he breaks this time, I'm shooting."

Tina nodded. "Don't hit Viper," she said. She gave Viper the release and heel command and she came off, flipping up tight against Tina's left leg—watching.

The suspect surrendered without reaching for his waistband a second time, saving himself from being shot or bitten again. When they searched him, they found his cell phone tucked in his waistband. No gun or knife or even a bomb, just the phone.

Idiot, thought Tina.

"You're lucky the dog had you," said Trebek. "If she hadn't

stopped you from reaching, I'd have shot you dead. And for what? A phone?"

"My one phone call," said the man.

Tina shook her head.

~

"YOU WANT WHAT?" asked Hearst.

We were back at the base, standing outside the barracks where Sarah and I had lodged.

"Your control room and all its assets."

"Look," said Hearst, "I said we'd get the people responsible, and I meant it. This is my bailiwick, and I know what I'm doing here a lot better than you do."

"When I said all the assets, that included you. I want your operators, drones, satellite coverage—everything."

"You can't expect to get all the bad guys rounded up tonight. It's a long process, takes time."

"I'm not looking for *them*—not yet."

"Who then?" asked Hearst.

"Her," I said.

"Her? Her who...?" he stopped in recognition. "Oh, man, come on. Don't do this to yourself. Don't, please. We have the DNA. *Her DNA*."

The sheriff's lab technician had been fast and thorough. Both the blood on the shirt and the samples taken from the corpse were compared against hair from Sarah's brush—hair that I had personally collected for them. A perfect match all the way around.

Didn't matter.

It wasn't her.

"You said anything I asked for."

"Yes, I know," said Hearst, "but I meant to find those responsible, not to go off on a wild goose chase. It's her—the body—it's Sarah Gallagher. You have to accept that."

"No."

"Mason, I had my best tech run a second test at the SO's lab himself. The results were the same."

"It's a trick," I said. "They set it up, somehow."

"Trick DNA? In the first place, that's impossible, and in the second, it goes against the whole *lack of time and flying by the seat of their pants theory* that you yourself came up with. And why? Why would they go to all that trouble? What do they have to gain? We're talking about a drug cartel. What do they need with a forensic lab tech that specializes in DNA? Not to mention they had no way of knowing from where on the body we'd take samples."

I had no answers, just my gut—that and what I'd seen from the video. I shook my head. "I don't know, but I know. And I'm asking for your help, your resources."

He took off his sunglasses and stared into my eyes. "You're talking hundreds of thousands—maybe millions—of dollars' worth of government assets being allocated to search for a woman whose body we have lying in a morgue a few miles away."

"Yes or no?" I asked.

"I think you're wrong."

"I don't care."

"I *know* you're wrong."

"I still don't care. Yes or no?"

He looked away, did the tick and suck thing, then looked back at me. I could see the wheels turning. He was thinking—going through his options. He could make the demand of me, and I would agree—anything to find my Sarah. If his terms were that I join his team in exchange for his support and resources, I'd do it, right then and there. And he knew it. He had me cold.

But he didn't.

Instead, he nodded and said, "Okay. What do you want?"

27

While Hearst gathered his techs and got the control room ready for my specifications, I met with Billy and Pappy at the barracks. Neither of them believed Sarah was still alive—I could see it in their faces, their eyes.

Billy kept tearing up.

Some gangster.

Pappy, who was used to the reality of losing friends and colleagues in combat, was stoic.

"She's not dead," I said to Billy.

I saw his big shoulders shudder. "Ah, Gil. The tests ..."

"I don't care about the tests. I know she's alive. I know it here." I touched my chest. "And I'm going to find her. *We* are going to find her."

About that time, Sammy and Dominic walked in.

"You think she's still alive?" asked Sammy.

"I do."

"What have you got? Tell me everything. And when I say everything, I mean *Princess Bride-wheelbarrow-holocaust cloak-list-of-assets-level* everything. Leave nothing out. We don't have a month to plan. If she is still alive, time is of the essence."

"You can't believe this?" Billy said to Sammy. "The DNA test ...?"

"Tests can be rigged or wrong or tricked. I've worked with Gil Mason—solved cases with him. If he says she's still alive, we check it out." Gunwood PD Investigator Sammy Rothstein, savant, perhaps the most extraordinary deductive mind in the world, looked back at me. "Show me."

So I did, starting with the video of the invasion at the lab. Hearst had sent me all the data he had, which included video surveillance—perimeter maps, footage of the lab invasion, what I observed the suspects doing with the evidence, the drone footage of the shooting, and the crime scene of the charred corpse *that wasn't Sarah*. Sammy seemed to zone out about fifteen seconds into my recitation, but that was just Sammy doing Sammy. When I finished, he zoned back in.

"You're right about the lab and the evidence. And if you're right about that, you might be right about the rest. If she's close by, we have to find her—no time to waste. Are Hearst and his team ready?"

"They should be," I said.

Without a word, Sammy stood and walked out the door.

The rest of us followed.

STILL IN THE BARRACKS, Sammy listened abstractly as Gil showed the videos and recounted his story, detailing what he had seen. Internally, Sammy's mind was at work—shifting, sorting, and flipping—turning images into musical notes, familiar smells into geometric patterns, and these patterns into mathematical equations that teased his senses as they tried to merge and weave and fit pieces until they formed a perfect harmony. After Gil finished and they moved as a group to the control room, Sammy only slightly emerged from his trance-like state. He appeared semi-normal to the others, but internally, his brain was in hyperdrive, directing, replacing, and refitting the shapes, smells, and sounds.

Hearst outlined their assets, their equipment and maps and consoles—what the satellites were capable of, their flight patterns and geosynchronous orbits—foreign resources—ground troops that had been deployed, both local and Hearst's own teams—video surveillance, weapons systems, drones—everything Hearst had at his disposal. When he finished, Sammy stood transfixed, staring at the perimeter map displayed on the monitor at the front of the room.

"There," he said robotically, pointing to a spot on the map. The shapes and equations in his mind had coalesced into a unified pattern. "Go back to nine minutes after the suspects fled from the jail. Show satellite number three's footage for that area."

One of the technicians clicked and clacked at a computer keyboard, and an instant later, the map was replaced by an overhead image of a dirt road with a single blue van driving along at nominal speed.

"Zoom in and get facial recognition of the driver," said Sammy.

"Can they do that?" asked Billy.

"Not much they can't do," said Hearst. "We're not quite Denzel Washington going back in time in *Deja Vu*, but almost."

The picture expanded, and the windshield zoomed into focus. A nicely dressed Hispanic man in his twenties was driving.

"Tats at the top of the collar," said Gil.

"Who doesn't have tats these days?" said Hearst.

"No," said Sammy, "he's right. It's a gang tat. Upper corner of the 'C' and the 'R' and the downward stroke of the top of the cross for the Cruz Cartel."

"What are you talking about?" said Hearst, pulling his sunglasses down and squinting at the screen. "You can't tell that—nobody can. There's maybe a total of an eighth of an inch showing. That's it."

"Don't doubt him," said Gil. "Sammy's never wrong about things like this."

As if he hadn't been listening, Sammy pointed at the tech who had keyed the satellite and said, "I need worldwide facial recognition on that driver."

The technician looked at Hearst for approval.

Hearst shrugged. "It's their game. Short of a nuclear strike, give them whatever they want."

After a few more keystrokes, men's faces began flashing across the screen for about seven seconds, too quickly for the human mind to decipher—*most human minds.* The flipping stopped, and they were all staring at a single picture—a mug shot of Juan Moreno, Columbian-born, twenty-five, a mid-level soldier in the Cruz Cartel organization.

"That's our man," said Sammy, his mind back at work, taking in all the data on the driver and cataloging it into the overall harmony that danced into place within and through his synapses.

"*Wow*," said Hearst, slack-jawed. "Color me impressed."

"Had they already made the switch by then?" asked Gil.

"Maybe," said Sammy, "but it would have been close. Still, my bet is she's in the van. Your call. You want to go back and look or keep going with the van?"

"Keep going. If they haven't made the switch yet, they will soon. And if they have, the car is unimportant. Only the van matters."

"Follow it," said Sammy to the tech.

Everyone watched in silence as the vehicle made its way along the winding road and out of the satellite's view.

"Is that it?" asked Gil.

"Expand," said Sammy, but the tech was ahead of him. The view zoomed out, revealing the roads, the landscape, and the van far below.

"How long will they be in range?" asked Gil.

"The satellite's in space, Slick." We can zoom in on almost any part of North America ... for as long as the satellite is *over* North America, that is. It's traveling at around twenty-six thousand miles per hour, so there is a limit—for this satellite, anyway."

Sammy walked up to the screen and touched a spot. "There."

The technician clicked, and the van zoomed up to meet them, still traveling along the road. They had to repeat this process three times before it stopped at a stop sign and then merged onto an asphalt street. A few cars passed it, but no police. Six minutes later, the van entered a subdivision of medium-income family homes. It made two turns and entered a garage as the door automatically opened. The door closed behind it.

"Address," demanded Sammy.

The tech shifted the picture on the screen and then zoomed in until he spotted the numbers by the front door. He listed the address.

"Dispatch cars to the area but keep them out of sight. Agent Hearst, we'll need a helicopter—no, two—one big, one quiet, ASAP. And a team."

Hearst clicked off his cell. "Already on it. And I can do it with one. It'll be ready in ten."

"Big *and* quiet?"

"The quietest ever."

"Good," said Sammy.

The picture zoomed out. Next door to the target house, two kids, probably around ten years old, could be seen throwing a football back and forth.

Mason turned to Billy and the others. "Go get ready. Bring my bag."

"Stay with it or advance?" asked Sammy.

"How long before the satellite's out of range?" asked Gil.

The technician punched a few buttons. "I calculate six minutes, thirteen seconds."

"Do you have another that can pick it up?"

The children continued to toss the ball in the yard.

After a furious clicking of keys, the tech said, "A Chinese bird is flying close ... in ... about nine. I think it will have coverage. Not certain, but I think so. Best I can do."

The ball flew past the one boy and into the yard of the house where the van had disappeared.

"Stay with it," said Gil.

All eyes were glued to the screen.

The boy scooped up the ball, laughing silently. Behind him, a slit appeared in the curtains. A face appeared, watching them.

"Zoom on the face," said Sammy.

"Tough angle," said the tech as the picture zoomed in rapidly. The face was a blur and distorted. "Let's see what you can do, AI."

Clickety-clickety-clack. The image suddenly sharpened and righted.

"Snap it," said Sammy.

"Done," said the tech. "Running it through facial recognition now."

The boy dropkicked the football. It bounced off the edge of his foot and sailed toward the window where the man stood watching.

In the upper right corner of the screen, a small picture-in-picture display showed faces blurring past as the database searched.

The boys watched the ball's flight, their small hands rising and going to their mouths as it bounced off the glass, making the man flinch, and the window and frame shake and vibrate.

The flashing images in the upper right corner of the screen came to a halt. One face stared out at them—a man they had all recently seen.

It was the face of Agustin Cruz, the drug lord they had gone to Mexico to kill.

"Son of a gun," said Steve Hearst.

28

Tina changed out of her uniform and put on sweats and athletic shoes. She'd pulled a muscle in her neck or shoulder, probably from tossing furniture off the stairs to get to the suspect. Speaking of which, *what an imbecile.* The paramedics had transported him to Swedish Hospital, where the staff made fun of him by downplaying his injuries and asking Tina if Viper needed a toothbrush to wash the *nasty* out of her teeth. The staff was collectively familiar with Tina, her K9, and the bite injuries. The doctors and nurses laughed right in front of the suspect, who looked like he was going to cry.

He did cry later while they were cleaning out the puncture wounds, which is understandable. Treating dog bites like his involves jabbing a needle directly into the wound at several spots to inject an anesthetic. Then, a transparent plastic cone is placed over the hole—in this case, multiple holes—and a high-pressure wash is injected straight in. It's rough, but not as rough as it was in the past when they used a bore brush to clean them out.

The forearm bite was pretty straightforward and was left unstitched to minimize the danger of infection. The stomach bite, however, had resulted in a good-sized gash. After cleaning the wound, the medical staff loosely stitched it closed, leaving space for oozing and drainage.

Tina had taken the required departmental photographs of the injuries before and after the stitching and bandaging and submitted them as evidence along with her report. She always took her most in-focus pictures after the cleaning—they looked better in court. It's incredible how a little blood can affect a juror who is unaccustomed to the violence of the streets. After that, the suspect was transported to the jail.

On her way home, Tina stopped at an Arby's and picked up a pile of roast beef—no bun—as a reward for Viper. It was their tradition—a reward. And, as the hospital staff had alluded, it helped eliminate the taste of *nasty*. All in all, a nice day's work.

As soon as Tina returned to her car after catching the burglar, she texted Billy to ask about Sarah. There was no response, leading her to conclude that he was busy helping Gil with the search. She checked with dispatch and received all the information they had on the case, which wasn't much—only the BOLO details and minimal information about an officer-involved shooting with suspects in a vehicle possibly linked to the kidnapping. The fact that the BOLO was still active indicated to Tina that Sarah had not been found in the vehicle.

Anthony Carlino knocked on her bedroom door and slightly cracked it open. "Okay to come in?"

"Sure," she said as she finished tying her shoe.

"I wanted to give you a heads up on Irmgard," he said.

"Irmgard? Why, what's wrong?"

"She's been acting a little strange—sort of goes off somewhere in her head. I've seen it a few times. Seems to be getting worse."

Tina nodded and stood up from the bed where she'd been sitting. "She's been through a lot. I'm thinking of having her talk with that therapist friend of Gil's."

"The guy who was involved with that psycho killer that tried to kill you and Billy?"

"Larry Gold," said Tina. "And yes, he targeted Rick while pretending to seek his help."

"Right, and the psycho doc didn't see him coming? You sure he knows what he's doing? I mean, I'd think he'd spot a nut job like that a mile off. Billy pegged him instantly, and he ain't got no fancy degrees."

"To be fair," said Tina, "Billy did have an advantage. Gold tased him, tied him up, and hung him upside-down while a partially dissected dead man lay in his living room. I think that qualifies as a clue."

"Okay, that's fair," said Anthony, "but still, you sure he's good enough for Irmgard?"

"I think so. He's good enough for Gil, after all."

"And then there's the other issue," said Anthony.

"The other issue?"

Anthony held up his hands, indicating the obviousness of the statement. "Irmgard's around *us*, and Billy and other relatives."

Tina shrugged her shoulders. "And?"

"She's young, but she's also smart. She hears things. When people talk ... she hears ... capiche?"

The realization of what he was implying suddenly dawned on her. "Oh! Oh, I never thought of that. Still, there's doctor-patient privilege—wouldn't that help?"

Anthony's lips curled. "Really? You want to get this doc killed because a nine-year-old girl leaked information without knowing any better? Some in the family might not want to risk him spilling the beans where he's not supposed to. Is that what you want?"

"I'm sorry," she said, "I didn't think it through. I'm not used to seeing things from the other side. But if she needs help, what can we do? Does your ... organization ... have therapists or doctors that might be able to help?"

"Mental health ain't our strong point. Guy gets sloppy in the head, we usually put him out to pasture."

"Pasture? Like retirement?"

"More like glue factory," said Anthony, pointing a gun finger at his head and pulling the trigger. "Dead men tell no tales."

"Well, that's horrible."

"So's being a nut. It's just trading one horrible for another horrible. Who's to say which is worse?"

"Then what can we do?"

"Maybe I'll go by this doc's office—have a little talk with him. See what he's all about. Then we'll decide."

"You won't ... you won't kill him?"

Anthony acted taken aback. "Not yet," he said. She looked shocked, and he broke into a smile. "I'm joking. I'll check him out, see if maybe she can talk to him without us having to snuff him later. If he doesn't check out, we don't send her to him, and it's all over before it even starts—no harm done. No need for extreme measures."

Tina nodded her head, feeling better—sort of. "I'll go talk with Irmgard."

"Good, you do that," said Anthony as she walked past him and out of the room.

Nice kid, that Tina. It hurt his heart to think about what he might need to do one day.

WHILE THE TECHNICIANS continued to play with the satellites in the control room, Hearst, Sammy, and I walked out to the barracks in time to meet our team—Pappy, Billy, Dominic, Montgomery, and some of Hearst's men from the first raid. Billy handed me my go-kit, and I started dressing. Behind me, I felt a shift in the breeze. A strange flutter weirdly vibrated my eardrums. Turning, I saw a copter landing maybe thirty yards away.

It looked like something out of a sci-fi show, maybe *Star Gate Atlantis*, but not one of Earth's clunky Daedalus-class battle cruisers. It was more like a Wraith Dart—sleek, fast, and stealthy. It had wings like a plane with tilted rotors at the end of each. The rotors were adjustable, allowing for VTOL (Vertical Take Off and Landing) like a helicopter, and could move fast when facing forward, like an ordinary airplane.

I heard Billy whistle.

"You can say that again," said Hearst. "You're looking at forty-plus million dollars' worth of state-of-the-art technology. That's the Bell V-280 Valor. Newest, fastest stealth helicopter in the world."

"Will she hold all of us?" I asked while putting on my armor.

"And then some," said Hearst. "Up to fourteen troops with two pilots and two rear gunners. She's got double Rolls-Royce AE 1107F turboshaft engines, can travel at close to 350 miles per hour, and has the biggest, baddest color cockpit touchscreen of any copter in the world, giving the pilots better visibility and situational awareness."

"Why are the props on the end of the wings like that?" asked Billy.

"Pretty cool, right?" said Hearst.

"Very cool," agreed Billy.

"And they're called nacelles," said Hearst in a lowered voice.

"Like in *Star Trek*?"

"Exactly like in *Star Trek*," said Hearst.

"Okay, that *is* really cool."

"I know."

"Weapons?" asked Pappy.

"None. Officially, she's not even off the floor yet. This is a loaner for testing. We need to bring her back in one piece."

Pappy gave him a look. "No weapons? What are all those pokey-looking things I see sticking out?"

Okay," said Hearst, "I might have added a couple of 12.7mm heavy machine guns on pintle mounts at the fuselage doors on each side, along with four laser-guided drop bombs, a couple of laser-guided rocket pods, and maybe a fixed 20mm forward-firing cannon, but other than that ... nothing."

Billy grinned.

"Hey," said Hearst, "I said I have to get her back in one piece, and I'm not taking any chances."

"That's what I thought," said Pappy.

"On this mission, though, the armaments are strictly for show. No way I'm explaining to my bosses how a super-secret stealth helicopter dropped *nonexistent* bombs on a neighborhood subdivision."

"Let's go," I said.

29

Sarah awoke in a dark room, the air thick with the pungent stench of urine mingled with the sickening odor of decaying matter and other unidentifiable foul smells. The floor was hard concrete, cold and dirty with grit and pieces of debris she couldn't identify in the nearly black surroundings.

Sitting up, she nearly passed out as the world shifted and spun inside her head. Nausea churned through her insides like wax in a sixties lava lamp. Her head throbbed, and she suddenly remembered the big man punching her, the spark of light, and then the darkness. There was nothing—until the car—and the same man who had punched her was pulling at her pants, stripping her. She tried to fight as he yanked them free, but he just laughed and tore her shirt down the front. She scratched his face with her nails, and he punched her again. Then, blackness—until now.

Where was she? Who had taken her? Why?

The face of the Double-Tap Rapist flashed before her. No—no, he was dead. She and Gil and Pilgrim had killed him.

She felt his hands, his lips.

Shuddering, she shook her head, sending waves of pain crashing through her skull. It did the trick, though—the DTP vanished from her mind.

Her throat, scratchy and swollen, ached with thirst. She reached out and touched a bucket—plastic from the feel of it—and from the smell, it was clearly meant to be a toilet. Still on her knees, she groped her way around the small, barren room, hands outstretched. The dizziness receded in slow waves, leaving her feeling weak, soft, and helpless.

But she wasn't helpless. She had to remember that. She'd lived through what the rapist had done to her. She had helped Gil kill him. She'd survived the bikers and the gangsters and had even defeated Tina—a tough cop—in the battle for Gil.

She'd had Gail murdered.

Yes, there was that, too.

And most important of all, she was to marry Gil in less than a month. Nothing would stop that. She wouldn't let it, no matter what.

And neither would Gil.

Thinking of him gave her strength. She knew he would come for her—she just had to stay alive until then.

She quickly took stock of her situation and realized she was dressed in different clothing than what she had worn at the lab: a plaid shirt, blue jeans, and no bra or panties. *What had they done to her while she was unconscious?* She had to push those thoughts aside for now—concentrate on escape.

No water bucket, no food, no weapons—she stopped herself. *That wasn't true.* She still had her greatest weapon—her mind. They obviously didn't want her dead, or they would have already killed her. The lack of food and water told her something. This meant they didn't intend to starve her or let her die of thirst, which also meant they would be coming for her soon. Why? She didn't know, not yet, but it had to have something to do with why they took her in the first place.

So why had they?

She remembered Gil telling her about stash houses—pollo farms, she thought he'd called them. Chicken farms—where the cartels kept prisoners while they extorted money from their loved ones. The thought brought another shudder. She'd read up on them, what the men did to their victims—torture, rape, murder, and mass graves—after bleeding the friends and relatives dry.

Was that it? Were they after money? No, that made no sense. They'd stormed a sheriff's department, jail even, to get to her. No, they weren't after money—*she* was the target. But again, that left a big question. Why?

Perhaps she needed to consider a different question before tackling the why. The five Ws in all report writing might be the key—who, what, when, where, and why. The *what* was already known—she'd been taken. The *when* and *where* were obvious. So, if not the *why*, then how about the *who*?

The obvious answer seemed to be the cartel, but which one? The most likely suspect was the Cruz cartel, thought to be responsible for the deputy's murder, as well as the attempted murder of her, Gil, and Hearst at the coffee shop. Not to mention that Hearst, Gil, and the gang had tried to kill the cartel boss, Agustin Cruz, in his own home. But what did any of that have to do with her?

Okay, if she had the *what* and the *who*, maybe it was time to go back and concentrate on the *why*. What was she doing when they attacked her in the lab?

The evidence.

She was processing evidence. But what exactly? It had to have been something she'd discovered—something the cartel didn't want exposed.

The casings?

No.

Prints?"

No.

DNA?

Yes, it had to be, but not just any DNA. Sarah remembered the strange discovery she'd made at the crime scene. The ice she'd seen in the pictures hadn't been there when she arrived—it had melted and evaporated. What had tested positive as human saliva—spit—

had turned to ice. The ice had melted, and the saliva was gone, but the DNA remained on the deputy's flesh.

Sarah hadn't thought it was of any real importance while gathering it or even later when testing it. She had assumed it was fluid from the dead deputy, but when the initial test for compatibility came back, it hadn't belonged to him. She immediately ran it through the DNA database, but it came up empty—no match on file. That would have ended it for most criminologists, but not Sarah. She submitted the sample for familial DNA testing.

Familial DNA testing labs, such as Othram and Parabon, search public genetic databases for shared chromosomal sequences between unknown collected DNA and previously tested family members. This technique had solved numerous cold cases, including that of the Golden State Killer. While it might take hours or even days for the results to come back, Sarah had a good relationship with both labs, always giving them credit for their discoveries. She hoped they could provide valuable information in a timely manner. If they did find a matching relative, Sarah was confident she could eventually narrow it down to their suspect.

A door burst open, and blinding light from the setting sun splashed across her eyes, making her wince and raise a shielding hand against the glare. A towering silhouette stepped forward, and she instantly recognized it as the big man from the lab—the one with the tattoos. He was the same man who had punched her and stripped her in the car.

Grinning and touching the scratches she'd left on his cheek, he came for her.

IRMGARD WALKED WITH TINA. They had the young cougar strapped tightly into his harness at the end of its leash, sniffing at trees, bushes, and rocks.

"Is something bothering you?" asked Tina.

"Bothering me?"

The sun was beginning to set, but at this altitude in the mountains, it offered a few extra minutes of light and warmth.

"Your great-grandfather says he thinks you are troubled. Bad dreams? Maybe other things, too?"

Unconsciously, Irmgard's hand slipped inside her coat pocket to touch the sharp edge of the paring knife. So far, no one had noticed she had it. She poked the soft pad of her pointer finger against its tip, feeling its potential to cause pain, strengthening her.

"I'm fine," she said, pressing just a little harder.

"No one's upset with you, darling. It's just that you've been through so many painful experiences—far more than any girl your age should have to endure. We're just worried about you, that's all."

A myriad of images flip-flashed behind her eyes—as fast as the machine gun's barrel had whirled back at her house when the bad man called the Ghost had strapped her to the chair.

Her father, the wolf, her mother dying, the peas, the man with two fingers, the dark, the cold, the blood, the screams, the fear.

The point bit deeper, bringing a spot of blood, chasing the images back, giving her strength.

"No," she said, "nothing to worry about. Grandpa's just being silly."

The cougar tugged at the leash, and Tina was momentarily distracted as she reined him in from chasing a squirrel that darted up a pine tree. In that instant, she missed the sudden glazed look that crossed the little girl's eyes as the Great Gray Wolf lunged at her.

More pressure, more blood ... not much ... not yet. That would come later when she was alone and could pull up her sleeves and make another line. For now, she just needed a little more—enough to keep Tina from seeing.

Tina turned back and caught just a glimpse, a hint of—*something* —something dark and terrifying. But then it was gone, and Irmgard was just Irmgard again. Had Tina imagined it? Had Anthony's words clouded her judgment, making her see things that weren't there?

"Sweetheart, really, you can tell me anything, everything. I love you. Billy and I both love you so much."

"Then why are you thinking about leaving me?"

That hit Tina like a slap in the face. She tried to form words that wouldn't pass her lips. Kneeling, she took Irmgard by the upper arms and pulled her into a tight hug.

"Oh, honey, no! Why would you think that? I'm not leaving."

"You and Papa are thinking about breaking up. I hear you talking at night when you think I'm asleep. I see the different way you are around each other—around me."

Tina shook her head, feeling lost and confused, not knowing what to say.

But Irmgard knew what to say—*what to do*—how to distract Tina from talking about the nightmares and the images and the monsters. *The knife told her what to say, what to do.* Her pocket was wet and sticky now, but it was getting dark enough that Tina wouldn't be able to see. She pressed harder, feeling the tip touch against the bone inside her finger.

It hurt so bad.

It felt so right.

It chased the monsters back into the darkness.

For now, at least.

"You're going to leave me, I know you are, just like my mother and father left me. And then I'll be alone. All alone."

Tina hugged Irmgard tighter, tears filling her eyes as she thought of the harm she and Billy might have brought on this precious child and the *future* pain they might still cause.

What had Tina gotten herself into?

30

I left Pilgrim in my room at the barracks. Max lay at my feet on the helicopter floor, unfazed by the speed, the banking, or even the fact that we were flying. The other men, seated on both sides of the fuselage, seemed to mean nothing to him as the helicopter rushed through the darkening sky toward the house where Sarah was being held. The speed and agility of the flight felt more like being in a jet than a helicopter. The tilting rotors moved forward and back, responding to the pilot's commands. When we started, they were almost vertical, the blades thrusting down against the ground, but now, as we cut a straight line toward our target, they were horizontal, creating speed and lift.

It would have been an exhilarating ride at any other time, but I could only think about Sarah and the need to control my rage until she was safe. I sent a continuous stream of prayer, asking God to watch over her and not let me be too late. The Holy Spirit is powerful and able to help in these situations, but He's working with and against free will agents, and the danger is ever-present and terrifyingly real.

I could tell Steve Hearst wasn't sold on the idea that Sarah was still alive, but I had to give him credit, he'd pulled out all the stops. I could only guess at the favors he had to call in to get access to this beast we were riding, not to mention the fallout if something happened to it. I'd do my best to ensure nothing did, but Sarah was all that mattered. Saving her was my only priority. If the forty-three-million-dollar aircraft got totaled, I'd have to give him an IOU, like Lloyd and Harry in *Dumb and Dumber.*

As we traveled, the sun fully set, leaving the earth below dark and foreboding. In no time at all, we arrived at our destination. Hearst, who was also a pilot—*go figure, dimples and a fighter jock*—set the helicopter down far enough away to minimize its noise signature but close enough for a quick assault. We had faced this drug lord before and should have known his tactics. But we were in a rush—my fault—and fell for the same mistake as before.

It was a trap.

~

"ANOTHER QUESTION," said Rick over the phone.

Nathan was home making spaghetti. Nothing fancy, just noodles and jarred marinara sauce—not even meatballs or sausage. When his wife was alive, she'd made the best spaghetti, rich and flavorful, full of spice, excitement, and love. But now that he was alone, he settled for the store-bought stuff, a pale imitation of what he had before, much like the rest of his life since she'd passed.

The sauce was done, the microwave having *dinged* him, but the noodles still had nine minutes to go. His cell was on speaker.

"Cooking dinner, but I've got a couple minutes."

"I'm home too," said Rick. "My wife's on her way, but she'll be a few. You sure this is a good time?"

"The noodles are still boiling. Go for it."

"What's the single strongest piece of evidence you have for your belief?"

"That's easy, the Resurrection. Having said that, it might not be the strongest evidence for you. Some people are more convinced by science, history, or philosophy ... different strokes for different folks. For me, it's the evidence of the Resurrection."

"I don't think that would do it for me," said Rick. "From what I can tell, the story of the Resurrection just seems like a story being passed down and changed through the centuries—basically myths and legends when you get down to it. Sort of a glorified fish tale, the fish getting bigger with each telling."

"Do you believe that George Washington was the first president of the United States?"

"That wasn't very long ago," said Rick. "And it goes to my fish tale comparison with little George not being able to lie and admitting he cut down the mythical cherry tree. Besides, there's plenty of evidence to prove Washington was the President."

"There's plenty of evidence to prove the Resurrection of Jesus Christ."

"Well," rebutted Rick, "nothing like what we have concerning Washington. Our very country exists because Washington won the war, signed the Declaration of Independence, and acted as the president."

"A declaration that refers to *nature's God*. Who would that be? Zeus? Allah? Gaia? No, it's the God of the Bible ... the Christian Bible. And what year was the Constitution signed? I believe it says, *In the year of our Lord*. Who were they referring to? That would be Jesus Christ, right?"

"That's not proof," said Rick.

"No, of course not, but it is evidence—as valid as your statement that our country is evidence for the existence of George Washington. The current political structure of the world is bent on hiding the truth of God. For example, the way we label years has recently changed from BC (Before Christ) and AD (Anno Domini-year of our Lord) to CE (Common Era) and BCE (Before Common Era). The funny thing is that while the labels have changed, they are still based on the birth and death of Jesus Christ—the two most important dates in all history.

"But the point is, just as you've never seen an actual picture of

Jesus Christ, you've never seen an actual picture of George Washington either. You've heard about him, read stories, and seen evidence, such as our country's existence, statues, monuments, paintings, and... cherry trees," Nathan laughed, "but you've seen much more evidence that there is a God. He's the one who made the cherry tree, by the way, and that's no joke. You'll find that the evidence Jesus Christ was born, lived, died, and was resurrected as foretold centuries before is undeniable once you look for it."

"Okay," said Rick, "so you have that piece of evidence. Personally, I think it's shaky, but okay—is that it?"

"Like Vizzini says in the battle of wits against Westley in *The Princess Bride*, 'Not even remotely.' Do you want me to start at the Resurrection, or do I need to prove that Jesus even existed as a man?"

There was a pause.

"I hadn't even thought of that—that He might not have existed at all. But now that you mention it ... can you?"

"You'd be surprised at how many youngsters today have been brainwashed against the existence of God. So much so that they believe there's no evidence Jesus ever existed. Yet they don't think twice about George Washington being a real person. I think this discussion is necessary, if for no other reason than to help refute the current culture's brainwashing."

"Okay," said Rick, "but I hope you have something other than our country's existence and the Bible as evidence because the Bible is only one book."

"Is it? Or is it rather sixty-six books written by forty different authors over fifteen hundred years? The authors ranging from peasants to kings, most never having met the others, and yet, telling a cohesive story from the beginning of Creation to its end and rebirth and on into eternity? Not to mention that it's the best-selling book of all time. Millions of copies have been sold every year since its first printing. And, as I'm sure you know, it was the first book ever printed on a printing press. I would argue that this is further evidence supporting its significance—not proof, but evidence. Despite numerous attempts, threats, and assertions that it would be eradicated from the face of the earth, its staying power is a testament to its influence and enduring impact on people."

The timer on the stove beeped, indicating the noodles were ready.

"I hear it," said Rick. "Go eat your dinner. We'll finish this later."

"Maybe at the reception."

"Isn't it an unwritten rule to never discuss politics or religion at important events?"

Nathan laughed. "The only things worth discussing ... except family, pets and food."

"Ha, finally, something we can unequivocally agree on."

WE LANDED in a field on the outskirts of the subdivision, maybe a hundred yards out. The copter was whisper quiet, sounding very different than any winged machine I'd ever heard. Hearst brought us down smooth as silk. The man was full of surprises.

Everyone was kitted and armed as we ran silently through the now-dark neighborhood. Only faint rustles, the quiet friction of clothing, and the occasional brush of metal against plastic signified our passage. We arrived at the target house within minutes—the football players next door no longer in their yard. There, we split up, all of us noting the security cameras but confident that the equipment Hearst's science guy had deployed moments before would render them inoperable. Half stayed in the front while the other half moved to the back.

Max, of course, was with me. He'd go in first, right after the explosive breach on the front door and the flashbangs. The team in the back would hold their position to prevent the enemy from flanking us or escaping and to provide backup and cleanup. I didn't want them to go in early since Max would be running free. He was good at distinguishing bad guys from good guys, but in the smoke and confusion, anything was possible, and I didn't want any of our guys getting hurt from friendly fire—or bite—or whatever.

We staged at the side of the footballers' house, nearest our target.

The stack in the front consisted of Max and me, followed by Sammy, Dominic, Pappy, and Montgomery. Hearst's best man was in charge of the rear team, along with Billy and the others. I also had an explosive breacher with me, a guy named Logan. When I gave him the signal, he ran up to the front door, attached the shaped charge, and returned to the back of the stack. The detonator was attached to my extra plated outer vest, my finger poised, waiting for the agreed-upon time… fifteen seconds.

Tic-tic-tic

A flashbang stood ready in my hand. I wasn't anxious, not scared. I was mad, enraged, and prepared to kill. I had to calm myself—not let my emotions get in the way of professionalism, but it was hard. So hard. They'd taken Sarah, faked her death, claimed to have raped her —maybe even had. *I thought of the trauma she'd suffered from the Double Tap Rapist.* They'd faked burning her body.

And it was all my fault.

tic-tic-tic

I had no right pretending I had any chance at a normal life. No right to put others in that kind of danger—certainly not Sarah. The knowledge only added fuel to my rage.

Max sensed it—I could tell.

And he was ready.

tic

Time.

I activated the explosive breach.

31

Sensing the Alpha's emotions, Max waited, certain he would be killing within seconds. The anticipation soothed him. Max's struggle never arose from the danger of combat—it was quite the opposite. His challenge was *restraining* himself from killing.

The sound of the directional explosive was weirdly sharp and muffled at the same time, and suddenly, they were moving. The Alpha, Max, and the others, ran to the door where the Alpha put him in a down before tossing the flashbang inside. There was another explosion, this one incredibly loud and bright—painful to Max's heightened senses. And then came the attack command.

Men were scattered around the room—some standing, some rolling on the floor—all concussed to varying degrees. Max attacked each one, targeting their throats when possible, biting deeply, and causing maximum damage with one *chomp and shake* before moving to the next viable target. He brought down all who were standing. The Alpha followed closely behind, shooting bullets into the men, killing them as he passed.

Something hot and fast burned through Max's rear right haunch, but before he could attack the source, the Alpha shot the shooter through the face. Max attacked him anyway, ripping out a chunk of his throat.

Suddenly, bullets were everywhere, pelting through the thick smoke—bullets and something else ... a grenade. Max had no real concept of what explosives were, but the Alpha had trained him to recognize their danger. Before the bomb could explode, the Alpha scooped it up and threw it into a side room.

As he finished the toss, a man came out and shot into his chest. Max caught the man in the thigh, spinning him back toward the room as the Alpha put a stream of bullets into his body. The room exploded, knocking Max off the bite. Parts of the man disintegrated while other parts splatted against a wall in the hallway. Max hit the wall with a powerful thud. He fell to the floor, where he lay dazed as the battle raged above him.

Through the smoke, darkness, and dizziness, he saw the Alpha standing over him, protecting him—shooting, ducking, and shooting again. His vest absorbed round after round, sending tiny puffs of dust and material vaporizing into the air. Max spotted a combatant and jumped to his paws. As he attacked, he felt another hot streak burn across his chest. He impacted his target, crushing the man's ribs and tearing through his flesh.

The man screamed, but that wasn't enough—he had to die. He had tried to kill the Alpha. He'd hurt Max. Max allowed his frenzy to go wild. Blood sprayed, and in the few seconds it took the Alpha to reach him, he had already completed his mission. The man was dead.

The Alpha shot him anyway—shot him and stepped over his body while calling Sarah's name.

Useless.

She wasn't here.

Never had been.

Max hadn't smelled her, but there was no way for him to tell the Alpha. He bypassed the Alpha and headed down the hallway, searching out danger before it could become a threat—there was still killing to do.

That was his job, his place in the pack. He would allow no harm to befall the Alpha.

~

PAPPY KNEW it was a trap almost instantly. Even so, the explosive breach, the flashbangs, and the lethal duo of Sammy and Dominic had stunted the effectiveness of the ambush, allowing them at least a chance at survival. They were like having twin machine guns with laser-guided bullets. *What Pappy could do with them on missions.*

It was a good thing the bad guys didn't have better bullets. He had taken several rounds to center mass, feeling the thuds and thunks but no pain through the vests Hearst supplied. Whatever they were, they were better than any ballistic armor he'd seen or worn before. He promised himself he'd snatch a few before leaving the base.

Mason's dog had distracted and incapacitated the combatants, opening a way for the rest of them to move forward even through the hail of bullets. Mason was a machine himself, finishing off the felled combatants with robotic efficiency, mercilessly popping rounds into their heads and moving on as if they were metal plate targets instead of living men.

Something sharp and hot nipped at the inside of Pappy's thigh near his knee. Spinning, he saw the shooter behind an island in the kitchen, still aiming at him. He put a stream of rounds into the man, obliterating his chest and the marble countertop.

Suddenly, everything got very quiet.

Sammy, Dominic, and Montgomery made it to him while Gil and Max finished clearing the bedrooms and hallway. Hearst's team came into the kitchen from the backdoor, guns at the ready, several covering their six behind them as they closed the door.

"I think we're clear in here," said Pappy.

"Not out there," said the leader. "They're coming at us from just about every house, every side, just walking with their guns—maybe fifty or more. No chance we take them all."

Gil walked back into the kitchen, Max at his side, blood drooling from his jowls.

"No basement," he said, "but there's a hatch in the back bedroom leading to a tunnel. No sign of Sarah, and it looks like Cruz escaped. They couldn't have gotten far. We need to follow."

"They've got a small army converging on us," said the rear team leader. "They must have been set up in the surrounding houses. What's the play?"

Gil looked at Pappy and said, "Drop a couple of flashbangs into the tunnel, then all of you go." He turned back to the leader. "Get Hearst's copter overhead—right overhead, close—then go with them and tell Hearst I need him to follow my commands. I'll stay behind until this is taken care of, then meet up with you at the end of the tunnel."

"Hearst doesn't take orders," said the team leader.

"I'm on the ground—I'm his eyes. He'll just have to trust me. Get on the radio and tell him."

The team leader shrugged. Pappy was at a window near the door, looking through the drapes. "They're maybe a minute away, tops. Still moving slow—very confident. I think they're going to shoot this place to pieces from out there."

"Go now," said Gil. "They're right where I want them."

Pappy and the others went to the floor hatch in the bedroom. The gangbangers started shooting into the house, bullets shattering glass and plaster and dishes. The couch erupted into puffs and fluffs of foam, feathers, cloth, and wood.

Gil dropped flat to the floor behind the island next to the dead man that Pappy had killed, Max beside him.

Max gave the body a quick bite for good measure.

The blades of the stealth-troop-attack helicopter suddenly whispered overhead, making Gil's lips twitch at the corners. *Perfect timing.*

"Light them up," said Gil into the radio. "Kill them all. Use everything."

And, as the bangers simultaneously entered the back and front doors, the copter did precisely that.

Hearst's copilot, a thirty-one-year-old Air Force Lt. Colonel named Roy Pickens, was on loan for this special project. He had a wife and three children and lived in Wisconsin. Roy could hardly believe his ears. He'd just been given the green light to use this juggernaut of war to its full capacity in a real-life, real-time situation where lives were at stake.

The Air Force would never condone such an operation or order, but he'd learned that Hearst operated on a higher level than the Air Force. Exactly what that was, he didn't understand and hadn't been told, but it was obviously true.

He turned to Hearst for confirmation, saw the look on his face, and knew they were about to go to war. An unstoppable grin spread across his lips.

Hearst's Heads-Up Display (HUD) and cockpit were beyond state-of-the-art—nearly Sci-Fi level sophistication, featuring the largest cockpit touchscreen in any war machine aircraft in existence, and Hearst had mastered it to the point of being a maestro. As his copilot managed their hover, Hearst went to work, sending commands to his two rear gunners and the computer that activated his missiles, bombs, and 20mm cannon under the nose.

Instantly, the great warbird shook and vibrated as hundreds of rounds, some as long as a big man's index finger and twice as thick, sprayed down into the advancing horde. Bodies turned into mist as tracer rounds stitched down from the heavens, exacting their wrath and illuminating the darkness.

Wing pods unleashed laser-guided, rocket-fueled destruction into the enemy ranks. Those who tried to flee were disintegrated, their heat signatures betraying them in the darkness and chaos. The rear gunners saw the enemy shooting up at them and returned fire with pinpoint accuracy, erasing them from the face of the earth.

A group of the bad guys ran into the street, hiding behind a car. One of them got in and started it up. Hearst gave his copilot and the gunners a heads-up and then rocked the V-280 Valor higher as he dropped the guided bomb directly on the vehicle. The car had made it about halfway up the street—but not far enough. The concussion was devastating, knocking windows out for blocks. The car, including its inhabitants, was simply gone.

The new vantage point gave the rear gunners the angle they needed to finish off the ground troops, and within ten seconds, they were done. The V-280 Valor had lived up to its name and hype.

So had Hearst.

As fire rained down on the men outside, I saw the bangers run through the back door. From a prone position, I fired on them, using the dead man's body as a shield to protect Max and me from possible return fire. There wasn't any.

I felt for Max at my side but realized he was gone. Men burst in from the front, heading straight for me, but Max intercepted them. Flipping onto my back, I fired at them with short, quick bursts, reducing the recoil and keeping the shots tightly grouped to avoid hitting Max with any stray rounds. They went down fast and then came the sound of a bomb exploding. The noise, the shaking, the dust, and a sensation like that of an earthquake vibrated through my teeth.

Max looked up at me from the man he'd just disemboweled as if the commotion were distracting him from his meal. I paused just inside the front door, checking for safety. There were pieces of the enemy everywhere. None of them looked alive.

When I stepped out, I saw a man and the two boys who had been playing ball walking out onto the porch of the house next door, stunned expressions on their faces.

"It's okay," I said, "we've got it all under control. You might want to go back inside until the police show up."

When the man noticed my kit, the rifle, and Max, his eyes widened. The boys were wide-eyed like their dad, but unlike him, they were grinning—excited. The man quickly grabbed the boys and retreated into the house.

I expected other neighbors to start poking their heads out, but none did. I didn't know if they were scared, indifferent, inattentive, or if the house with the boy footballers was the only ordinary, non-gangbanger house on the block. It didn't matter—I had to find Sarah.

Max and I headed for the tunnel.

32

Pappy tossed the flashbangs into the gaping hole in the floor. He waited for the light and noise to do their job, then dropped straight down, landing lightly despite his heavy gear. He scanned the area with the night vision goggles attached to his helmet, anticipating incoming bullets, but none came—not yet, anyway.

The bangers probably didn't expect anyone to find the hatch hidden under the rug. Either that, or they believed their troops would successfully kill all of them. But Gil was experienced in dealing with tunnel rats and knew all their tricks, so the rug game hadn't fooled him. Pappy had helped train Gil and couldn't help but feel a bit of pride in how skilled he had become.

Pappy had one goal—to find Sarah for Gil—but he knew Hearst had another. Hearst wanted to find Sarah too, dead or alive, but he also wanted Cruz, the drug lord they had failed to kill in Mexico. Pappy motioned for Sammy and Dominic to take point, as they were the best guns. The two moved forward without lights, relying on their night vision, Dominic leading and Sammy close at his shoulder.

Montgomery was next. Pappy had watched him during both raids and liked what he saw. The man was good. He was strategic, cautious, quick, and didn't ask stupid questions. Despite the saying that there are no stupid questions in combat—and in most of life, actually—that wasn't true at all. Most questions were stupid. Good, useful questions were rare. In combat, stupid questions could easily be fatal.

Hearst's team leader was next, and Billy was at the rear with two other soldiers.

Pappy noticed recent footprints in the dust. They belonged to one man, with nothing to indicate Sarah was with him unless he was carrying her. However, the length and depth of each stride made that unlikely. The man had taken long, quick steps, running on the balls and toes of his feet—at full speed. It would be difficult for a man to run like that while carrying a grown woman, even one as light as Sarah. No, Pappy didn't think Sarah was with him.

Did that mean she was dead?

Most likely.

Gil had been right about the change in cars, but that didn't mean he was right about her still being alive. The banger's story seemed legit, not to mention the discovery of Sarah's clothing, blood, charred remains, and DNA that had been validated—*twice.*

Pappy hoped he was wrong and acknowledged, at least to himself, that he might well be. After all, he was a Marine, not a PI. Gil had a lot more experience with this type of thing. He'd continue looking for her as Gil requested, but inside—inside, he thought it a wild goose chase.

Topside, something detonated, shaking the tunnel's ceiling and hailing dirt and small rocks down on them. Pappy, familiar with explosive ordnance, knew it was a bomb. He hoped it wasn't the house exploding. The bad guys could have rigged it with a timer, or maybe the copter had missed its target or misunderstood their orders. The fog of war was an ever-present danger.

Gil hadn't made it to the tunnel yet.

Shaking it off, Pappy continued down the passage.

Gil was Gil—he could take care of himself.

~

IRMGARD PULLED AWAY FROM TINA. There were tears in Tina's eyes, but Irmgard couldn't let that sway her. She had to make sure Tina didn't discover the truth—the truth about the pinches, the scratches, the cuts ... and the knife.

What Irmgard was on the inside.

She was finally beginning to understand that the things in her dreams weren't the monsters—she was the monster. Everything that had happened was because of her. All the hurt, the hate, the fear, the death—all because of her.

Even what was happening to Tina and Billy now. They wouldn't be having problems if it weren't for her. She was the real problem. She messed everything up, just like when she wouldn't eat her peas. She didn't mean to, didn't want to, but that's how it always was. Irmgard was just bad, and because she was bad, terrible things happened to the people around her—the people who loved her.

She had to make it stop, somehow.

"It's okay," Irmgard said, "I understand. I'm not your real daughter. Not yours or Pa—*Billy's*. Me being here is making it harder for you—for both of you. I'm sorry."

"No, Irmgard, that's not true. It's not—not at all. Our problems have nothing to do with you. It's because of our jobs and our lives. You know that I'm a police officer. Well, Billy's family has a different kind of job—like Billy used to—and it's kind of at odds with my job. That's why we're having problems. That's why we've been in strange moods and acting weird. It has nothing to do with you.

"If anything, you are the main thing holding us together right now. We both love you and want what's best for you. That's why we've been fighting. We're trying to come to terms with our differences and the differences in our lifestyles. I doubt we would still be together if it weren't for you."

Irmgard listened as best she could while the visions and flashbacks invaded her mind, touching her brain with their dirty fingers. It felt like unwashed hands sliding around the inside of her skull, squeezing and slithering—like worms or snakes writhing around, forcing the pictures and words deep into the recesses of her brain, reminding her of what she had done and how many had suffered. She feared how many more might suffer because of the badness lurking inside her.

Tina was trying to take the blame from her, but Tina didn't know the real Irmgard. The Irmgard who had secretly wished her mother would die and who had disobeyed her father. The Irmgard who had brought the bad men to their farm because she wouldn't eat her peas—bad men who had murdered her father and chased her. Tina didn't know that the wolf had been sent to punish Irmgard, just like the bad man they called the Ghost had been sent to punish her.

Punish her for all the bad that lived inside her.

All the guilt.

The images were coming too fast—too fast for Tina not to notice. Irmgard's hand had slipped back inside her pocket for the knife. It was her only hope. If Tina saw, *if she really saw,* Irmgard didn't know what she would do or what might happen to her.

She pressed down on the knife tip with her finger, blood still seeping. The bright, hot point of pain pushed back the thoughts, the images, the memories, and the hurtful accusations that assaulted her—thoughts that pressed in so forcefully she could think of nothing else. The intensity of the pain helped—not as much as before, but a little. Enough, she thought, enough to hide her true self from Tina. But the bleeding went too far. It started wetting her pocket, seeping to the outer layer of her coat. She could feel it.

Thankfully, she could tell that Tina hadn't noticed—that she was still unaware of what Irmgard had to do to cope. Her surrogate mother just kept on talking, trying to reassure her the fault was theirs and not hers. *The point grated against bone.* They loved her and would do anything to protect her. *The blood soaked and flowed, warming her through the thin material of her pants as it ran down her leg.*

Suddenly, Thor was there at her side ...

growling at her.

~

THOR WALKED ALONGSIDE THE COUGAR. Occasionally, one would nip at the other's ear, shoulder, or back of a leg. They would then roll and tussle, breaking apart and coming together in a ball of fur, teeth, and claws, biting, scratching, and snarling. It was mostly light play, but sometimes it escalated until Tina or Irmgard had to tell them to knock it off.

The two girls stopped, and Atlas went to a bush. Thor moved to a tree and lifted his leg, but as he did, he heard something in Irmgard's voice. Something strange.

And the scent.

Blood.

Pain.

He sensed ... cortisol release, adrenaline dump, and increased heart rate and perspiration. Dropping his leg, Thor stared at the two of them, watching. He didn't understand what Irmgard was saying, but he didn't like what she was feeling.

He walked back to her slowly. They were so absorbed in conversation that they didn't notice him—not until he nudged Irmgard's leg. He brushed against her so lightly that she didn't register the contact, just that he was there. She looked down at him, her eyes glazed... *with pain?* Maybe. Maybe something else.... *It didn't matter*. Not to Thor. He didn't like it.

He growled. The scent of blood was more pungent now, but there was something else. Something inside the pocket, where her hand was—where the blood was.

A knife.

It was hurting her, causing pain and triggering chemical changes throughout her system. Atlas noticed that Thor had returned to the humans. He spun around and bounded their way.

Tina noticed Irmgard's change of posture and realized Thor was standing next to her. She didn't like the way he was looking at Irmgard or the way he growled. Tina had never heard Thor growl at Irmgard before. She started to reach for him but was too slow. Atlas was too slow, too. Before he could get to them, Thor moved like his namesake, striking with lightning speed, his teeth digging into the fabric, tearing and gripping. With a mighty snap of his neck muscles, he flung the knife away into the bushes and the dark.

Irmgard grasped her wrist and stared at the blood streaming down her finger. It trickled into the sleeve of her coat and shirt, staining them red. A two-inch gash was clearly visible.

"NO! Bad dog!" screamed Tina. She wedged herself between the two, protecting Irmgard with her own body.

Thor had struck precisely and flawlessly, ripping the coat and grabbing the knife from the pocket without touching Irmgard's flesh. But unintentionally, the blade caused more damage as it was torn free. Tina was yelling at him now, gripping Irmgard's hand and inspecting the injury with frightened eyes.

"Platz-platz-platz!" she screamed at him.

Thor did as she ordered, dropping to his belly. Irmgard was safe now, the thing that hurt her gone.

"How bad did he get you?" Tina asked Irmgard, looking closely at the wound.

Irmgard started to tell her that it wasn't Thor, that it was her—like everything else—*her fault*. But Tina was so mad, so scared, and Irmgard was only nine and she was scared too.

She didn't say anything.

"It looks like it went to the bone," said Tina, tearing a strip from the bottom of her own shirt and wrapping it around Irmgard's finger, applying direct pressure. "That's going to need stitches. Let's get you inside. Can you walk? Don't go into shock on me. It's a lot of blood, but you'll be fine. Just stay with me."

Tina scowled at Thor, thrusting a chin at him as she walked away. "I'll deal with you later." She pulled the cougar behind her, the leash wrapped around her wrist.

Thor stayed in the down position, watching as they hurried back to the house. As she was dragged along, Irmgard threw a look at Thor, a look that said she was sorry, tears spilling. Twice more, she tried to gather the courage to tell Tina the truth—that it wasn't Thor, that it was her, that he had only wanted to save her, but that he couldn't—that no one could. Because nothing could save her from the badness, the darkness, the evil.

Because the bad wasn't in the knife, or the thoughts, or even the images.

The bad was in her.

The bad *was* her.

33

Hearst yanked back on the controls, pulling the warbird high overhead so they could avoid ground fire while safely surveilling the area. He'd received word from Pappy that their secondary target, Cruz, had escaped via a tunnel, much like he had in Mexico. But in the Valor stealth copter, they had something they hadn't had in Mexico—GPR (Ground Penetrating Radar).

A sophisticated piece of equipment that emits electromagnetic radiation in the microwave band of the radio spectrum, it sends high-frequency polarized radio wave pulses into the ground. When these pulses encounter an object or a boundary between materials with different permittivity (a property that reflects how a material interacts with an electric field, essentially an insulator's electric polarizability), the energy is reflected, refracted, or scattered back to the surface. The helicopter's receiving antenna captures these variations in the return signals. This process is akin to seismology, but GPR utilizes electromagnetic energy instead of acoustic energy.

The data is then instantly processed by an advanced military computer program, which displays it as real-time video to the pilot. Commercial GPR is often limited to low-resolution, static images, as it uses either very high frequencies (which limit depth penetration) or lower frequencies (which go deeper but reduce resolution). The Valor's onboard equipment overcomes these limitations by rapidly alternating pulses of extremely high and low frequencies. These signals are then extrapolated by an advanced algorithm and displayed on the helicopter's HUD on the windshield, providing a clear and detailed real-time view.

Hearst saw a complex network of tunnels originating from the target house, extending in three directions to neighboring houses, and then branching out further to numerous other locations. It was astonishing, even to Hearst, and on a scale he had only seen in the tunnel systems used by Hamas during their operations against Israel.

How many of these houses and tunnels were there?

Assuming they were primarily used for housing and transporting kidnapping victims, as well as for sex trafficking, narcotics processing, and delivery, just how far did they extend? It infuriated him. The tunnels suggested a full-scale invasion was underway, hidden just beneath the surface.

Hearst flipped a switch, activating his thermal and infrared imaging capabilities. The GPR computer program seamlessly integrated the new data into the video images on his HUD screen. Instantly, he saw glowing silhouettes of bodies moving through the tunnels. He identified Pappy's men by the transponders they wore, approaching another structure—a house across and several houses north of the initial target. He spotted what he believed to be Max running from the initial target location, followed by Gil, also running ... and something else. Approximately thirty combatants were lying in wait, not far from Pappy's advancing position.

Another ambush.

DROPPING through the hole hidden by the wooden hatch and rug, Max landed ten feet below and hit the ground running. The drop was nothing to him.

The tunnel was nearly pitch-black, illuminated only by the shafts of light streaming from the square opening above. The darkness ahead was too deep, even for his enhanced vision. It didn't matter. Max didn't need to see. He could smell them, hear them. The path was clear.

The Alpha's pack was ahead, moving cautiously—slowly. Max would catch up to them quickly.

But there were others.

The enemy.

The Alpha had dropped into the tunnel behind Max and was running to try and catch up with him. He wouldn't make it—not before Max passed the pack and reached the others.

Max's prey.

ANTHONY CARLINO WAS furious as he opened the front door and stepped outside the cabin. Irmgard's hand was covered in blood, her face pale with shock, her eyes wide and terrified.

He knew those dogs were dangerous.

And now it had happened.

Thor had attacked her.

And there he was, maybe twenty yards away, lying in the dirt as he had been commanded by Tina. Anthony checked the fifteen-round magazine of the Sig Sauer P320 in his hand. *Fully loaded.* He slipped it back in, smoothly slid the slide back, and let it snap forward, loading the first round.

Mason would be angry—an understatement—furious. He'd probably want revenge, but Anthony didn't care. The dog had hurt his great-granddaughter, maybe even maimed her, and Anthony knew all too well about the pain of losing a finger.

Any dog that would attack a little girl was worse than dangerous—it was crazy. *Mad.* And, like the missing finger, Anthony knew all too well about mad dogs. He'd had to deal with more than a few of them—guys who, after tasting blood, became addicted to it.

There was only one cure—a bullet through the head.

Too bad, so sad. He'd liked Thor.

~

THE NIGHT VISION goggles attached to my Kevlar helmet illuminated my way through the cavernous tunnel. Ahead, I could hear Max's claws scraping against the hard-packed dirt. I ran after him, but he was doing about fifteen miles an hour, slow compared to the thirty-plus he could reach on a straightaway. But this was no straightaway. The tunnel was filled with curves, bends, and corners, and he was working in complete darkness without any enhanced night vision technology.

There were no bodies along the way, which told me that Pappy and the boys had encountered no resistance. Cruz must have high-tailed it with Sarah, who was probably unconscious, to wherever this tunnel led.

He wouldn't get away.

Not this time.

Not from me.

Up ahead, I could hear the muted jangles and snaps of uniforms and equipment—men trying to operate in stealth but dealing with the reality of movement, physics, and acoustics in a contained, echoing environment. I was getting close.

But not close enough.

A scream.

A growl.

Gunfire erupted.

~

WITH DAWNING HORROR, Hearst saw the throng of men at the end of the tunnel, their heat signatures glowing an ominous green against the darkness of night behind the windshield display. Despite their advanced skill and professionalism, there was no way Pappy's small contingent of men could survive an encounter against this many combatants. Out in the open, maybe, but not in the confines of that space. There was no room to maneuver or take cover. They would be sitting ducks once they rounded the last bend.

It would be a massacre.

Activating his throat mic, he yelled into the radio, "Pappy, stop! Ambush-ambush-ambush!"

But before he could finish the warning, the sound of automatic weapons blasted across the two-way radio.

He was too late.

Pushing down on the stick, he put the copter into a dive, knowing in his heart that his men were already dead.

THE ALPHA'S pack didn't notice Max until he streaked past them in the dark. Startled, most of them jumped, some pointing weapons uselessly as he silently increased his speed, overtaking those in the front and rounding the corner before them. The enemy was directly ahead, waiting in ambush, just as Max had waited in ambush for the boar. The difference was that the enemy was not Max.

They never saw him coming.

They didn't even know he was there—until he impacted the one closest to him, his teeth crushing through soft flesh and crunching cartilage, his body slamming into two more men.

And then came the screaming.

Chaos erupted.

Gunshots exploded.

Death enveloped the enemy like a shadowy figure as they tried to fire at Max but instead shot each other at point-blank range. Blood, panic, and darkness did the rest as the untrained men tried to flee, crashing into those behind them and creating a bottleneck.

Pappy and his men, joined by Gil Mason, rounded the corner and saw what was happening.

"Don't hit Max!" Gil yelled.

And then they all opened fire.

34

Tina held Irmgard's hand under the faucet, letting the cold water wash away the blood and bacteria. It helped to quell the fear and shock Tina felt about what had just happened. She couldn't believe Thor had attacked Irmgard, but she'd seen it herself. *Why?* Irmgard hadn't done anything to provoke him.

Why would Thor attack like that? Tina's mind raced through her understanding of dog psychology—their traits and drives—but came up empty.

Now that Irmgard's wound was cleansed, Tina could see it was far less serious than she'd initially thought. The cut was a little over an inch long but deep, resembling a single, precise slice as if made by a razor. It looked more like a knife wound than a dog bite. But Tina knew how sharp dogs' teeth could be. She'd been involved in several incidents where paramedics and even doctors were convinced a blade rather than Viper's teeth had caused the wounds on a suspect.

Tina, of course, knew better. And, as with those incidents, she'd witnessed what happened between Thor and Irmgard. She'd been there—seen it with her own eyes.

She called to Anthony, asking him for a towel, but he didn't respond. He wasn't there.

Where had he gone?

~

IRMGARD SAW the anger in her great-grandfather's eyes and the fear and determination in Tina's as she rushed her to the bathroom sink. She wanted to explain, to tell them everything, but she didn't know where to begin—*what to say*—how to say it. They would hate her.

The cold water washed away the blood but not the guilt. Nothing could remove that—not from her. Tina grabbed a hand towel from under the sink and wrapped it tightly around her finger, so tight it hurt.

Good.

It's what she deserved. She'd let Thor take the blame for what she'd done. Tears welled and spilled, not because of her finger but because of her betrayal. She tried to think of a way to explain what had really happened, but again, she couldn't think of how to do it. Instead, she stayed silent, tears flowing, not cold like the water that had washed away her blood, but hot, like the shame she felt.

Poor Thor.

~

THE BREEZE HAD INTENSIFIED into a cold wind laced with tiny shards of icy snow. Anthony had to squint his eyes and hunch his big shoulders against the barrage. He would finish the job quickly.

He screwed the suppressor into the barrel so the girls wouldn't hear. Later, he'd tell them he couldn't find Thor—that he'd run off. They'd never see him again, never find the body. They'd think he just ran away after attacking Irmgard. Watching Anthony from under his brows, Thor looked perfectly relaxed, even as the wind rustled through his fur and ears.

Anthony wasn't afraid of the dog. Thor had grown compared to the pup he had been, but he still wasn't that big—not yet, anyway. And, of course, he'd never get any bigger. Anthony figured he could handle Thor's forty or so pounds if necessary. Even though Anthony wasn't as big and strong as he once was, he still weighed well over two hundred pounds. Plus, he had the gun.

As he approached Thor, he raised his arm, pointing the weapon at the dog's head, his finger wrapped around the trigger. Before pulling, he looked back at the cabin to ensure the girls were still inside and not at the window.

A pang of guilt nagged at him, something he hadn't felt in decades, not even when he had to kill men. But Thor had committed the gravest of sins, and Anthony couldn't let it go. He couldn't take the risk, not with his great-granddaughter. "Sorry, buddy," he said, turning and taking the last of the trigger's slack.

But the dog was gone.

Thor watched as Anthony Carlino left the cabin and began walking toward him. The wind had picked up, turning cold and wet, interspersed with ice crystals that slashed at the eyes. Thor was unbothered by them. They meant nothing. The wind meant nothing.

Only the man mattered now.

His smell had changed. He was no longer Thor's friend, a member of the Alpha's pack. Now, he was a threat.

As the man turned away to look at the cabin, Thor moved fast, silent, and not in the way a predator might expect. He moved out and around until, as the man turned back, he was sitting directly behind him, waiting for the man to turn again.

Ready for the man to look for him.

Ready to attack.

Anthony was stunned—the dog was *just* there. It was as though he had vanished. But Thor hadn't vanished. A sixth sense, or maybe just a lifetime of experience, told him the dog was still here.

It told him something else as well.

It told him he was in mortal danger—that he had made a terrible miscalculation—one that might well cost him his life. Holding the gun steady, he slowly turned.

And there was Thor, unfazed by the wind and the coming storm.

Anthony Carlino stared into the animal's eyes and saw something he had only seen once before. Something he had seen, not in an animal, not in a dog, but in Gil Mason's soul. Anthony's blood ran cold, and it had nothing to do with the ice or the wind.

He thought that if he moved smoothly—slow and easy—he might just have a chance. One shot, that was all it would take at this distance. Just an inch to the right and a few inches down, and Thor's head would be in line with the barrel. Yes, Anthony thought he might just make it.

His hand moved.

But, like before, he had miscalculated.

THOR KNEW what the man was thinking. He didn't know how he knew, but he knew. A complex mix of chemicals and electrical signals flowed through the man's central nervous system and veinous pathways, flooding organs, synapses, and tissues, emitting scent molecules through his pores and surrounding his frame like an aura.

Thor struck.

TINA HAD JUST FINISHED WRAPPING gauze, slathered in triple antibiotic cream and secured with medical tape, around Irmgard's finger when the little girl's sleeve slipped toward her elbow, revealing the pale skin of her forearm. Being who she was and doing what she did, she instantly recognized the cluster of thin, straight lines sliced into Irmgard's flesh.

Tina froze, her eyes locked on the wounds, each in different stages of healing—some almost scarred, most scabbed, and some still fresh. Irmgard noticed Tina's reaction and cringed as if expecting to be struck.

"Sorry," she said quickly, her voice tiny and scared, "I'm sorry."

She tried to pull her hand away, but Tina held it firmly, so firmly that it hurt. Terror slashed through Tina's heart like a slap.

"What? What are you doing?" Tina's lips felt numb, the words almost garbled. And then came the scream from Anthony Carlino outside. Both girls looked toward the cabin door.

"Thor!" cried Irmgard, still sounding frightened and guilty.

"Stay here," said Tina, letting go of Irmgard's wrist and running for the door.

As Tina rushed out, Irmgard stood still, so frightened she couldn't move.

Tina knew—that meant they would all know. The horror of it pressed in on her so heavily that she felt like she was suffocating. She couldn't bring air into her lungs, and for an instant, she hoped she would die right then and there.

At least then, she wouldn't have to face them.

It would all come out now. They'd think she was crazy, or worse, they'd learn the truth—they'd know what she was on the inside.

How she hadn't eaten the peas.

How she'd wished for her mother to die.

Unconsciously, her hand went into her pocket to grasp the knife, but it was gone. It didn't matter, really. Like the pinches and the scratches, the slices from the knife had begun to lose their effect. They weren't enough anymore and certainly wouldn't be in the future. Irmgard understood that now—the images, memories, and thoughts were too strong.

Besides, now that they knew, they wouldn't let her have knives anymore. Irmgard needed something else—something more. She saw Tina's gun in its leather holster hanging on the coat rack. Tina would notice if it went missing, but her great-grandfather had guns—lots of guns—rifles, pistols, shotguns. She could sneak one, hide it for later. If the thoughts got too bad—so bad she couldn't stand it—she could *make* them go away.

She would make them go away forever.

And then it wouldn't matter if they knew.

TINA SAW THOR ATTACKING ANTHONY. The old man was on his back, a gun in the dirt beside him. Forty-pound Thor was dragging him back and forth, the muscles in his neck and shoulders bunching and bulging like shifting granite as he effortlessly jerked him this way and that.

The wind was wicked, its icy crystals slashing at her. She yelled for Thor to release and platz, but the storm whipped the sound away, making it unlikely he could hear her.

Tina hadn't closed the door behind her, and now all the animals came rushing out—Viper, Petros, Arrow, and even Atlas. They flooded around her, watching the conflict on the ground. Tina ran toward Anthony and Thor. The other animals ran with her and quickly surpassed her, reaching the scene before she did...

...where they joined Thor in the attack.

35

I fired into the throng, taking careful aim but shooting fast—fast for me anyway. Sammy and Dominic were something else.

The bangers were in total disarray, those closest to us clawing over the ones behind, tripping and screaming and crying as we slaughtered them. They had high-powered flashlights, probably intended to blind our night vision, but they were useless against the panic and Max.

I was reminded of a story in the Bible, from the Book of Judges, when Gideon's forces were vastly outnumbered, just as God intended. One of the Midianites had a dream about a loaf of bread tumbling into their camp and overturning a tent so that it lay flat. The story of the dream spread through the ranks, causing fear. When Gideon's small army lit their torches and sounded their horns, the ensuing panic routed the multitude, giving Gideon the victory.

It was like that now, but instead of a loaf of bread rolling into their camp, it was a dog named Max.

~

Hearst saw the battle beneath the surface of the earth, but even with the enhanced video provided by the computers and the embedded responders each of his men wore, he couldn't tell who was winning or even who was who. The locations of the opposing forces were overlapping, and their movements too fast.

Pulling back on the stick, he came out of his dive and hovered the big copter just above the roof of the target house. Men came running out of the residence and started shooting up at them, bullets *plunking* and *spanging* off the ship's thick armor.

"Take them out," he said to his rear gunners.

The two men angled their big, mounted machine guns down and blasted away.

We were pushing ahead through the chaos when enemy reinforcements began dropping into the tunnel from the house. Two side tunnels began filling with men as well, diverting our attention and allowing the troops from the house to advance unopposed. We were suddenly flanked on both sides and taking fire.

Grenades were out of the question. They might well bring the whole tunnel down on us. I pointed to the advancing forces on the right.

"Pappy, Sammy, take those!" I pointed to the left, "Everyone else, them! Max and I'll concentrate on the house."

As I began spitting bullets into the horde, I saw Max still inflicting damage and provoking fear.

Good boy!

We needed the edge. Still, it might not be enough.

But I knew Sarah was up there, in the house, and nothing would stop me from reaching her.

I started killing again.

TINA SCREAMED at the dogs and Atlas to stop as they dragged Anthony Carlino from one point to another. But the wind, the sleet, the chaos, the growls, and the blood lust rendered her commands ineffective.

She waded in, grabbing fur and collars, pulling and shoving with all her strength. Something hit her hard in the chest—a shoulder or hip—and she lost her balance, tripping over a body and landing awkwardly on her shoulder and neck. She managed to roll and ended up on her seat, half inside a bush, her hand resting on something cold and sharp. Looking down, she recognized the short paring knife, its blade and handle smeared in red. Tina felt her blood run cold.

She looked up at Thor, still growling and biting into Anthony Carlino's forearm as he dragged him around, the other animals latching onto various parts of the old man's body.

They would kill him if she didn't act quickly.

But, as she struggled to devise a plan, she was caught between the horror of the attack and the sudden realization that had blossomed in her mind.

Thor hadn't bitten Irmgard at all—he'd been trying to protect her. He'd ripped the knife from her pocket, stopping the thing that was hurting her—the thing that was making her bleed.

How long had Irmgard had been cutting herself? *Oh, that poor, sweet girl.* How had Tina missed the signs? She felt sick—ashamed.

Suddenly, the cop in her took over, and she shoved those thoughts aside. She had to save Anthony Carlino. Her gun was inside and would take too long to retrieve. If she tried to get it, the animals might kill or horribly maim him by the time she got back. Besides, what was she going to do? Shoot Thor? Petros? *Viper?*

No, she couldn't do that, not even to save Billy's grandfather.

And then she remembered seeing Anthony Carlino's gun lying in the dirt next to him when she first came outside. There it was, just a few feet away.

Tina grabbed it.

~

Hearst realized they were losing. His thermal sensors detected over two dozen heat signatures in the house, indicating a significant number of soldiers—and that didn't account for those still alive and fighting in the tunnels.

His copilot had visually identified at least five houses from which the combatants were emerging. His rear gunners were making mincemeat of anyone who showed their face outside, trying to shoot at them. But what could he do for his men underground?

Hearst didn't like the answer to that question, but based on what he saw, he had only one choice—one chance. Jerking up on the controls, he soared high, praying he wasn't about to kill them all—Gil, Pappy, his own men.

Leveling high enough so they would be safe from the blast, he dropped the bomb, but this time, it wasn't a car he was targeting.

It was the house.

~

I was a machine now, killing without thought, without emotion, not even rage. It was the only way. Pain was meaningless. Bullets tore and plucked at my vest and clothes, taking little nicks and chunks from unprotected flesh.

I ignored it all, feeling nothing—just doing what I needed to do to get to my Sarah. Men were dying all around me, falling as I pumped round after round into their bodies, heads, and limbs. They piled up beneath the ladder protruding from the tunnel's entrance. As I reached it, I started clawing my way over their corpses to make my way up, firing one-handed at the men trying to come down to me, dodging their dead weight as they fell.

I'd almost made it to the top of the ladder when Max caught sight of me. He ran toward me and leaped. Just then, the world exploded. My hearing, sight, and thought were instantly blanked. A wave of searing heat slapped me back and away like the hand of God, sending me sailing across the tunnel, where I slammed into a dirt and rock wall.

Everything went black, and when I opened my eyes, everything was still black, my senses dead. Gradually, muffled sounds began to penetrate the deafness, and then a high-pitched whine escalated from nothing to a deafening scream that hurt my brain. I rolled over from my stomach, which was difficult since I was buried in dirt and bodies, and pushed myself to a sitting position.

The fighting had stopped, or at least the sounds of fighting had stopped. My helmet had been knocked askew, the mounted night vision goggles twisted to the side and away from my eyes. I felt for them and pulled them back into place.

The tunnel, what was left of it, glowed green before me. The dead were everywhere. Streams of dirt pattered down from above, popping against my helmet, neck, and shoulders. The air was clogged with dust, filling my lungs and making me cough and gag. Feeling disoriented, I scanned the tunnel.

Where were the others?

Pappy, Sammy, Dominic—Billy?

Where was Max?

But then my thoughts came back into focus, filling me with terror. I looked to where the ladder leading into the house should have been and saw only a wall of impenetrable dirt and rock.

"Sarah."

Irmgard took the smallest one from inside the dresser across from her great-grandfather's bed. There were three, so she didn't think he would miss just the one. It was surprisingly heavy compared to its size. Probably because of the bullets, she thought. Billy had once explained that they made up a good portion of a gun's weight, especially the ones with lots of bullets. He said it was worth it, though, because the more bullets you had in a fight, the better.

She would need only one.

As she turned the metal and plastic object in her hands, she liked how it felt—the same way she had liked how the knife felt. It promised protection. Protection from the pictures in her mind, the memories that assaulted her repeatedly, like the lyrics of a half-forgotten song that wouldn't stop playing—over and over and over—until she couldn't stand it.

Now, she'd be able to stop them—stop them forever. She pointed the hole toward her face and slipped her thumbs around the trigger. The hole looked so small, so dark, so deep. She thought she could see something way down inside. Something almost bright at the bottom of the darkness. She couldn't be sure—it might just be a trick of the light, but maybe—just maybe—there was something.

An answer?

She looked closer, her thumbs tightening reflexively, angling the barrel slightly so the light from the desk lamp could shine down a little further. It looked pretty, whatever it was.

The answer to everything.

She hadn't planned on using it yet—she was sure she hadn't—it was just in case. Just in case. But Tina knew, and she would tell everyone, and then they would all know.

Irmgard looked closer, her eye just above the hole.

36

Thor tore at Anthony's arm, blood flooding his mouth through the scant protection offered by the man's sleeve. His mother, siblings, and even Atlas joined in the attack. Not that he needed them—he would have killed the old man himself. The old man had been about to kill him.

Self-preservation demanded he act in kind.

Although his young, inexperienced brain didn't comprehend this in sequential terms as humans do, he understood it nonetheless. Perfectly. More perfectly than most humans. His drives, traits, genes, and heredity drove his thinking.

He'd heard Tina's orders, but Tina was not the Alpha. Tina was not his father.

And the blood lust had a hold on him.

The entire pack had joined him, almost as if he were the Alpha.

It felt right.

It felt good.

Atlas was gnawing on one of Anthony's calves, Viper had his other arm by the bicep, and Arrow had a thigh. Petros ran around the group, sneaking in for a quick nip and jumping back before finding another open point of attack.

Thor eyed the old man's throat and, at just the right time, released his bite on the forearm. Opening his mouth wide, he adjusted his head, turning it to the side, to grip the kill spot, deep and full.

Death would be swift.

~

ANTHONY CARLINO KNEW he was about to die. He could accept that. For most of his life, he'd expected to die a violent death. But never, not in his wildest nightmare, did he think he'd go out like this—torn apart by a pack of dogs.

Suddenly, the bone-crushing grip on his forearm released, and the cold wind of the storm blowing at his neck was washed away by hot breath. Needle-like points closed over his throat.

Three gunshots shattered the night, louder than thunder and as bright as lightning. Everything came to a standstill. Thor, Viper, Petros, Arrow, and Atlas looked toward the source.

Tina stood tall, her hair blowing in the sleet-laden wind, her arm stretched high, the gun pointed to the sky like some god calling power down from the heavens. The silencer lay at her feet in the dirt where she'd dropped it.

"*Platz!*" she screamed.

And they all did.

~

AGUSTIN CRUZ KNEW it was time to leave. He had watched the destruction of the house from a safe vantage point eight structures to the south. Even so, the blast had shattered the large picture window he had been watching from, cutting him in several places. The lacerations were minor, but he was vain about his looks, and a piece of glass had sliced his jaw near his left ear.

The destructive force of the bomb had flattened houses within a thirty-yard radius, leaving only a crater. His men were dead, but so were those who had been searching for him. The tunnels could not have survived. They were strong, well-built, and supported, but nothing could withstand that level of devastation.

He never imagined the Americans would use this level of force. Their leaders were primarily a weak and cowardly lot, afraid to do anything that might cost them votes or raise accusations—easily bribed or blackmailed, subject to the most juvenile forms of entrapment.

Theirs was a failed form of government that would collapse within a few years, leaving a power vacuum where the strong could seize control.

He and his brother were strong—leaders of the most powerful cartel in South America. Even the Colombians dared not challenge them. However, this group of American soldiers, led by Hearst, was proving to be a problem. Twice now, they had managed to survive the ambushes he had set for them.

Agustin touched his jaw, and his finger came away wet with blood. His teeth clenched. The wound, though minor, might well leave a scar. Agustin did not like scars. The señoritas were attracted to his boyish face. They liked him, and he liked them liking him. His older brother often joked that they only came to him because of his money, power, and influence, but Agustin knew better. He knew that, unlike his brother, he was handsome.

They were akin to Jacob and Esau, the two of them. Agustin was smooth, soft, and refined, like Jacob. His brother was a man of the fields—hairy, ruddy, and brutish—like Esau. His brother sometimes thought Agustin was weak, but like Jacob, Agustin knew his inner strength. He knew his worth. After all, didn't the Holy Book say that God loved Jacob and hated Esau? And who could argue with God?

Sirens could be heard in the distance. Yes, it was time to leave.

Besides, he had a treasure to uncover.

I HEARD SOUNDS—COUGHING, the rustle of clothing. The dust that hung in the air made it difficult to see, even with the night vision.

Using my hands, I shoveled my way out of the dirt and bodies until I could stand. It was still hard to breathe, and streams of dirt constantly trickled from the tunnel's ceiling, making me wonder how long we had until the whole thing collapsed.

"Max?" I called. "Billy? Pappy?"

"Over here," came Pappy's voice.

I made my way toward him. There was no response from Max, Billy, or the others. Pappy was buried even deeper than I had been, though not with bodies. Using the butt of my rifle, I dug him out and helped him to his feet. The explosion had knocked off his helmet and goggles, but I found them a few feet away and brought them to him.

Once he put them on and had vision restored, he looked around. "The others?"

"Around here somewhere," I said. "Let's get looking."

A clatter of small rocks and dirt rained down on Pappy. He shrugged them off. "This tunnel's going to go."

"Yeah," I said, searching for Max and the others.

I found Billy first. He was unconscious. I noticed a large scuff on his Kevlar helmet where something hard must have hit. After giving his cheeks a good smack, I dragged him to his feet, where he stood, swaying.

"What happened? Did I win? Did he knock me out? Did he choke me out?"

"It's okay," I said. "You're in a tunnel helping me look for Sarah, not in a cage fight. You took a hit to the head, but you look okay."

"Why can't I see?"

"No lights. Your goggles probably got bonked. See if you can turn them on."

Billy fiddled with them. "Ah, that's better. I see Pappy. Anyone else?"

"Start digging," I said. "We may not have much time."

"What happened?" asked Billy for the second time.

"I don't know. They must have had the tunnels rigged to detonate. Strange though—they were winning."

"I've got Miles," said Pappy from down a side shoot. Miles was Hearst's team leader. "He looks okay. Groggy, though."

That accounted for four of us, but where were the rest?

Where was Max?

Max had been right behind the Alpha when the bomb hit. The blast wave sent him tumbling through the air, back down the tunnel he'd just come from. He landed hard on his shoulder, neck, and head, rolling like one of the tennis balls Pilgrim loved to play with. Somewhere during the tumble, he lost consciousness as parts of the tunnel ceiling and walls crashed down, covering him in dirt, rocks, and splintered wood from the support beams.

Upon waking, he'd tried to stand but felt an enormous weight pressing him down, confining his movement. Dust was choking his lungs, and the pressure from the debris was suffocating him, but he flexed his massive neck and shoulder muscles, pulling and pushing with his muzzle until he created a small pocket, allowing him to breathe.

A lesser dog would have panicked and died.

But Max was not a lesser dog.

Max was Max.

Once he established the pocket, he stayed still, contemplating his situation. He was trapped and blinded by darkness. He could hear nothing, and the dust-filled air made it impossible to detect odors.

Max did not like Atlas, the cougar, but he had observed the creature's antics—its strengths and abilities. He had studied Atlas and added what he could to his own arsenal of weapons. Although Max could not retract his claws and spring them out like knives, seeing Atlas use this tactic made him consider incorporating it himself.

Stretching his thick claws as far as he could, he flexed his wrist (carpus) joints, moving them slightly back and forth, just as he had done with his neck and muzzle. His claws were far more efficient, and the space quickly grew. Max repeated the process with his back legs and paws until he had enough room to pull his knees (stifles) up to his stomach. Once there, he shoved back—hard. The dirt shifted.

He repeated the process three more times and then began to *walk*, or at least he made the motion with his rear legs, clearing dirt and rocks from under and around his belly and hips. Still lying on his side, he *ran*, using his front legs too, shoveling dirt quickly.

Twice, avalanches caved in on him, once around his legs and once around his face. Both times, Max stopped, refusing to panic, and repeated his earlier steps to gain air and room.

Some ancient instinct alerted him that his actions might well bring down the rest of the tunnel and kill him, but he didn't stop. He didn't stop to rest, catch his breath, or relax his muscles—he just kept moving. Max had to get out.

He had to get out and find the Alpha.

37

At the last instant, Tina's gunshots halted Thor's attack on Anthony. She looked powerful standing there in the wind and sleet. Thor's mother was watching her, too, as were the others, none of them moving. On the ground, the old man moaned.

Tina walked through the dogs, all of them observing her every movement. Thor could have attacked—attacked and finished the old man, but he didn't. The danger had passed, as had the bloodlust.

Tina held a higher position in the pack than he did—higher even than his mother. He and the others backed away when she shooed them. In true pack behavior, they all turned in unison to see what she would do next.

Atlas did as the others, standing next to Thor as if he were just another dog. Thor looked at his brother cat, licked his cheek, then turned to watch Tina.

If the old man tried to hurt her, Thor would finish him.

~

TINA TRIED to pull Anthony Carlino to his feet, but he was unable to help, and he was too big and heavy for her to lift by herself. She remembered the ranger roll and fireman's carry she'd learned as a cadet, but she'd never been very good at them. With the wind, the wet sleet, and the possibility of exciting the dogs to another attack, she didn't think trying was plausible.

Giving up on the attempt, she grabbed both of his wrists and started dragging him toward the cabin. Anthony groaned. The animals watched, silent and unmoving.

Tina yelled for Irmgard to come and help, but the wind had intensified in strength. She doubted Irmgard could hear her.

Why hadn't Irmgard come out? she wondered. She had to have heard the attack. There had been barking and screaming ... and the gunshots.

Tina thought of the knife, the cuts, and that horrible look of shame and dread in Irmgard's eyes as she saw the dawning realization creep across Tina's face.

A gunshot, as loud as the sound of death itself, exploded from inside the cabin.

WHEN HEARST SAW the carnage the bomb had delivered to the tunnel system, he feared he'd killed them all, including his men. But what other choice did he have? If he had done nothing, the bad guys would have overrun them. It had been a risky move—the type of thing Hearst had done numerous times in the past. More often than not, he'd made the right decision, saving many lives and winning the day for his side. But this time, it might have been too big a gamble. Yes, he got the bad guy, Agustin Cruz—*no way he could have survived that blast*—but at what cost? Technically, it would be chalked up as a win—but what about his men? What about the others?

Miles? Mason? Pappy?

Sarah Gallagher?

No, he didn't believe she'd ever even been there. She was already dead, shot, and burned after being brutalized by Cruz's men, just as they said.

But what if he was wrong? What if she had been in the house?

Hearst shook his head, refusing to dwell on it while he still had a job to do. And he did still have a job to do. His men were down there, somewhere under the collapsed tunnels. He whipped the copter in a circle and flew low above the crater where the house had been.

He activated the GPR and started searching.

IRMGARD SAW IT THERE, way down at the bottom of the barrel, shiny even in the darkness. She knew about bullets, of course. While living in Germany, her father had taught her about them. So had Billy, her great-grandfather Anthony, and even Tina had explained how they worked. She learned that tiny bits of metal shoot out of a gun and are very dangerous. They can kill you. She was told never to play with them or handle any gun unless she was with one of them—but that was okay—she wasn't playing.

Tina knew the truth.

There was really only one answer, and there it was, way down in the hole—so very close and so easy.

Because the images were flipping through her mind again. The images, thoughts, memories, and the new knowledge that Tina would tell everyone. They would all hate her. They would send her away forever, and there would be no way to stop what she felt. Not ever.

The thought of being alone, trapped with those pictures in her mind, was too horrible to contemplate. To have them spinning around and around, flashing, reaching, and groping at her with tendrils that stretched and wrapped themselves around her every thought.

Outside, the wind slammed the cabin like a fist, rattling the windows with powerful gales. But inside the cabin, within Irmgard's mind, there were only terrible nightmares come alive—*and the answer.*

"I'm sorry, Billy, Tina, Petra, Petros, Uncle Gil ... *everyone*. I'm so sorry."

Her thumbs squeezed.

The blast sounded.

But Irmgard never heard it.

WE'D ACCOUNTED for everyone in our crew except for Max. As we progressed through the tunnels, we encountered little cave-ins everywhere—piles that sometimes stretched from wall to wall and varied in height and density. We climbed over and, when possible, around them, calling for Max, but there was no response.

I kept expecting him to appear magically next to me the way he usually does, but he didn't. That worried me. He'd been right below me when the blast wave hit. He should have been somewhere close, but I'd dug through the mound where I'd been buried, and he wasn't there. He had to be someplace else.

Blown to bits? The thought kept sneaking into my mind—and there were plenty enough *bits* scattered about for that to be a possibility. I saw hands, legs ... other parts ... but no paws or fur— nothing I could identify as belonging to canine physiology.

He had to be here.

And he had to be okay.

I poked, prodded, and dug at every mound of collapsed tunnel, praying that I would find him alive. The others helped, but progress was slow. The air was hard to breathe, and continued leaks and small ruptures of pattering dirt hinted at how little time we had before the whole tunnel gave way, trapping or killing us all beneath tons of earth.

And every second, I worried about Sarah. Had she been obliterated in the explosion? Was Cruz escaping with her while we wasted time fruitlessly searching?

It didn't matter, I couldn't leave until I found Max. Those thoughts were just distractions, so I shoved them away.

Shoved them away and continued digging.

~

MAX FELT a rear paw break through, but the movement sent a cascade of dirt into his face, choking him. It reminded him of the day he was first captured in Germany, riding in the bed of the truck over bumpy roads—bloodied, beaten, burned, his lungs filled with pneumonia. Helpless.

Only he wasn't a pup now, and he was not helpless. Slowly, he repeated his muzzle sweep until he could breathe once again. The trick had kept him alive so far, but he was running out of time. The air he did manage to inhale was stale and thick with dust and becoming clogged with his exhaled carbon dioxide.

Despite the risk of continued avalanches, he dug back with his rear paws, scattering dirt and allowing a trace of fresh air to seep in from the outside. But his victory was short-lived. A rumble sounded as something let loose in the tunnel ceiling, and rocks, boulders, and dirt crashed down. Something heavy impacted the mound across his chest, compressing his lungs and making it nearly impossible to inhale.

Once again, panic tried to rule his actions, but once again, Max refused to let it. Slowly, he resumed digging, walking front and rear legs while lying on his side, as much as the oppressive weight would allow. Little by little, the dirt and rocks fell aside until he had short arcs around each limb.

And then he heard a sound ... his name ... *Max*.

It was the Alpha.

And then again ... and again. Unconsciously, his tail wagged.

He resumed digging, wanting to let the Alpha know he heard him and that he was there. But then a new fear arose, threatening to give final victory to the panic he had fought so hard to vanquish.

The Alpha's voice ... *was fading* ... moving away from him.

Steeling himself, ignoring the danger of another collapse, Max dug faster.

"We have to go," said Pappy, gripping my bicep. "This whole place is going to come down on top of us. Maybe Max made it topside already and is waiting for us at the original target house."

I shook my head to the negative. "He would have come to me."

"Either way, we have to go. You know we do. Besides, there's Sarah to think of."

He gripped tighter, and I turned on him, my voice as dead as my eyes. "Go. Take them with you. I'll come when I've found Max."

"You know that's not happening," said Pappy. "And if you stay, you'll be risking all our lives."

"That's what we do, right? What we always do as soldiers, Marines, and warriors. We put our lives on the line for each other. I'm not leaving him. You do what you need to do." I turned away and started calling again. Moving down a side tunnel, I saw blood and parts of the bad guys scattered across the dirt. Behind me, I saw Pappy hang his head, then motion to the men, sending some this way and others that way, directing them to keep searching.

Montgomery Byrne, Billy's friend, came up beside me.

"I'm with you," he said. "We leave when we find the dog. He saved my bacon like three times back there."

"Thanks," I said as I started digging at a mound. Byrne joined in, both of us coughing in jerky spasms as we shoveled away the earth with our hands and rifle butts.

Nothing.

And then I heard Billy cry out.

"Gil! Here, over here! It's him!"

I'd never been happier and more terrified at the same time. I ran to him, overjoyed that he'd been found but frightened of what I might discover when I got there.

Because if Max had been able to come to me, he would have.

~

Tina dropped Anthony Carlino where he was, letting his wrists thump to the sleet-soaked dirt as she ran for the cabin. The dogs were still there, still watching, and might resume their attack the moment Tina made it inside, but none of that mattered to her now. All she cared about was Irmgard—*her daughter.*

The instant she heard the gunshot, she realized what a vital part of her Irmgard had become. Tina wasn't just playing house and family or trying to make the little girl into something she wasn't. They had formed an inseparable bond, as close as any mother and daughter. No matter what happened between her and Billy, Tina knew she could never endure a time when Irmgard wasn't in her life. Whatever happened to Anthony would just have to happen. All that mattered was her daughter.

When she burst through the door and found the living area empty, she ran through the large cabin, screaming Irmgard's name.

No answer.

Tina's professionalism evaporated despite having been in dozens of similar situations during her career. Equally unimportant was the fact that she had counseled countless frantic parents, telling them that calming themselves was essential so that she and the other first responders could do their jobs and bring about the best possible outcome. Because just like with Anthony Carlino, none of that mattered now. Tina was now living through the nightmare herself, and all the knowledge she had ever shared with them, as true and accurate as it was, was utterly useless.

There *was* no calm.

There was only the mind-numbing terror that the unthinkable—the irrevocable—had happened, and nothing she could ever do would change it.

Tina took the stairs, three at a time, and ran into Irmgard's room.

Empty—just like Tina's.

Stopping at the threshold of Anthony's doorway, she saw Irmgard, the gun on the floor. The smell of burned gunpowder heavy in the still air.

Tina froze.

The blood—so much of it.

Tina had never screamed in her professional career, despite all the horrors she had seen. Not even when she'd been shot at the bridge or when she watched Gil robotically shove gauze into her stomach as if she were nothing more than a mannequin. Never, not once.

But she screamed now.

She screamed and ran to the lifeless body of her daughter.

38

Thor watched Anthony lying on the ground, close to the open front door of the cabin. The urge to attack and kill him was gone. He was no longer a danger to the pack, not to them, and not to Thor. Tina had ordered them to stay where they were.

If Viper moved, then Thor would follow suit, but she didn't. His siblings followed their mother's lead. Only Atlas violated pack rules by slowly standing and stretching. He padded over to Thor, the wind and sleet slicking his ears back along his head, making him look even more sleek and graceful.

He nuzzled against Thor, first rubbing his cheek, then the underside of his chin, and finally his shoulder along the dog's muzzle. Thor licked the cougar's neck and head, and the big kitten flopped down on its stomach, hunkering against him in the storm.

At the sound of Tina's shriek, Thor stopped. Viper stood and darted into the cabin, ignoring and leaping over the moaning man to get inside. Thor stood, looking after her. Should he follow? The others stood with him. Atlas alone stayed down, eyes closed to slits, purring louder than the wind.

Making up his mind, Thor followed his mother, as did Petros and

Arrow. They crowded into the downstairs living room just as Viper reached the top of the stairs and disappeared into a room at the end of the hall. All the dogs ran after her, with Thor in the lead.

Each stopped upon entering, watching Tina as she alternately pumped on Irmgard's chest and then switched her position to puff air into her lungs.

Thor was young and still lacked experience in life, but he knew the scent of fresh death.

He smelled it now.

~

ANTHONY CARLINO OPENED his eyes to pain—pain in so many places. He'd been bitten and clawed too many times to count, and the storm was slashing at him with icy gusts. In his struggle with the animals, he'd injured ligaments, tendons, and joints he didn't remember having and others he hadn't used in years.

But he'd experienced worse. Once, in his early thirties, he was ambushed and shot five times. After killing both the men who'd been gunning for him, he'd driven himself to the hospital. In the heat of the moment, the pain hadn't seemed as bad as this, but once the excitement, fear, and adrenaline had worn off and his body had time to register his injuries, it had been excruciating. It made him a little afraid to think how bad he'd feel tomorrow.

He suddenly thought of the dogs. Slowly, he forced his neck to move so he could look about.

No dogs.

He saw the open cabin door and light spilling out at him. *Why had they stopped?* He'd thought he was a dead man, but here he was, and he wasn't dead. *Soon enough, they would be,* he thought. He'd shoot the lot of them—once he got better, anyway. Especially Thor, the one who attacked his Irmgard.

Anthony looked at the open door again. Why was it open? Where were the dogs? Where was Irmgard and Tina?

The dogs.

Had they left him to attack the girls?

Forcing himself to his belly, he tried to push up from the ground. Everything hurt. His muscles felt like grape jelly, and he fell down onto his face. He heard a sound from behind, and when he craned his neck to look, he saw the cougar. It was licking blood off its claws—*Anthony's blood.* It was watching his every movement as though waiting for the right moment to strike.

But Anthony's concern for Irmgard outweighed his fear of the cat. Ignoring the beast, he pushed up again and, this time, made it to his hands and knees, the wind howling around him like a banshee. After resting for a few seconds, he managed to get one foot underneath him and shakily rose to his feet, swaying against the tempest.

The cougar continued to lick at its paw. Anthony pointed a finger at him. "Your time's coming, kitty. You just wait."

He saw the gun lying a few feet away, where Tina had dropped it when she grabbed him by the wrists to drag him to the cabin. Noticing the missing silencer, he picked it up and looked at the cat. *Not yet—it would alert the dogs.* Anthony staggered his way to the cabin.

It was time to kill some dogs.

STEVE HEARST SAW the transponders embedded in his troops' communication gear activate on the GPR display, showing their placement and movement. They were alive—most of them, at least. He knew the computers could be programmed to do the math and provide him with exact numbers, but he didn't have time to deal with that now. Instead, he whipped the warbird up high and around.

There was nothing he could do for the men underground. The best way to help now was to locate other potential combatants and prepare to protect his men from new threats. Since he'd pretty much leveled an entire neighborhood, he figured there wasn't much he couldn't do.

Too bad for them.

Flipping up the protective cover to his rocket pods, he searched in all directions. *Nothing out in the open ... back to thermal and GPR.* And there they were, some of them anyway—heading away from the action toward another set of houses. *Just how many were under their control?*

Hearst felt indecisive, and he never felt indecisive. Should he go after the bad guys—maybe Cruz himself? Or stay with his men—act as a medivac for his injured?

Every fiber of his being urged him toward the seek-and-kill solution. That was the *fighter jock* in him, the warrior. But the leader in him won out, and he swerved back to his troops.

He had already taken a chance that could have easily killed or severely wounded the soldiers under his command, not to mention possibly killing Sarah Gallagher. There was no way his conscience would allow him to abandon them now when their lives might depend on getting swift medical attention.

But he promised himself Cruz would be his. And soon.

BILLY WAS ALREADY DIGGING when I reached him. I saw Max's rear legs sticking out of a huge mound of dirt twenty yards down the original tunnel we had traveled. The tunnel was piled almost to the ceiling with a four-foot diameter boulder and chunks of splintered wooden beams, creating a shoulder-level mess. Max's legs were moving, scattering dirt in a sizable radius as he tried to free himself.

How much air could he have left?

I frantically joined Billy in digging, and Byrne did the same. Others began to join us, and soon, everyone was helping. I started digging where I thought Max's head would be, and when I broke through, I saw the cavity he'd somehow created that allowed him to survive.

Of course he had—he was Max.

Once he was free, he shook himself mightily, sending dirt flying. He had a few nicks and holes, like mine, but they didn't seem to bother him. Everyone patted him and cheered with grins on their faces, and for once, Max let them.

I interrupted the celebrations and ordered everyone back down the tunnel.

Sarah was waiting.

WHEN ANTHONY CARLINO pushed through the pack of dogs, he saw Tina working on Irmgard. Without thought, he dug into his pants pocket, pulled out his cell phone, and called Sal, ordering him to send a medical helicopter immediately.

Sal knew better than to tell the old man that the storm would make it nearly impossible for a copter to fly. He would just have to make it happen—he had that ability.

Knowing that help was on the way, Anthony dismissed his own injuries and knelt next to Irmgard's body. He saw the gun, the pool of blood, and the hole in his great-granddaughter's face. Recalling her recent strange behavior, he instantly realized what had happened.

"I can take over breathing," he said calmly.

"You know CPR?" Tina asked between counts.

"I know lots of things," he pointed to Irmgard's chest, "You keep up compressions, I'll breathe. My wrists and arms are messed up, but I'll take over if you need me to. I've got help on the way."

"I heard," she said as she checked Irmgard for signs of life. "No pulse." She resumed pumping the little girl's heart. "Breaths every fifteen."

Anthony nodded.

They worked in near silence for the next twenty minutes until, at last, they heard the helicopter landing out front. Paramedics pounded up the stairs and into the room to take over. The dogs stood aside as though sensing the urgency.

Tina calculated in her mind—*twenty, maybe thirty minutes since the sound of the gunshot.* That was a long time, but she'd started compressions almost immediately. Twice in her career, she'd had to perform CPR on people with no detectable heartbeat—neither had survived. *Third time's a charm,* she thought, as tears welled and flowed.

Following the paramedics, she ran for the helicopter, and for the first time in as long as she could remember, she prayed to the God of the Bible.

She prayed for Irmgard to live.

39

A mile from the house the Bell V-280 Valor Stealth Helicopter had obliterated, Agustin Cruz sat across from Sarah Gallagher. A bruise running from temple to cheek decorated her face, where Cruz's man had punched her, but she was still by far the most beautiful woman he had ever seen. No wonder his brother wanted her.

He had to admit, he wanted her for himself and had it been anyone else who had laid claim, he would have taken her. But he wasn't about to challenge his brother. He had often been accused of being rash, but stupid? Nobody ever called him that.

Agustin had taken the time to clean himself of the dust and grime from his journey through the tunnel—he was very vain about his appearance. His brother considered this a flaw in his character, but Agustin didn't care. After all, he didn't need to kidnap his women. They came to him.

His brother was older and had a better mind for business, crime, and controlling other men. Women were not his strength—he was too rugged, too rough. The comparison between Jacob and Esau came to mind again. However, Agustin doubted his brother would be foolish enough to relinquish any part of his inheritance for a bowl of red stew, no matter how hungry he might be.

Although gazing at the woman's beauty, he wondered. After all, food was hardly the only form of hunger. And his brother had made it clear that he wanted this woman for more than a night. The wedding dress tucked in the bedroom closet was proof of that.

"What do you want from me?" asked Sarah.

Agustin shrugged. "What do all men want from women who look like you?"

Sarah's face went pale. She leaned back in her chair away from him.

The young brother smiled and shook his head. "No, you have nothing to fear from me, señorita—not that I don't want you. Of course I do. And once you got to know me, I think you would not object so much as you might think. I'm very gentle. But it is not for me that you have been brought here. You are for my brother, Matias, the most feared and powerful man in all of Mexico."

"But I don't know him. I've never even heard of him," said Sarah.

"My brother demands the best of everything—the prettiest of flowers, the best guns, the biggest hacienda, the most beautiful of women. He owns Mexico, the politicians, the policia, the military, the cartels. And soon—soon he will own all of North America as well. It seems you are the most fortunate of women since the Virgin Mother herself. You should rejoice. I have never seen him so captivated by a woman."

Sarah shook her head. "This is a mistake. It has to be. I'm getting married next month."

"No," said Agustin, "not next month, tonight. Tonight, you will be married—married to Matias. It has all been arranged. You must accept this."

"This is insane. This is ...," but before she could finish, the front door opened, and in walked her future husband, Matias Cruz.

Except Sarah knew him as Sheriff Matt Adams.

~

We made it to the house we'd initially targeted and climbed back up from the tunnel. Outside, I saw the man and his two sons on their front porch, their house untouched amidst the destruction, sirens wailing in the distance and disbelief on their faces. Across the street, Hearst had landed the copter in the deserted crater where a radius of houses, now obliterated, had stood less than an hour ago.

"Gas explosion," I said to the trio, feeling like Agent K from *Men in Black*, minus his handy electro bio-mechanical neural transmitting zero synapse repositioner, better known as a neuralyzer. From their incredulous looks, I think it would have gone better if I'd had one after all.

The group of us, Max included, boarded the stealth helicopter, and up into the sky we went.

"I had a read on escapees in the tunnel heading to the west, but I lost them," Hearst said through the radio system. "A team is on its way to the houses I nuked to conduct a search. If Sarah's body is there, they'll find her."

"She's not," I said. "If Agustin got away, he took her with him. He wouldn't have gone to all this trouble just to let her get blown up in a house or leave her behind. But I don't believe she was ever there. And it wasn't *her* body that they burned. Just like I said."

I could see from the look on almost everyone's faces that they didn't believe it.

I didn't care.

"Where to then?" asked Hearst.

"The Sheriff's Office. There's something I need to check. Get the wounded to the medics in the jail and be ready to leave fast. We need to be quick."

Hearst's team leader, Miles, pointed at me. "You better get looked at yourself. You're leaking pretty bad," he said, referring to the dozen or so nicks and holes I'd gotten in the house and tunnels.

They were nothing ... nothing compared to what I was about to do to the men who had taken Sarah.

~

ADAMS WAS DRESSED as she'd always seen him—sheriff's shirt with the badge over his pocket and stars on his collar, blue jeans, gun belt with a tie-down holster, and cowboy boots. Only one stark difference stood out—his cowboy hat was black.

He saw that she noticed and grinned.

"Not because I've suddenly become the bad guy," he said, flicking the brim with his forefinger. "Not like in your American TV movies and shows. I'm always the good guy. In Mexico, we have no such silly differentiations. Black is the color of strength. Under my leadership, Mexico is strong, unlike your so-called United States. Your people are easily fooled by false symbols—a white hat instead of black, blue instead of red, a simple trick during an election newscast, tools to play the idiot masses. Nothing more."

"But ... you're the sheriff," said Sarah incredulously.

"A role that serves its purpose, as it has for nearly a decade. My brother," he smiled at Agustin, "manages my empire in Mexico while I set up the fall and eventual takeover of your country."

"Impossible," said Sarah. "You're nothing but a ... a drug dealer."

"Oh, Sarah, I am ... so much more. I am a visionary. I am America herself. The new America—what America was meant to be—powerful, untouchable, the earth's rightful ruler. I am everywhere, in every state, in your banks, at the highest levels of government, Congress, the Senate, and, who knows, maybe one day even the President himself. After all, county sheriffs are elected officials, a steppingstone to something greater. Do you think it mere chance that Agent Hearst and his *special* unit are headquartered here under my watch, where I can observe their every plan and move?" He shook his head, amused. "All coordinated by me. Because, in America, money talks—and I have lots of money. But you will have time to learn this. All the time you need ... as my wife."

Sarah shook her head. "I'm marrying Gil."

"Gil Mason is dead," said Agustin. "He and his men. Agent Hearst bombed them while they were in the tunnels chasing me."

Sarah stared at him wide-eyed.

"No," she whispered.

"It's true," said Adams, feigning sympathy. "I'm sorry for the hurt, but it's necessary. Loss is sometimes required to show us what we truly need—what's important. You were meant for more than Gil Mason. You were meant for me."

~

SURROUNDED BY MY ENTOURAGE, I stopped at the lab, grabbed the baggy with the evidence that hadn't been taken, and then went to Sarah's computer on the desk. I punched in her password to call up her last entries and emails. The fourth one was from Parabon Nano-Labs. A stream of data rolled down the screen, complete with a digital mugshot of the suspect.

I nodded, feeling the rage. I clicked the print icon and, a few seconds later, retrieved the page. Then, I rushed out of the lab and up to Sheriff Adams' office, with Billy, Pappy, and Hearst following.

"What is it you're looking for?" asked Hearst.

Before answering, I paused to kick in the locked door with a front kick that splintered the wood and destroyed the frame.

"Three things," I said as I went behind his desk and jerked the drawer open. The sudden movement propelled all the loose and heavier items to the front, just like it had the last time I was here.

And there they were.

A handful of tokens.

Grabbing one, I held it up next to the baggy containing an identical coin so they could all see.

Hearst took both. "Tokens from Shooter's Showdown. So? It's a tourist attraction. There are thousands of these all over down here."

"I said *three* things. That's the first." I turned and pointed at the gun and belt high over Adams' desk. "That's the second."

"I've seen guns like that before," said Pappy.

"Yeah," I said, "we both have. Above the fireplace at Agustin Cruz's mansion in Mexico. Only they weren't *like* this one ... they were *exact* replicas—right down to the pearl handles and silver bullets."

"What are you saying?" asked Hearst.

"That Sheriff Adams is our leak. He works for the cartel... *no* ... more than that. He *is* the cartel. You said that Agustin Cruz had a brother who was assassinated about a decade ago. When did Adams get voted in as sheriff?"

Hearst did the eye tick and tooth suck. "About the same time."

Pappy and Billy looked at each other.

"Still," said Hearst, "it's weak. I mean ...."

I cut him off. "It also explains the fake DNA—tested in Adams' lab by his men. They didn't take samples from the burn victim—they used samples from Sarah, who is very much alive. And last, there's this." I nodded toward the papers I'd printed. "Sarah sent the DNA from the spit she found on the dead deputy's face to a lab that matches *unknown* DNA signatures to relatives with *known* DNA signatures. Agustin Cruz was arrested twice in Mexico, so we have his DNA on file. Matias Cruz has never been arrested and had no DNA on record ... until now."

I held up the papers along with the picture. "Ninety-five percent probability that the man in this picture is brother to Agustin Cruz."

They all stared.

Facing them were two pictures—an AI-generated digital mugshot and a recent photograph taken at an award ceremony that had been posted on social media. AI matched the two images from an Instagram photo. Despite slight differences in the AI colorized version, they were unmistakably the same person—Matt Adams, Sheriff of Baros County, also known as Matias Cruz, the true leader of the Cruz drug cartel.

40

Irmgard was rushed from the helipad into the emergency room, with paramedics still performing CPR as they moved her. She had been without a pulse for nearly forty minutes. Despite medical staff administering shocks and injecting epinephrine, there was no response.

Anthony's world-class limo driver took Tina, Anthony Carlino, and a few of his men to the mountain hospital, arriving twenty minutes after the helicopter. Security attempted to stop Tina from entering the emergency room with Petros in the dog crate, but Anthony's men took the guards hostage when her badge failed to grant them access. Tina then took control of the crate, and she and Anthony proceeded to where Irmgard was being treated.

Emergency room personnel were frantically working to save her life. The sight of her daughter's body being treated so roughly—with tubes, wires, blood, and compressions—was almost too much for Tina. But with Irmgard's life hanging in the balance, she forced herself to stay strong.

Noticing his ripped and bloodied clothing, a nurse approached Anthony to see if he needed medical assistance, but he shooed her away. He had been upset with Tina for insisting on bringing Petros with them, but she had been adamant, and there was no time to argue. Instead, he had sucked it up and let him ride with them, but secretly, he wanted to pull out his gun and riddle the crate with bullets. Once this was over, he promised himself he'd do just that—and that would only be the beginning.

Tina felt sick. She'd been in so many emergency rooms over the course of her career—too many. She'd watched helplessly, as she did now, while the medical staff worked their incantations and administered their potions in their feeble attempts to save life—modern versions of ancient witch doctors or tribal medicine men. Tina wondered how much difference there was between the two. In both cases, the outcomes often felt like a coin toss. Sometimes, they succeeded, sometimes not.

Too often not.

She'd watched so many die—car crashes, heavy equipment accidents, knives, fires, falls... *gunshots*. And here she was again, only this time it was different. This time, the outcome mattered—truly mattered—to *her*. The way it had mattered to them, the families of the victims she'd cared for professionally.

So different now.

So much more horrible and terrifying.

Trembling, she prayed to Gil's God. She'd been praying nearly non-stop since she found Irmgard lifeless on the floor, begging God to take her instead—anything—only don't let her daughter die—not like this—not at all. A part of her called out *hypocrite*, but she didn't care, not now. All she cared about was saving Irmgard.

She would say anything, pay any price, only please God, don't let Irmgard die.

And then she heard the words.

"Call it," said one of the doctors, touching the shoulder of the man performing compressions. He looked at his watch, about to speak the time.

Tina had seen it all before.

"NOOOOO!" she screamed, her knees unhinging and the room tilting.

We were all back in the Valor stealth copter, moving as fast as the blades could beat the air. Many of us were wounded, but not a single man stayed back for medical care. Despite the impossibility of Sarah still being alive, they all came—bleeding, hurt, tired, and risking death—yet they still came. I would owe them forever. I could never repay them, but I'd be there if they ever needed me.

Hearst flew us back to where he'd seen the men running through the tunnels, but according to the ground-penetrating radar, they were all empty now. Heat signatures still glowed faintly in places, proving he hadn't been wrong.

I had him set down to drop off Max, the rest of my crew—Pappy, Sammy, Dominic, Miles, Anders, Luthor, Billy, Byrne—and me. Then I sent the copter back into the air with the rest of the men to act as cavalry in case we needed them and to cover and pick us up if my plan failed.

Only it wouldn't fail.

I wouldn't let it fail—not with Sarah's life on the line.

Besides, Max was with me. And Max never fails.

Sheriff Adams—no—Matias Cruz asked Sarah to put on the wedding dress. She refused at first, but when Agustin suggested he could help her, she agreed to go into the other room and change.

They didn't give her long.

She removed the white wedding dress and veil from an elegant garment bag, which must have come from a high-end clothier somewhere in Mexico. It wasn't gaudy, nor was it simple. She took a moment to admire its intricate lace and sleek lines—a work of art that would have made a fine testament to an act of love under different circumstances. But here and now, in her situation, it made her want to throw up.

When she came out, both men whistled and clapped.

Nausea continued its slow roll through her.

Sarah would never go through with the wedding—not the wedding and certainly not the wedding night. She'd kill herself first. Kill herself—or better, kill them. After all, she'd done it before. She'd helped kill the Double Tap Rapist, and of course, there was Gail Davis.

No, she would not let the sher ... *Cruz* ... take her. Either she'd end him, or she'd end herself.

If only Gil were out there, somewhere, anywhere. They said they'd killed him, but was it true? Others had thought they'd killed him in the past, but Gil was Gil—tough to kill. She wanted to believe he was still alive, but they were so convincing.

"Beautiful," said the sheriff. "But now we must hurry. We have a date at a church. Everything has been arranged."

Sheriff Adams waved a hand toward the dozen SUVs waiting outside. "In case Hearst still has his fleet of drones and satellites out searching—an armada of identical vehicles, three passengers each, to fool the heat signatures. All will simultaneously travel in separate directions—not that Hearst would have any reason to be still looking, let alone know where to start. He's a brilliant man though—a sneaky man—with powerful resources at his fingertips. I never sell him short. That's why he hasn't found me out. That, and certain connections I have in very high places."

"I'll never go through with it," said Sarah. "You should let me go now. If you do, and you flee to Mexico and never return, I'll stop Gil from killing you."

Adams and Agustin both laughed.

"We told you he's dead," said the sheriff.

"No," said Sarah. "Gil's not dead. But you will be if you don't leave —leave me. Gil will kill you. You won't be able to stop him. Not you, your brother, your fast draw, or even your army. I promise you that. So just leave me here and run. It's your only chance."

"You see why I want her?" Adams said to his brother. "She has grit ... along with her other qualities. My perfect mate."

"You should be honored," said Agustin to Sarah. "Matias is not a ladies' man. He's obviously picked you because you are the very best. That's all he ever chooses."

Sheriff Adams opened the rear door of the closest vehicle. A big man with tattoos sat behind the wheel—the man who had punched her. The man who had stripped her.

Adams noted her recognition. "It's okay. I know what he had to do. I'm sorry for that, but there was no other way. He won't hurt you again. You have my word on that."

"If you really want me," said Sarah, "kill him now."

For the first time, Adams looked surprised. So did Agustin.

"See what I mean?" Adams said to his brother. "Grit." He smiled.

"I mean it," said Sarah. "Kill him."

"I believe you."

Adams peeked in at the driver, and Sarah saw fear on the man's face. For just an instant, she thought the sheriff might actually do it.

She wanted him to.

Instead, he turned back to her. "He was following my orders—something you will learn to do. I admire grit, but only so. Even the most spirited horses must be tamed to know the master's voice." He held out his hand for her to enter the car.

Sarah canted her head, shrugged, and moved to get in, brushing Adams as she passed.

"You should have taken me up on my offer," she said. "Mexico is better than Hell."

41

The helicopter set us down directly over the last location Hearst had seen the cartel members running through the tunnels. He had recorded the scan taken with the GPR, so we were able to land perfectly along the latitude and longitude coordinates. I then had him lift off and beam the waves to ensure we were on target. Max was skilled, but the tunnel was ten feet underground—a lot of earth for a dog to detect odor. Since I didn't have an article from Agustin for Max to lock onto, I decided the best approach was to have Max search for any fresh human scent. This was both good and bad. The good part was that any underground human odor would most likely be his. The bad part was the depth and the time elapsed due to my sidetracking to the sheriff's office.

I could have gotten us a more precise time estimate by having Hearst fly us to the next tunnel junction, knowing they couldn't have entered a house or turned off since there were no branches yet. However, I decided it would be better to let Max get a strong fix on the odors before encountering any potential obstacles like turns or elevation changes.

I needn't have worried.

This was Max, after all.

He spent about fifteen seconds sniffing around, dug his nose into the dirt, scented for a few more seconds, then shot off like a rocket, nose scraping the terrain as he ran.

We were outside the neighborhood running over primarily flat yet rutted, ankle-breaking terrain—ankle-breaking for us, not for Max. But then again, he did have four-wheel drive.

It was time to test the stamina of these Special Forces guys, because Max wasn't holding back. Luckily, he was slightly hindered by his need to stay in odor, but not by much. Our only job was to follow him, but our thirty-plus pounds of armor, weapons, and fancy gadgetry didn't make it easy.

Training and past encounters with the Cruz Cartel dictated that we move slower in anticipation of a possible ambush, but I didn't think it necessary. They had no way of suspecting Max's superpowers, and besides, they had a good jump on us. We needed to make good time—Sarah was waiting for me to save her.

And I would.

~

MAX WATCHED the Alpha as he moved out from under the helicopter's blade wash, taking them several yards further away before touching the ground with the palm of his hand and motioning for him to scent the dirt, moving in a forward motion. Not having trained for this, Max didn't understand exactly what the Alpha wanted him to do. However, he did know the scent search command, so he sniffed the earth where the Alpha had touched.

Dirt.

Vegetation.

Scattered markings from other animals.

Bugs.

And ... *something else.* Something faint ... not on the surface where it should be. *Deeper* ... human scent.

Fresh.

Difficult to locate, but now that he had it, his remarkable scent receptors and olfactory memory storage capabilities worked in unison to form a type of 3D mapping system, aligning and outlining the path of his prey. And off he went, needing only the barest of odors to follow accurately.

Sensing the Alpha's urgency, he wasted no time. Experience told him that good things followed the Alpha's search commands.

There would be prey.

There would be fighting.

There would be killing.

DESPITE THE DIFFICULT conditions under which Max was working, we made unbelievably good time. We'd covered more than a mile at a near-dead run, turning three times as Hearst radioed that we were off the main tunnel and now following branches and offshoots. The only assurance we had that we were still going the right way was Max's nose.

Good enough for me.

When we entered another housing subdivision, we had to slow down—Max included. There were new and changing scent patterns for him to decipher—people in houses, food cooking, paint and rubber and car exhaust.

It took Max all of five minutes to adjust. Before we knew it, we were stacked on the back porch of a two-story house with a three-car garage—a cookie-cutter version of every third house in the neighborhood.

But this one was different.

Because this was the house Max said the bad guys had entered from the tunnel.

I didn't waste time with a flashbang—I just kicked the door, splintering its reinforced dead-bolted doorframe, sending pieces of wood and metal flying. We entered fast—ran the rooms—the upstairs, the basement, and garage.

Empty.

But Max wasn't wrong.

We found bullets, boarded windows, blood stains, smells—*nasty smells*—decomposing smells.

This was a pollo stash house.

Then I found something else—tiny words scratched into the paint of a bedroom wall that read, *'Find me, S.'*

We were too late. Sarah was gone, but she was alive—and she had been here. That was all that mattered.

"No cars in the garage," said Pappy as we stood in the bedroom looking at the message scratched in the paint. "They could have gone anywhere. We're back to square one."

Sammy spoke up, "We can go back to Hearst's command post—see what the satellites might have caught."

"No," I said. "She would have left me something ... something to tell me where they were taking her." I looked around the room.

It was empty.

"Maybe she didn't know where they were going," said Billy.

I went to the closed closet, remembering how Elio Colombo had left a clue for me in a closet so I would find him. Sarah knew all about it, just like she knew about Paula and Janice, the two women who were abducted by Sid, the kidnapper robber. Majoqui Cabrera's henchmen subsequently murdered Sid, taking the women with them and stashing them in a pollo house as bait for me to follow. The women left me a clue, scratched near the baseboard in the closet of the room where they were locked.

I had told Sarah the entire story, and genius that she was, she'd used the same tactic, scratching a message with her nails, knowing I would put two and two together. Simple math, even simple enough for me. Opening the door, I found her second clue—a long box with fancy writing. The now-empty box had held a wedding dress.

I reflected on everything—how Adams looked at her, how he leaned toward her in the lab, the things he'd said, the token, and his obsession with a particular movie set town.

The church.

And how Sarah had said Adams was getting married there.

"I know where they are."

~

SAMMY OBSERVED Gil Mason as they rode in the helicopter. Gil and his dog—what an amazing pair. He was even more impressed with Gil's deductive reasoning skills. Sammy wondered what he, himself, would have been like had he not died that day in the water only to come back weaker physically but so much stronger mentally. Would he have his savant abilities? Probably not, but who could say? Perhaps he would have become an Olympic athlete instead of being burdened by his slight limp and frail constitution.

The one thing he knew was that life wasn't like comic books, where everything turned out great. In real life, gaining spider-like abilities would mean having eight arms and needing to liquefy your food before slurping it up. If you could fly, you'd likely suffer from vertigo and constantly crash. Super strength wouldn't come with the necessary invulnerability. Your tendons, ligaments, and skin would tear whenever you exceeded their tensile strength limits. And if you could teleport, you'd probably lack navigation capabilities, risking your molecules reassembling inside a wall, rock, or piece of playground equipment.

Because that was what real life was ... give and take. The God who created everything had a weird sense of humor.

Sammy's intellect compelled him to recognize the intelligent design present in the code of life, embedded in the structure of the DNA molecule itself, with its sophisticated language and the intricate micro-machines interacting with it—far more complex than anything humans can create. The idea that these complexities could arise by random chance, regardless of the billions of years often cited to make this notion seem plausible, struck him as willful ignorance at best and an insidious lie at worst.

Of course, there was a God, and through Sammy's research, he had even come to accept that it was the God of the Christian Bible, with its reliance on the Trinity, the Father, the Son, and the Holy Spirit. Yes, Sammy accepted all of it.

But he hated the God of the Bible.

God had put Sammy through more pain than any little boy should have to bear. He'd killed him, then brought him back—*changed, warped*—a mutant, a freak to be laughed at, humiliated, and picked on by every schoolyard bully.

And there were a lot of them.

And that was only what God had done to him. What He had done to Sammy's poor wife, Cinnamon Twist, was truly unforgivable.

It seemed strange that a man as brilliant as Gil Mason could see the same God in such a different light. But then, Mason was handsome, strong, and physically superior to most of the male population—no limp, no glasses, no palsy. Still, the God Mason claimed to love had murdered his wife and daughter. Sammy wondered how Mason could reconcile that with his beliefs. He'd have to ask him someday.

But not today.

Today, they had a job to do.

A queasiness in his lower stomach told him they were diving, and when he looked down, he saw the small movie-set town rushing toward them in the distance.

Electric lights on the streets and shining from windows.

The place was supposed to be closed for the winter.

Looked like Gil was right again.

Well, God had better get ready because they were about to send Him a whole bunch of souls for judgment.

42

Dominic watched Gil Mason as they landed outside the town, far enough away and downwind so the whisper-quiet blades chopping at the air couldn't be heard. That last stroke of genius had been Mason's contribution. Somehow, he knew the wind patterns and told Hearst where to set down.

Dominic had a lot in common with Gil—both Marines, both cops, both Christians.

Both in love with women named Sarah.

Dominic knew Sammy respected Mason, which carried a lot of weight with him. Dominic respected Sammy. And over the last few days, Mason had proven himself more than capable in combat. That was also important to Dominic. He'd worked with many who were not—men who could get you and your friends killed—cause your mission to fail.

What was Mason's Sarah like? he wondered. He'd seen her, of course, and she was incredibly beautiful. Brilliant, too—CSI, forensics, computers, DNA. Yeah, she was smart on a scale way beyond Dominic's pay grade. She was also more intelligent and more physically beautiful than his own Sarah. Still, if he had to bet money on it, Dominic's Sarah would win if it came down to a fight—guns, knives, or fists—any way you called it, his Sarah would make mincemeat of Mason's Sarah.

Besides, his Sarah had her own strengths—stellar tactics, common sense, and street smarts. She also had an uncanny knack for reading people.

And she loved him, which made all the difference.

Dominic thought it must be like that for Mason, so he would do whatever it took to help him save *his* Sarah—and Dominic could do a lot.

Once outside the copter, they all ran toward the town, Mason's dog leading the way, ensuring there were no traps or ambushes.

And there weren't ... not *outside* the town.

MAX STREAKED FORWARD at the Alpha's command, the men following as the helicopter raced back into the night sky. He was downwind and had already scent-located a large number of enemy forces. They were scattered around the buildings—some of which were partially constructed, others complete. They were at ease, relaxed, smoking, talking, joking.

They were not expecting an attack.

They were not expecting Max.

They should have been.

Max smelled something else ... *someone* else.

Sarah.

WE FORMED a stack at the back of the first building we encountered, with Max in a heel at my side. I could see structures along the dirt street, some little more than storefronts, others finished, looking like something out of a traditional Western movie. I heard a generator running in the distance, and several strings of lights were draped along and around the small town on high poles. I spotted recognizable buildings—a post office, saloon, barber shop, general store, Sheriff's Office, and the church. All were lit on the inside.

There was a multitude of cars parked at the far end of town. That meant troops—cartel thugs—lots of them.

"How many men, Sammy?" I asked.

He zoned out, doing his thing, and came back in about six seconds. "I calculate between thirty and seventy."

"What's our best move, Pappy?" I asked.

"Take out the generator, go in with night vision, kill everyone but Sarah. Should be a cakewalk."

"Yeah," said Byrne, "seventy of them—in their town, their turf—against the nine of us and a dog. Cakewalk."

"You could turn around and go home," said Pappy.

"I didn't say it wouldn't be fun, just that it doesn't sound exactly like cake."

I pointed at Billy, then at Byrne and Miles. "You three take out the generator. Do it quiet."

I clicked my radio mic. "Hearst, stay high so they don't pick you up, but watch us close in case I call you in. If I do, come fast, but no bombs like you used at the houses. Sarah *is* here. We need precision to keep her safe—a sniper round instead of a shotgun."

"Copy that, Slick," said Hearst in my helmet earphones. "I'll be careful. You all do the same."

I tapped the next three on their shoulders. "Anders, Luthor, and Pappy, you go right. Your job is diversion. Draw as many as you can to you while Sammy, Dominic, and I go left to the church. That's the final meeting point for everyone."

"Why the church?" asked Luthor.

"Because that's where Sarah and the sheriff will be."

"Looks like you're taking all the heavy firepower with you," said Anders as he nodded toward Sammy, Dominic, and finally, Max.

"Sarah is the mission," I said.

He shrugged, nodded, and said, "Yeah, yeah, right."

"So, what are we, chopped liver?" asked Miles, grinning and punching Anders in the arm.

"You're okay," said Anders, "so am I and the rest of us. But come on—them? Anyway, Mason's right. She's the mission."

Most of us were wounded and bleeding as we acknowledged each other with a nod, looking into each man's soul. Warriors about to walk into battle, knowing we would face death, that we would have to kill to live, and all of us were okay with it.

It was time.

"Go," I said.

MATIAS CRUZ GRIPPED THE SMALL, nearly bald priest by the back of the neck and drag-walked him to the altar at the front of the church. Sarah cringed in the arms of the big man with the tats and her scratches on his face. The priest saw the terror in Sarah's eyes. "I won't do it," he said. "You can't make me. God will not be mocked."

"Yes, you will," said the Sheriff. "We have the five parishioners who were with you at your church in town. If you refuse, my man will shoot one of them. And after every additional minute you refuse, he'll shoot another." He looked at Sarah. "My bride-to-be doesn't want their blood on her hands or yours. We don't need anything fancy, just the part about her swearing to obey me in all things, the 'I do's,' and the 'kiss the bride' part. Quick and easy, and you can all go home ... after you sign the marriage license, of course."

"But ... but you're a sheriff. How can you do this? You must know it won't mean anything ... not when I tell." The priest stopped suddenly, realizing that none of them were getting out of this alive.

Sheriff Adams smiled sadly. "Yes, Padre, it's true, you will have to die. But if you stay brave and strong and do what I say, the others—those from your church who haven't seen me—can live. It's the best I can do. Will you do this? For them?" He looked at his watch. "Hurry, please, the first minute is almost up."

The priest nodded slowly.

"Good," said Adams, motioning the tattooed man to bring Sarah to the altar. "Agustin, you'll act as my best man. The rest of you will be witnesses," he said to the assembly of soldiers standing by.

"Of course," said Agustin, coming forward to stand next to him.

"I'm sorry, my child," said the priest to Sarah.

Sarah shook free of the big man and walked up beside the Sheriff. "It's not your fault." She looked Adams in the face. "Gil will kill you for this."

"Dead men can't kill anyone," he smiled.

The generator suddenly died, plunging the church into darkness.

One of the men looked out a window. "Whole towns down," he said.

"It's Gil," she said.

"It's gas," said Agustin, "or rather the lack of it. The backup will kick on any second."

As if in response to his words, the lights flickered back to life.

"See?"

"You are all going to die," said Sarah. "Your only chance is to leave us now and run away. That way, you get to live at least another day."

Adams and Agustin both shook their heads, smiling.

"Your belief in Mason is admirable." The sheriff looked to the priest. "Get on with it."

"I don't have a Bible," said the man, trying to stall.

"Pretend," said Adams. "Your time is up. Start the ceremony, or I'll have my man kill the first parishioner, and we can start the clock all over."

The priest nodded and started, "Dearly beloved …."

Sarah felt disembodied, detached from the reality of the situation, as though she were in a movie—the set she was standing in, the priest, the Sheriff, and everyone else were all actors playing parts.

A week earlier, at Gil's insistence, he and Sarah had watched *The Princess Bride*. She had never seen it, thinking the premise seemed silly, but about ten minutes in, she changed her mind, realizing it was a love story, a comedy, a fantasy, and so much more. Now, in this moment, she couldn't help but think of the wedding scene where

Princess Buttercup is forced to marry Prince Humperdinck and how the priest hilariously pronounced the word "mawage."

It didn't seem quite so funny now.

"The vows," said Adams, hurrying things along.

The priest gave Sarah a last, kind but sorrowful look, then nodded in surrender and said, "Do you, Sarah Gallagher, promise to love, honor, and obey Matias Cruz till death do you part?"

Snapping back to the reality of where she was and what Adams was forcing her to do, Sarah stared deeply into his eyes, smiling slyly.

"Till death do us part," she said. "I do."

43

Billy brought up the rear, Byrne in front of him and slightly offset, Miles taking point. When they came upon the generator, they saw one man standing guard—sort of. He was smoking and looking at his cell phone, the screen's glow illuminating his face, while he shuffled his feet as if he were cold or fidgety.

Miles double-tapped him in his left temple with two nine-millimeter rounds, the rumbling growl of the diesel generator drowning out the suppressed rifle signature. As Billy stepped over the man's body, he saw a high-velocity scarlet mist of the man's blood sprayed across the phone's screen. He'd been part of the Mafia his entire life, participated in several shootouts, had beaten people up, and even killed a few. Yet, the mechanical proficiency of these elite soldiers—the way they killed without hesitation, as though the people were nothing more than targets on a range—made him feel a little sick.

Byrne clicked the generator off, then sliced through the gas line for good measure. The town went dark. They expected to hear a commotion, maybe gunfire—the diversion Gil's team needed to make it to the church unobserved. Instead, they heard another generator roaring to life at the other end of town.

The lights flared back on, and men started coming out of the saloon to look around. A few began walking towards them.

"What do we do?" asked Billy.

"Same job," said Miles, "at least for now. We take out the other generator. Anyone gets in our way, we take them out too." He winked at Billy and moved to the corner of the closest building, hugging the shadows.

Byrne and Billy followed.

~

PAPPY HELD UP A HAND, signaling for the others to stop. He was about to toss a grenade into the saloon when the lights flickered back on, another generator starting up at the far end of the strip. Ah, the unexpected—the stuff of combat. Like Mike Tyson used to say, *"Everyone hath a plan until dey get punthed in the mouth."* The important thing was to take the blow and get back to work. Adapt and overcome.

They wouldn't have the advantage of night vision in the dark, but there was still the element of surprise, not to mention *first blood.*

Pappy pulled the pin on the M67 fragmentation hand grenade as enemy combatants rolled out into the dirt street from the saloon. He let the handle pop free and tossed it through the pane of a side window. All three ran toward the back as the explosion sounded, shattering more glass outward.

Screams erupted as Anders, Luthor, and Pappy came around the far side of the saloon, shooting. They took out the three men who had wandered outside when the lights went out, as well as two more who stumbled out, bleeding and holding their ears. Flashes sparked from inside, and bullets whizzed past Pappy and the others as the remaining bad guys, those still able, returned fire.

Luthor took a round in the side, just below his vest. He grunted but kept firing. Anders, Pappy, and Luthor, shooting fast and with as much accuracy as the situation and environment allowed, backed around the building the way they had approached. Pappy pulled the pin from another grenade, grinned at his companions, and tossed it through another window.

"Diversion accomplished," he said. "How bad?" he asked Luthor.

"Through and through my love handle. Hardly bleeding."

"See if you can get one on the other side," said Anders. "Save you the cost of liposuction."

"Funny," said Luthor.

They headed toward the church.

HEARST WATCHED it all from above, feeling useless and restless. He wasn't one to sit the action out while his men were in danger. A red light blinked across the HUD (Heads-Up Display) spanning his windshield's lower portion.

Finally.

After dropping Gil and his men off, he had called in a fleet of drones from his command group. And here they were. They weren't armed, as they had been used in the search for Sarah Gallagher during the roadblock checks, but they would serve as eyes and ears—and perhaps even more if necessary.

He saw one of Gil's teams take out the first generator, extinguishing the town's lights. Then he saw a different generator fire up, powering the lights back on. He also saw Pappy, Anders, and Luthor hit the saloon. So far, so good—not exactly as planned, but good enough.

Now, if only Gil, Sammy, and Dominic could make it to the church to rescue Sarah. His telescopic infra-green imaging showed them converging on the target. As they arrived at the church, the doors burst open from the inside, spilling men out at them.

And just like that, the plan fell apart.

The shooting began.

As we came around the corner of the barber shop, three doors down from the church, we ran into four cartel thugs in their mid-twenties, armed with rifles and a shotgun. They were shocked to see us. We weren't. Marines engaged in forward advance movements are always ready for contact with the enemy.

Max hit the closest man in the thigh.

Sammy took the man out before he had a chance to scream from the pain. Then he took out two more, Dominic the other. I was still locking in on the closest as they fell lifelessly. I called Max off and helped drag the bodies around the corner, where we stashed them in the shadow of the building, so I guess I wasn't entirely useless.

And then the lights went out.

It hadn't taken long to dispose of and hide the three bangers, but they had delayed us—not by much, but enough.

And then the unexpected happened. The lights came back on just as the planned diversion began. It was supposed to happen in the dark, and we were supposed to already be at the church.

Which we weren't.

I put Max in a down. This was about to turn into a shooting match, and I didn't want him to get hit.

"Let's move," I said.

We sprinted across the street and advanced until we reached the chapel just as the front doors burst open, releasing a tide of cartel soldiers. The first man out the door was the big guy covered in tats I had seen on the jail video feed from when they'd taken Sarah—*the one who punched her.*

I saw that he saw me, but before he could complete the grin that pulled at his lips, I put a bullet through the bridge of his nose. I would have shot him again, but there were too many men I needed to kill to waste the time or the bullet. My thumb clicked the selector switch from semi to full auto, and I sprayed into the bodies as they rushed at us.

Something hot and fast clipped my helmet, and another hit me in the chest, but the bad guys were going down fast. Dominic and Sammy were blasting away faster than I could track. Of course, I was busy myself. All three of us were forced to back away to avoid being swamped while taking care not to trip down the stairs … with is a lot tougher than it sounds, what with men charging and lead flying everywhere. Needless to say, we were going the wrong way.

Sarah was inside.

Throwing caution to the wind, I called Max, gave him the attack command with a hand gesture, and blasted my way forward.

Somehow Max was already there.

And he hit the crowd like a missile.

WHEN COMMANDED, Max went into the down. He didn't like it, but the Alpha was the Alpha. Absently, he licked the blood off his lower jowl, watching as the others ran across the street to approach the church.

Sarah was inside.

Max could smell her.

The Alpha and his men ascended a short set of steps and were about to breach the entrance when the doors exploded outward, men pouring out. Max should have stayed in his down until commanded otherwise, but he didn't. The Alpha was in danger, and his pack mentality overrode obedience training and protocol. By the time he closed the distance, the gun battle was already in full swing.

Hearing the Alpha's attack command a second after he launched from the bottom of the stairs where his companions had retreated, he vaulted over their heads, slamming into the crowd and smashing the men back into and onto each other, causing massive confusion and chaos. Max bit into the cheek of his first victim, released and ripped at a bicep, released and tore into a throat, released and shredded a thigh, released and fell and lunged up into a man's groin, released and took out a hamstring.

And then bodies were falling all around Max, with Gil in the lead, and Sammy and Dominic coming up strong from behind. Bullets and blood and shrieks and cries and ricochets filled the air, scorching his fur, stinging his nostrils, and screaming in his ears.

Max loved it.

The thrill of the fight.

The danger.

The victory.

And then he saw Sarah, the men beside her, and an army filling the space between Max and them. His powerful leg muscles bunched and corded, preparing to go through the crowd, but the Alpha gestured to the left and shouted a command. Max's battle-sharpened mapping instincts recognized the tactical soundness of the Alpha's plan.

Dodging an elbow while delivering a snapping bite to a man's ribs, Max disengaged, then dove between a pair of knees and went up and under and through and around. He met resistance as he cleared the pews to the left and had to fight his way forward. There were fewer of them here, but still, it was a fight.

And just ahead was Sarah, the men, and the priest.

44

Miles, Byrne, and Billy had almost reached the backup generator when they spotted the commotion at the church. Billy could see that Gil and the others would not survive without help. He turned and started toward them.

The single guard stationed at the generator heard the shooting and came forward. Montgomery Byrne stitched him from hip to throat with automatic gunfire. Miles took a step toward the generator, saw that Billy was headed to the church, started to order him back, then shook his head and followed—too late for the dark to help much now anyway.

All three made it there just as Max plowed through the crowd and into the church. The advantage of having three extra shooters saved Gil, Sammy, and Dominic from being slaughtered.

Sometimes, plans must be ditched in the heat of combat, and this was one of those times. Even so, without the advantage of the dark and night vision, Billy saw they were fighting a losing battle. The tidal wave of cartel soldiers surged again and would soon outnumber them.

Pappy and his men exploded around the corner—*literally.* A hand grenade landed mid-church, detonating and scattering men and furniture in all directions. Billy shook his head to clear his vision. Seizing the opportunity, he opened up, firing in short bursts, as his phone vibrated unnoticed in his pants pocket. It was his uncle, Nick Carlino.

But he wouldn't know that until later.

~

THE FORCE of the exploding grenade knocked Sarah, the sheriff, and his brother off their feet and into the body of the priest, throwing them all to the hardwood floor. If Pappy had tossed a fragmentation grenade instead of a simple concussion grenade, they could have been killed. But instead of being pelted by razor-sharp pieces of jagged metal and ball bearings, they were hit by a shockwave that rocked their senses and blunted their perceptions.

Sarah's head smacked the wood floor so hard that everything went white and then black. She drifted peacefully into the world of dreams, surrounded by friends and family as she and Gil stood at the altar, the two of them finally to be wed. Everything was perfect—joyous.

But then the dream ended, and the horrible truth of reality broke through as she felt the cold metal of the pistol pressed against her head. Blood ran down her face from where she had struck the floor. Her dress was bloody, torn, burned, and dirty, and the world tilted like an amusement park ride.

Craning her neck, she recognized Agustin Cruz as the man with the gun.

"One move, and she dies," he said.

Nothing made sense. Where was she? Why was she here? What had happened to her beautiful wedding?

And then she saw Gil, bodies strewn about his feet as he threw his rifle away and faced the man holding the gun to her head. There was a look on his face she'd never seen before—a look that frightened her. No, it terrified her.

He didn't look human.

He looked like a feral animal.

Soulless.

Without mercy.

And in that instant, she realized her fear wasn't for herself—it was for everyone else in the room.

Gil was about to kill them all.

I FOUGHT INSTINCTIVELY, relying on my training, combat experience, and sheer force of will. I took hits, primarily to my armor but to other places, too. None of them mattered. The pain was nothing. My blood was nothing. I would gladly forfeit my life if it meant getting to Sarah.

And I would get to Sarah.

I could see her in front of the altar, next to Adams—Matias Cruz. But there was still a wall of men separating us.

Walls were made to be knocked down.

So, I kept on knocking.

And then a grenade floated through the air from behind me. It disappeared into the crowd of enemy forces, halfway between me and Sarah. I jammed my rifle into a man's stomach, fired a burst, then grabbed him, ducking low and using his body as a shield.

The explosion was deafeningly mind-numbing, even with the shield. We were close enough that the concussive force shredded the man's clothing and sent his already spraying blood all over. I dumped him off of me and tossed my empty rifle on the floor.

Everyone was flattened.

Almost everyone.

Agustin Cruz was already on his feet, one hand gripping Sarah's hair, forcing her to look me in the face. His other hand held a pearl-handled .45 pressed against her head.

"Move, and she dies," he said.

I would have shot him dead without hesitation, but I was still dizzy from the concussion grenade. To prevent his hand from convulsing after a headshot—which might make his finger spasm on the trigger, killing Sarah—the shot had to be perfect, instantly exploding the medulla.

Thankfully, I'd planned ahead.

"Strike," I said quietly.

And Max did.

~

MAX HEARD the command from his hiding place on the far side of the pews.

He'd been waiting.

Most dogs need time to get up to speed—to launch and strike with real force—but, once again, Max was not most dogs.

His teeth crushed into the bad man's wrist, snapping the bones into pulverized splinters, severing tendons, and shredding ligaments and muscles. A millisecond later, his full ninety pounds of weight smashed into Agustin Cruz, knocking him away from Sarah and twisting him around just in time for the Alpha to draw his Smith & Wesson 4506, and put three .45 caliber bullets into Agustin's chest and face.

Max let the dead weight drop.

~

AS HE ROSE from the body of the priest lying beneath him, Matias Cruz saw his brother die. Jumping to his feet, he stood, rage and horror filling him with one mission.

To kill Gil Mason.

And he was just the man to do it.

He was the fastest shootist in the world.

He'd kill Mason, then the dog, then the others.

"You killed my brother, Mason. Your turn."

He went for his gun, and even though Gil already had his out, Matais was faster.

Sarah screamed.

~

Irmgard felt at peace. She was floating up out of her body toward the brightest, most beautiful light she had ever seen—too bright to look at directly. But somehow, she could, and she did, and it didn't hurt at all. The light was wonderful, alive, and pulling her toward it.

Irmgard wanted to go to it.

Go to Him.

Somehow, she knew that the light meant the end of the terrifying images, thoughts, shame, and guilt. The end of fear. She was so happy she wanted to cry but couldn't—she didn't need to. She would never need to cry again. The light promised her that.

For a moment, she saw her body below, surrounded by doctors, Tina, her great-grandfather, and the crate. A part of her wanted to stay with them, to tell them it was all right, that she was free now. She was happy. The light would take care of her—they shouldn't worry about her, miss her, or be upset. There would be no more bad men, dying mothers, murdered fathers, or even wolves.

She was happy now, and they needed to let her go. She would miss them, but one day, they would join her, and they could all be together forever.

A tear rolled from her eye, and fell, landing on her still face. Doctors and nurses stuck needles into her lifeless body, shocked her cold flesh with electric paddles, and pumped on her chest, trying to bring her back.

But they would not bring her back.

They couldn't.

Irmgard didn't want to go back.

The light called to her again, and her *oh-so-light body* rotated to face it. She began moving faster than the fastest car, plane, or even a bullet, racing up and out of the building and into the sky and past—moving as fast as the light. Irmgard smiled.

She was going home.

~

"CALL IT," said the doctor, looking at his watch to pronounce the time of death.

"NOOOO!" screamed Tina, her knees unhinging.

Anthony Carlino held her up, whispering harshly in her ear. "Stop it. You said *he* could help. This is your chance—your last chance. Irmgard's last chance. Do it!"

Tina, shaking and on the verge of fainting, felt the pain of his iron grip ... heard the steel in his voice. Through the fog of despair, she drew strength from his words.

"Get them back, now," she said.

Carlino motioned to his men. They shoved their way into the cramped space, forcing the doctors and nurses up against the walls and holding them there. Tina unlatched the crate and let the dog out, praying again for a miracle, but knowing no such thing existed.

Petros tore out of the crate, running straight into the room, jumping up on Irmgard's stomach and chest.

Tina ran behind him, seeing a tear roll down Irmgard's cheek.

Petros barked—loud and hard, not stopping until Irmgard sucked in a breath. Crying out weakly, she opened her eyes. Seeing him, she reached out with trembling fingers and stroked his head, neck, and chest. Petros wagged his tail, licking her face and quivering even more than Irmgard's unsteady hands.

"Petra," she whispered, mistaking Petros for Max. "My sweet Petra, I missed you."

The medical staff stood in stunned disbelief as Tina and Anthony ran to the little girl, stroking her hair and kissing her cheeks and forehead and lips—*crying*—both of them.

"Let us to her," said a doctor, "she still has a head wound. We need to treat her immediately."

Anthony nodded to his men. They backed away as Tina grabbed Petros from Irmgard's chest. Tina prepared to leave the room when the doctor stopped her.

"You can stay," he said. "You and the dog. I don't know what just happened, but I want him in here with us."

While the doctors cleaned the wound and sewed their sutures,

Anthony and his men stood guard, ensuring none of the staff slipped out or made a call to the police. Tina and Petros stayed close in case they were needed again, with all the staff sneaking glances at the miracle dog who had just brought a dead little girl back to life right in front of them.

But Tina and Petros weren't needed.

The light was no longer calling.

45

He could shoot me a thousand times, and still, I would kill him. Nothing was going to stop me. A lifetime ago, I made the same promise concerning Majoqui Cabrera. I had failed then, but this time I wouldn't. Sarah's life was at stake.

The sheriff's gun was out of its holster and pointing at my face just as I was lifting mine. Two shots rang out, snapping mists of blood from his chest. The double impacts prevented him from firing, his barrel still pointing at me, eyes wide in shock.

There's truth to the saying, *He who hesitates is lost.*

I didn't hesitate.

I was no longer dizzy, and Sarah was no longer in my line of fire, so I put a .45-caliber hollow-point bullet through the center of his forehead. His head snapped back, and he dropped dead right there. Looking to either side, I saw Sammy and Dominic bracketing me. They'd beaten me to the draw, each hitting the sheriff once in the chest and stopping him from shooting me in the face.

Still, I decided to take Thanos' advice from *Avengers: Infinity War*. After Thor slammed his new enchanted axe, Stormbreaker, into Thanos' heart, fatally wounding him, Thanos still had enough time to snap his fingers and end the lives of half the beings in the universe. In his not so final words, Thanos told Thor he should have gone for the head.

I didn't make the same mistake—not this time. I went for the head, instantly delivering the fatal wound that killed him. No snap of the fingers or pull on the trigger. So, technically, even though Sammy and Dominic hit him first, it was me who killed him.

"Nice shot," said Sammy.

"Yeah," said Dominic. "Little slow, but good placement."

I went to Sarah while Sammy, Dominic, Pappy, and the rest finished cleaning up. Hearst landed on Main Street and oversaw the surrender of the remaining men. His tail gunners and the rest of our crew stayed onboard, ensuring no one escaped while we waited for men from the base to arrive for transport.

Sarah appeared to be in shock at first. She had some scrapes, bumps, and a laceration on the side of her head that had already stopped bleeding, but she looked more beautiful than ever. Seeing her in the wedding dress broke my heart. I had to tell her right now, or I would never regain the courage.

"I'm so sorry," I said. "This is all because of me. And this is why we can't ...."

She stopped me with an upraised hand.

"Don't," she said. "Just don't. Not now, not ever again. None of this was because of you. This is all on me. They didn't call you down here, they called me. They wanted me, not you. This happened because of my job, not yours. Adams—Matias—whatever his name is, didn't raid the Sheriff's Office because of you. He did it because of me and the evidence I uncovered, evidence that would have revealed who he was. And he didn't kidnap me because of you. He kidnapped me because he thought I would make a pretty trophy to hang on his arm and show off, like the gun over his desk.

"None of this was about you. It was all about me. It wasn't you who put me in danger—it was the other way around. I almost got you killed. But you don't see me calling off our marriage or saying we can't go on with our lives just because there might be danger ahead. That we should live in fear, denying ourselves the happiness we both deserve, just because something, someday, might threaten us. No, I refuse to live like that. And I won't let you live like that either."

Sarah turned, went to the little priest standing by the wall, and pulled him by his arm to stand before us.

"Marry us," she said to him. "Right now."

"Sarah," I said, "it's alright—you've made your point. Next month will be fine."

"No, right now. I'm not waiting. *I'm not*. Marry us, now." She grabbed my arm and turned me until we were both facing the small man, his glasses bent and mangled.

The priest shrugged his shoulders, straightened his glasses, and cleared his throat.

"Are you Catholic?" he asked.

I started to say no, but Sarah broke in. "Tonight, we are."

"Dearly beloved," he started, but again, Sarah cut him off.

"Same rules as before, short and sweet, before aliens show up."

"Do you have a ring, at least?" he asked me.

I patted my pockets.

Nothing.

Pappy, acting as best man, came to the rescue with the pin from the concussion grenade he tossed a little while earlier. I held it up for inspection.

"Good enough," said Sarah, staring hard at the priest. "Go."

And he did.

"You may kiss the bride," he finished in record time.

And I did.

And just like that, after all we'd been through, Sarah and I were married.

I looked around for Billy, wishing we'd waited for him, but he was gone. Pappy told me he'd gotten a phone call from his uncle, something about his daughter, and that Hearst managed to arrange transport for him to the airport so he could fly back. I gave Sarah a look that told her I was worried. She looked worried, too.

"See?" she said, slipping her arm through mine, "That's why we didn't wait. Now let's go find out what happened, Husband."

Husband—I liked that. It had been so long.

Less than an hour later, we were at the hospital in Aspen. Only it wasn't aliens.

No, it was so much worse.

EPILOGUE

The water was beautiful—enchanting—a sparkling blue that grew deeper and darker the farther you looked out from the shore. Irmgard splashed in the surf with Atlas and the puppies while Pilgrim, Max, and Viper stood watch from the shore. It seemed like an unnecessary task, considering we were on a secluded island in the middle of the Pacific, looking out over paradise and protected by a giant dormant volcano that poked through the clouds, housed in million-dollar bungalows reserved for the wealthiest politicians. The trip was a month-long wedding present from Steve Hearst and the United States government.

The day before, a five-foot tiger shark had somehow slipped through the underwater netting meant to protect the cove. It had sped like a torpedo toward Irmgard and the pups. I pulled my gun—never leave your bungalow without it—and ran full out toward the water to get the shot. Before I got there, Max magically appeared, diving into the water without so much as a ripple. He killed the shark and dragged it ashore.

A Tiger Shark, in the water, moving at full speed—killed it without a fight.

Of course he did.

He's Max.

As soon as Max dropped the predator on its back, the pups and Atlas pounced, eating their fill and making short work of their first taste of seafood. Afterward, the lot of them flopped to their sides, backs, and tummies, relaxing on the warm sand, their bellies full. They slept most of the afternoon, legs running and muffled barks, growls, and whines escaping their dreamlands.

Billy and I snorkeled the perimeter and found the hole. We fixed the netting, ensuring it wouldn't happen again, but Max stood watch anyway.

We'd been here for two weeks, and the trip was doing wonders for Irmgard—the sun, the waves, the peace. Rick had started working with her as soon as she was released from the hospital, as well as in the days before we flew out to begin our double honeymoon. Since then, he'd flown out twice to spend time with her, courtesy of the Carlinos.

She claimed not to remember that night or the events leading up to what happened—not the knife or the cutting or the shooting. Whether the memory loss was from the trauma of the head wound or a form of mental protection of sorts, Rick couldn't say just yet. He didn't know if she was being honest or just saying what she thought we needed to hear. Rick said that she seemed sincere, but only time would tell. She did admit to the dreams and the bad memories, but those, too, seemed to have faded.

On the night we arrived at the hospital in Aspen, she had just returned from an MRI scan, and my father-in-law, Nathan, was already there. I had called him from the jet. Tina and Billy pulled him aside, and a minute later, we stood with Irmgard as he performed an impromptu wedding ceremony in the emergency room, using the sermon and vows he had written for me and Sarah, pronouncing them man and wife. They kissed each other and then kissed Irmgard, promising her they would never separate and that they would never leave her. Irmgard cried. So did they, so did we.

The scans all came back good. The .22 caliber bullet had hit Irmgard with a glancing blow just above the eyebrow. A reflexive jerk at the last second, probably due to the strength it took to pull the trigger even with two thumbs, caused it to slide under the skin, where it skimmed along the bone and exited behind the top of her ear. The doctor explained that it was the shock that had stopped her heart—the shock to her body and the concussion to her brain from the impact. Exploding gasses had caused some cosmetic damage that would require plastic surgery to repair. Still, there was no swelling of the brain, and due to immediate and continuous CPR, there was no brain damage from lack of oxygen.

Godfather Great-Grandpa Anthony Carlino would see that Irmgard received the best plastic surgery money could buy. The prognosis for a full recovery was very high.

Somehow, Anthony Carlino and Steve Hearst had used their influence to keep the story of the Aspen Hospital invasion and staff hostage situation out of the press while also avoiding a police investigation.

Hearst told me that his team, along with numerous local and state law enforcement agencies, had raided over eighty Cruz Cartel operations involving narcotics, sex trafficking, and money laundering while rescuing hundreds of victims and making dozens of arrests in the process—and that was just on our side of the border. The impact would be immense.

He'd also had the entire Baros County Sheriff's Office patrol and detective divisions arrested and investigated. People had talked, revealing that the dead deputy had been planning on turning states' evidence against the Cruz Cartel's involvement in Sheriff Adams' control over the county, as well as his true identity.

Hearst again asked me to join his team, and again, I refused, but with a caveat. I held out my hand and shook his. I told him we were friends and thanked him for helping me save Sarah. I told him I was always there for my friends and that I'd be there for him if he ever needed me.

He smiled, nodded, ticked the eye, sucked the tooth, then said, "Good enough for me, Sport."

The honeymoon surprise came next, with a note that read, *From one friend to another, no strings attached.* And so, here we were, enjoying the island, the sand, and the peace.

Irmgard finally opened up to me this afternoon, sharing what she remembered of that night. We were sitting on the beach watching the dogs playing in the ocean while Atlas chased a bird and climbed a tree. After body surfing, we were drying in the sun when she looked up at the sky and smiled.

"I was higher than those clouds," she said.

I gave her quizzical.

She nodded, pointing. "Not quite all the way to space, and not all the way to Heaven, but way up there."

"I don't understand," I said.

"When I died. I could see everyone. I could even see me. I floated, then I flew." She turned to face me. "I was going so fast—faster than surfing, faster than sledding on the snow. And I wasn't afraid. I wasn't afraid of anything. I didn't want to come back."

"Why did you?" I asked gently.

"I knew you'd be sad—that Tina and Billy would be sad. Everyone would be sad. Great-grandpa Anthony and Uncle Nick, even the puppies. Max would be sad."

"How did you know?"

"Max told me."

"Max told you?"

She smiled at me. "It sounds silly. That's why I haven't told Rick or anyone else. They wouldn't believe me. They can't understand. But you won't think it's silly. You know God, and you know Max. You will understand."

"Tell me," I said.

"I was flying so fast and so high—flying to the light. I couldn't see the doctors or Tina or me anymore. I couldn't see them with my eyes, but I sort of *could* see them ... maybe with my soul. And then Petra jumped up on me and told me to come back. He told me he loved me—that you all loved me—and how sad you would be without me, so I came back."

I nodded slowly. "Tina says it was Petros, not Max. Max was with me."

She smiled bigger. "She's right, it *was* Petros, but not really. It was really Petra—it's *always* Petra. Like me not seeing the doctors when I was flying to the light, *but still seeing them too.* It was Petros' body on top of me, but it was really Max—Max that called me back. God sent him to me. Just like before, in Germany, when the bad motorcycle man took me, and the man that tied me in the chair. God always sends Max to save me."

I almost couldn't speak, but I forced myself. "I have a friend I want you to talk to when we get back. He's like you."

"Like me?"

"His name is Sammy, and he died once when he was even younger than you. He said he floated, too. I think maybe you can help each other."

Max was suddenly there, sitting next to her. Irmgard smiled and hugged him tight. Max let her. She looked deeply into my eyes, deeper than any nine-year-old should ever be able to look, tears welling.

"See? God always sends Max. Max and you. I love you, Uncle Gil."

Crying was beginning to become a habit for me. "I love you too. Thank you for not letting me be sad."

That night, as Sarah and I made our bed under the full moon on the beach, the waves and the warm breeze lulling us with their peace, I told her what Irmgard had said.

"She's a blessing," Sarah wiped at a tear of her own. "And she's right to love you. Thank you for not making me sad."

She kissed me, and we stayed there the night, content, sharing each other's warmth and touch, enveloped in our love.

As slumber finally wrapped me within the comfort of its gentle embrace, I thanked God for this second chance at happiness—a chance that I didn't deserve, that I could never repay. But that's the point, isn't it? God gives us what we don't deserve, what we could never earn, because He loves us and wants only the best for us. We are His glory, just as our children are ours. Like my Marla, like Irmgard.

God is the loving Father.

Thank you, Father.

ACKNOWLEDGMENTS

Hello, fellow Pack Members. First and foremost, thank you once again for purchasing and reading the latest installment in the Gil Mason series, *Twice Shy*. The phrase "once bitten, twice shy" has ancient roots, dating back to Roman times and possibly even originating with Aesop himself. William Caxton, who brought the printing press to England, is credited with introducing this phrase into the English language through his translation of *Aesop's Fables*.

"He that hath been ben ones begyld by somme other ought to keep hym well fro(m) the same."

The meaning here is that once a person has been hurt by something, they become reluctant or fearful of experiencing that pain again. For example, if someone tried to pet a dog and was bitten, they would be very cautious before trying to pet another dog. In Gil's case, after losing his first wife—the love of his life—he was understandably hesitant and fearful of ever feeling such pain again, making him unlikely to consider marriage a second time.

A similar outcome can occur during K9 training. If a young dog experiences an overly harsh correction, it may develop an intense fear associated with that experience, causing the dog to refuse to participate in future training sessions, anticipating the same harsh treatment. We refer to this as *supernatural dread*. There are usually ways to counter this negative experience, but it can be difficult and time-consuming, not to mention stressful for the puppy. It's best for all not to let it happen in the first place.

That's what good trainers and handlers do—they make the training process positive, fun, and exciting. Our dogs are more than just tools or partners ... they're our friends, and we love them. We strive to ensure every experience is a good one for our dogs. They always win. No decoy ever beats them. If they fail on a track, trail, or evidence search, we have an easier task ready to go. We immediately put them on that one so they still succeed. This approach makes them feel invulnerable and infallible, much like the dog Bolt in the Disney movie. It reinforces their genetic strengths and drives, amplifying their already incredible attributes and confidence, which sustains them when things get really tough—and believe me, things can get very tough and very dangerous.

In *Twice Shy*, I delve into some painful and dark themes, particularly Irmgard's mental state, her self-harm, and even worse scenarios. Having responded to more suicide and attempted suicide calls than I can count, I can sadly say that the descriptions and elements in the book are both accurate and tragic. We're living in a challenging time, especially for children, and I believe the only true answers lie in God and good parenting. I sincerely apologize if any scenes in the book were disturbing, hurtful, or brought up painful memories. I draw from my experiences when writing, and I recognize that I may have a somewhat hardened perspective on subjects like violence and gore—it's something that comes with the territory for cops, paramedics, firefighters, doctors, morticians, and soldiers.

As I mentioned in the acknowledgments of book nine, *Silent Dog Still Water*, Gil has been becoming progressively darker and more violent. It will be interesting to see how things unfold now that he and Sarah are married. I'm hopeful marriage will soften him somewhat, but then again, I'm an eternal optimist, much like God, who hopes all things.

As for the next book in the series, *The Wrong Tree*, things are getting wild. I'm already over 40,000 words in, and while I wish I could give you a publishing time frame, I've learned that I always underestimate. Because of that, I've been forbidden from even speculating. That being said, whatever you do, don't tell my wife or daughters that I'm hoping to have it done in time for Christmas. Just don't hold me to that because, like I said, I'm an eternal optimist.

Finally, as with all my books, I had a lot of help writing and finishing *Twice Shy*. Just as catching murderers, bank robbers, home invaders, and perverts is a team effort, so was publishing *Twice Shy*. I want to extend my heartfelt thanks to my wife, Becky (my editor), my oldest daughter, Athena (who creates all my covers—this one is the best yet!), my son, Anthony (who handles all my marketing and advertising), my dear friend Barbara Wright (who, along with her daughter, has helped me find K9s for the Sheriff's Office), and our wonderful editor Betty Fisher, who gave the manuscript a final review and fixed everything we missed.

I thank God (not an expression of speech) for both the ability and the opportunity to write, for encouragement from my readers, and for being able to introduce small pieces of His Word to reach and encourage others.

Any incorrect, outdated, or misapplied information is wholly on me, either because it worked for the story or because I messed it up. Also, my editors give me constant grief about my use of ..., —, and italics. I break some grammatical rules while writing, but that's because I write to tell the story and make it flow as smoothly as possible. I apologize to those who find my use of these tools a distraction. I feel they add an effect for the average reader (me) that mere commas don't, and for me, it's all about the story experience. I don't think I'm a great writer, but I try to tell a fun, inspirational story that leaves you happy at the end.

Once again, thank you, dear reader. Thank you for buying, reading, spreading the word about *Twice Shy,* and making the Gil Mason novels a best-selling series. I hope to see you soon as the excitement continues with *The Wrong Tree*. Thanks for howling at the moon with me, and hopefully, I'll see you around Christmas! Ho-ho-ho.

Until then...

ABOUT THE AUTHOR

Gordon Carroll is the author of *GUNWOOD USA* and *The Gil Mason Sheepdog* series. Gordon grew up at the foot of the great Rocky Mountains in Colorado. Joining the United States Marine Corps at eighteen, he served for seven years, achieving the rank of sergeant (selected for staff sergeant). After that, he became a police officer in a small (wild) city nestled snugly in the middle of Denver, Colorado, before moving on to become a sheriff's deputy.

Gordon became a K9 handler, trainer, and instructor, training and working four separate dogs for over three decades (a hundred-twenty-pound German Shepherd named JR, a ninety-pound Belgian Malinois named Max, a fifty-six-pound Belgian Malinois named Thor, and a sixty-pound fur-missile named Arrow). Gordon retired from police work in 2020 to focus on writing and spending time with his grandchildren. K9 Arrow retired with him.

Over the years, Gordon and his K9 companions assisted the DEA, FBI, and numerous other local, state, and federal law enforcement agencies in the detection and apprehension of criminals and narcotics. Together, Gordon and his K9 partners are responsible for over two million dollars in narcotics seizures, three thousand felony apprehensions and were first responders to both the 2012 Aurora Mall shooting and the 2013 Arapahoe High School shooting.

He has been married to the same wonderful woman (his high school sweetheart, Becky) for over forty years. Together they have four adult children and a whole *pack* of grandchildren.

Gordon's love of books began while he was in sixth grade when he became captivated by Jack London's *White Fang* and *Call of the Wild*.

From there, he branched out, gobbling up everything from Robert E. Howard to Steinbeck to Brand, King, Wambaugh, Irving, Craise, Hunter, Rothfuss, Lowry, Card, Emmerich, and on and on.

After years of telling stories to his children and friends, his wife insisted he write some of them down. After that, he just couldn't stop. Sending short stories out, he was quickly published in several magazines in genres ranging from Si-Fi, horror, mainstream, mystery, and Christian. He then wrote *GUNWOOD USA*, followed by *Sheepdogs* (Book 1 of the Gil Mason and Max series), fictionalized compilations of real-life scenarios that he has seen, heard of, or been involved in over his years with law enforcement and military service.

The *Sheepdog* series, as well as *GUNWOOD USA*, became instant bestsellers.

Gordon is a member of Rocky Mountain Fiction Writers (RMFW) and served on speaking panels for years, as well as performing K9 demos at the annual conferences.

ALSO BY GORDON CARROLL

Gil Mason Book 1: Sheepdogs

Gil Mason Book 2: Hair of the Dog

Gil Mason Book 3: Feral Instinct

Gil Mason Book 4: Old Dog New Tricks

Gil Mason Gook 5: Sleeping Dogs

Gil Mason Book 6: A Dog Returns

Gil Mason Book 7: Dog Eat Dog

Gil Mason Book 8: The Hand that Feeds

Gil Mason Book 9: Silent Dog Still Water

Gunwood USA

Bone Hill

Made in the USA
Columbia, SC
29 December 2024